"Do you always sleep with this many pillows?"

As she spoke, Emily snuggled into the fluffy depths and pulled the sheet over her naked body.

"Nope," Ned said from the adjacent bathroom. "K-Mart had a sale and I thought it would be neat, having all those pillows."

"It was...." She sighed dreamily.

"And will be," he murmured, climbing back into bed. He eased her body into the curve of his and cupped her breast. "You can do all sorts of interesting things with extra pillows."

"Oh, and where did you learn that?"

"Books," he teased, nuzzling her ear. When she only laughed, he said, "Why do you doubt me? You know I'm a scholar."

"Then I guess you could show me the book where you learned this...."

ABOUT THE AUTHOR

A fear of heights didn't keep
Vicki Lewis Thompson from tackling a story
about ironworkers. "These people are so
brave," she says. "Day after day they work
twenty, thirty stories in the air." Vicki herself
is quite happy to write in her ground-floor
office. A talented and prolific author, she lives
in Tucson with her husband and their
two teenagers.

Books by Vicki Lewis Thompson

HARLEQUIN SUPERROMANCE

HARLEQUIN TEMPTATION

£H

Connections
VICKI LEWIS THOMPSON

Harlequin Books

TORONTO • NEW YORK • LONDON
AMSTERDAM • PARIS • SYDNEY • HAMBURG
STOCKHOLM • ATHENS • TOKYO • MILAN

Published January 1990

First printing November 1989

ISBN 0-373-70389-9

For William T. Moncada,
my connection to the world of ironworkers.
Thanks, Willy.

CHAPTER ONE

QUITTIN' TIME. In an air-conditioned coffee shop across the street from the construction site, Emily watched men in hard hats abandon the open girders of the fifteenth floor. Most of those climbing down from the top were ironworkers, men who erected the steel skeleton that eventually would poke thirty stories into the cobalt sky. By Tucson standards, the building would be tall.

When the ironworkers reached ground level and filed through the opening in the chain-link fence surrounding the site, they wandered by twos and threes to a bar several doors away. Emily noted the name of the place— Suds and Subs. So that was the "watering hole." She had the necessary information to begin her research project.

She could leave now, but not until her brother, Danny, supervisor for Johnson Construction, drove away from the site. If Danny noticed her and called out, he'd blow her cover and spoil the project. Finally his truck pulled away from the curb.

Emily tipped the coffee-shop waitress thirty percent of the meager bill before trading the restaurant's iced air for a blast of summer heat. The pancake-griddle sidewalk toasted the soles of her red pumps, yet she lingered, filled with nostalgia.

Slipping her Ray-Bans over the bridge of her nose, she tilted her head back and looked up through the smoky lenses to the fifteenth floor. A fall from that height could kill a man, yet this afternoon members of the raising gang had balanced on the narrow girders with the non-chalance of boys playing on a grade-school jungle gym. Emily had forgotten the physical bravery required of ironworkers, especially those who made the first erec-tor-set connections of the giant beams.

Back in the days when her father had worked the iron, Emily had visited a construction site with her mother. Emily had been about five, she remembered, and look-ing up at the rust-red beams had made her laugh and feel so dizzy she'd nearly toppled backward.

"Your father is connecting on this job," her mother had said, pointing out a man balanced on a top girder. "Connectors lead the way to the top."

The sun had glittered on her father's hard hat far above them, and Emily had decided that he was some sort of god. Over the years she'd learned to mute her admiration, however, especially in her father's pres-ence. Ever since she'd begun dating he'd insisted that a mere ironworker, or anyone with a blue-collar job for that matter, wasn't good enough for her.

All of the men had left the construction site except for a group of four who remained by a corner of the fence talking, their tanned faces shaded by white hard hats. Emily covertly studied them while pretending interest in the bus schedule posted nearby.

One man, taller than the other three, had the narrow hips and wide shoulders of a college fullback. His un-buttoned shirt revealed a tank top molded to his broad chest with sweat. His flat stomach contrasted with the slight paunches of the other three, who obviously en-joyed their round of beers after work at the Suds and Subs bar.

Emily stood too far away to catch the scent of a hard day's labor on the ironworkers, but her memory filled it in from all the nights her father had come home, swung her up in his arms and plopped his hard hat over her dark hair. Just then the tall man glanced in Emily's direction and she turned away, but not before she caught his smile acknowledging her covert assessment. The smile stayed with her as she hurried down the street away from the construction site to the underground garage where she'd parked her red Corvette.

As Emily drove toward her foothills apartment on Tucson's northwest side, she thought about the chance conversation with one of her sociology students a week ago that had changed her summer plans. For some reason Curt Tucker had wanted to talk about his brother, who was helping finance his education.

According to Curt, his brother was a paragon who also supported his widowed mother and read classic literature on his lunch hour. The unusual part about his reading, Curt had said, was that his brother was an ironworker. Curt was impressed with his brother's ability to be "scholarly" and yet fit in with his buddies when they all went to a bar for drinks after work.

Curt's story had aroused Emily's curiosity, both as a sociologist and a woman. When she'd casually inquired where this brother was working, Curt had mentioned the new high rise downtown. Emily's father had the ironwork contract for that building, but Curt, like everyone else on campus, was ignorant of Emily's connection to Johnson Construction. Emily hadn't enlightened him.

With Curt's brother as inspiration, she had conceived a project that would be more fun than teaching summer school and might earn her some academic brownie points in the bargain. As a first-year instructor at the University of Arizona, she could use them.

Her father would hate the idea, of course, but she'd overcome his objections by taking him to lunch at his favorite Mexican restaurant and breaking the news gently. After all, she needed a certain amount of his cooperation or her plan would fail.

"I HAVE AN EXCITING research project planned for this summer, Dad." Emily had waited to spring her news until the waitress had cleared away their plates and her father was stoking his Meerschaum with his beloved Borkum Riff.

"Oh? What's that?" Settling back after his lunch of tamales and beer, Dan Johnson passed the match flame over the bowl of his pipe and puffed slowly while he waited to hear the latest scholarly adventure his daughter had dreamed up.

"I'm conducting a two-month study of the social patterns established by ironworkers in a temporary watering hole."

Her father snapped out of his complacent position and leaned across the table. "You're doing what in a bar?"

"It's a natural, Dad. The sociology paper I write following the study will be a cinch for publication, which will help my standing at the University. The subject matter is perfect for me, don't you think?" She flashed him a smile.

"You're gonna study ironworkers?"

"Exactly. You may not have thought about it, but I'm sure they establish definite relationship patterns, choose leaders, and so on. The bar becomes a miniature world, a social experiment almost, until the construction is finished and the social fabric disintegrates.''

Her father stared at her in puzzlement. ''Yeah, I guess. So what?''

''I'll document that world in a sociological context. I think many of my colleagues will find the subject fascinating.''

''Hold it. You don't have to study anything. Just ask me. I'll fill your ears full of more than you ever wanted to hear.'' He leaned back again, as if he'd dismissed the matter with his offer. ''Hanging around those guys is no place for you, Angel.''

''Dad, I'm a scientist. I have to obtain my data firsthand.'' She paused and tried a different tactic. ''Would you rather I chose a gay bar?''

''A *what*?'' Dan jerked forward and glanced around nervously. Then he lowered his voice. ''Watch what you say, please, will you?''

''I only made a suggestion.''

''Suggest something else, for crying out loud. Why can't you study little kids on a playground? What's the big deal with bars all of a sudden?'' Dan's pipe had gone out. Pulling it from his mouth, he gazed at the seasoned Meerschaum and shook his head. ''Bars, for crying out loud.''

''I don't know much about little kids, Dad. I understand construction. I understand ironworkers.''

''Not the way I do, Angel.'' He jabbed the pipe stem in her direction. ''If you think you can waltz into a bar, plunk down on a stool and start asking questions, you've got mush for brains. These guys will either clam up or make a pass.'' He sighed. ''Nope. This is one terrible idea. I didn't send you to Stanford so you could hang out in bars with ironworkers.''

Emily reached over and patted his large hand where it lay clenched on the table. "Relax, Dad. You don't understand what a study like this could do for my career. How many sociologists could bring a background like mine to such a study? This is exactly what I need to launch myself as a respected member of the faculty."

"I don't like it, Angel. Those guys are rough. I oughta know. Besides, they don't take kindly to college professor types interfering with their drinking time, even beautiful ones like you."

"That's the fun part, Dad. They won't know I'm a college instructor, or even about the study. I've got a job as a waitress."

"Oh, hell, Angel. You're gonna be a barmaid?" Her father put down his pipe and massaged his eyes while mumbling what might have been a litany of four-letter words. Finally he looked at her with a tired expression. "Where is this job?"

Guilt, delayed but swift and agonizing, washed over Emily. He wanted so much for her to remain above the dirty struggle of everyday existence as he'd experienced it. How could she explain to him that she needed more action, more color, more *life* in her life? The brilliant blue of his eyes, so often compared with hers, looked as faded as old jeans. He'd be sixty in November, and today he looked every year of it. When had his hair become completely gray, his cheeks networked with lines? She began to question her entire plan.

"Let me guess," he said when she hadn't replied. "Suds and Subs, right?"

Emily nodded.

"I suppose you've seen the getup those girls wear?"

She nodded again, not even bothering to correct his "girls" to "women."

Dan Johnson sighed heavily and put his pipe and to-bacco pouch in his breast pocket. "You're twenty-five years old, Angel, and I can't force you to do, or not do, anything anymore. But I wish you'd think again about this study. My idea all along was to keep you out of places like that bar, and here you are getting a job there, like you had no advantages at all."

Emily opened her mouth to tell him that she'd forget the whole thing, but he continued speaking.

"And another thing. You'll hear all sorts of bellyach-ing about me and Danny if you stay around those mugs very long."

"Dad, I wouldn't listen to that kind of talk. I know you're a good boss."

"Spoiled punks these days that I'm hiring," he con-tinued, almost to himself. "Got to grouse about every little thing."

"Perhaps that will fit into my study," she said, al-though her father's comments surprised her. In the past he'd seemed to get along well with his workers.

"So I guess you really hafta do this, huh?"

She paused. He'd accepted her plan, after all. If she caved in now, she'd be snatching defeat from the jaws of victory. "Yes, I do," she said. "And I have to ask you not to give me away, either you or Danny. Does he go in Suds and Subs much?"

"No." Her father's answer was abrupt. "He got tired of the grousing, too."

"Well, would you tell him what I'm doing, so he won't be surprised if he does stop in."

"Why don't you tell him?"

"You'll probably see him first," Emily said quickly.

"Yeah, I know." Her father looked away. "You just don't want to call his house and maybe have to talk to

Gwen. I don't know why you two girls can't hit it off. You're sisters-in-law, for crying out loud.''

"We don't have much in common, that's all," Emily said, figuring that much was certainly true. "She has the house and kids and I have my job. We're neither of us very interested in what the other does all day."

"Humph." Her father took his pipe out again, as if reconsidering lighting it. "I thought by now both you and Danny'd be married. We all thought you'd end up with that professor you wrote us about. The one you took the graduate course from."

Emily sighed, remembering the pain of Michael. She'd have been miserable married to him, but she'd loved him, nevertheless. "He never stopped treating me like his student," she said, thinking her father was waiting for some explanation.

"What's so bad about that? You were his student."

"Yes, but—" A glance at her father's face told her that further discussion of Michael was futile. Dan Johnson could see no problem with a man's feelings of superiority over a woman.

"Well, since you've moved back here, there have been some others," he said, pursuing the subject. He'd love to marry her off, Emily knew, especially to a "suitable" man. "What ever happened to that Brian guy?"

"Dad, can you imagine spending a whole evening analyzing the trajectory of a tennis ball?"

"I didn't know he played tennis."

"He doesn't. At least we never finished a game. After I scored the first two points, he called me over to the net and spent well over an hour describing why the ball left my racket the way it did and why he'd been unable to return my serves."

"Oh." Her father looked perplexed and then he brightened. "What about whats-his-name, Edward? He seemed to like you. Are you still going out with him?"

"He got so wrapped up in studying Asian cultures that he started dating only Asian women."

"John?" her father ventured hopefully.

"Dad, come on. You want me to marry somebody who made the whole family sit through five hundred slides about the pottery of the Anasazi Indians?"

"The first fifty were kinda interesting."

"Face it, all the guys I've dated recently have been terminally boring or have had immense ego problems."

"Your mother and I wish you'd settle down, that's all."

"I know, Dad. But I haven't found anybody who's right for me. To tell the truth, I'm a little tired of the scholastic types I meet at work."

Her father raised his eyebrows before lowering them in a scowl. "Just keep your distance from them iron-workers."

She gazed at him, her face, she hoped, the picture of academic objectivity. She banished thoughts of Curt's brother and the tall ironworker she'd seen on the street. She smiled at her father. "Dad, this is a scientific study."

Dan Johnson clenched his unlit pipe between his teeth once more. "Yeah," he muttered.

EMILY STOOD in front of the rust-stained sink in the cramped women's rest room at Suds and Subs and struggled with her hair. The manager, a man who had introduced himself simply as "Bailey," hadn't bothered to mention when he hired her that she couldn't let her hair hang loose.

"Especially that mop," he'd added, rolling his eyes in amazement at the dark tresses that fell in a straight line past her shoulders to the middle of her back. The other waitress, Monica Spangler, had rummaged through her large purse to find a few hairpins and Bailey had contributed a rubber band.

Emily coiled her hair on top of her head, a style that added another two inches to her already considerable height. Her required three-inch black heels combined with her barefoot height of five-eight put her over six feet tall, counting hair.

When she reemerged from the bathroom and walked into the kitchen, Bailey gaped. "I've gone and hired me a skyscraper," he muttered.

"Maybe I should wear lower heels," she suggested hopefully.

"Nope, nope. Got to remember we have ironworkers in here this summer. They like anything that's tall, from a glass of beer to a dame."

Emily started to object to "dame," but thought better of it. He didn't seem like the sort of man who was used to corrections from women. Instead she smiled and pretended he'd given her a compliment. "Thanks, Bailey."

Monica, a dyed redhead with slightly crooked front teeth and a warm smile, had come through the swinging doors from the bar in time to catch the last of the exchange. She handed the cook a sandwich order and waited for Bailey to leave before she spoke to Emily. "Don't let him bug you," she said. "You look great. Wish I had legs like that."

Emily glanced down at the black shorts and white blouse tied at her midriff that made up the Suds and

Subs waitress "uniform." "This is the most sexist outfit I've worn in my entire life," she complained.

Monica chuckled. "Sexist? This ain't nothing, honey. Some places I've worked you're lucky to get a few bows and sequins." She eyed Emily more closely. "Ever waitressed before, honey?"

Emily shook her head.

"Then be grateful for those long, glamorous legs, because Bailey didn't hire you for your experience. If I was you—" She stopped speaking as Bailey pushed through the swinging doors and called over to them.

"You two ladies finished with the coffee klatch? It's quittin' time at the construction site and I had in mind the silly idea that you might serve the customers some refreshment when they arrive. Of course," he continued with exaggerated courtesy, "if you have more pressing matters than the matter of keeping your jobs..."

"We'll get right on it, chief," Monica said, and Bailey left the kitchen once more. "Okay, Em," she began, automatically assigning Emily a nickname. "Here's a crash course in being a barmaid." She turned her order pad over to the cardboard back and began sketching a rough floorplan of the bar.

"I appreciate this, Monica."

"Don't mention it. You can do me a favor sometime. Now, see, the customer part is an L-shape, with the bar here, five booths along this wall, and the pool room in the short part of the L."

"Right," Emily said, nodding.

"We'll divide it up, I'll take the three booths on the left as we go out, and you take the two on the right and anybody playing pool. Got it?"

"I think so."

"We'll start in the middle and work out. Take your orders clockwise or counterclockwise, but get a system and stick to it, or you'll get your orders mixed up. Now the pool players will move around, so you have to put down something about them, like color of shirt, until you learn who is who."

"I see. Monica, I hope I won't be more liability than asset around here."

"Are you kidding? Before you came along I was doing this job by myself. We had another waitress for a while, but she quit and Bailey decided I could handle it alone. Until you showed up, anyway, and he figured a looker like you would help business."

Emily smiled uncomfortably. In the academic world her looks had counted against her more often than not, and she'd had to prove her intelligence. Here she was valued only for her outward appearance. Having never traded on that before, Emily found it difficult to do so now. "I want to be a good waitress," she said to Monica.

"Don't worry, honey. Stick with me and you'll be the best darn waitress in Tucson. Ready?"

"Might as well get it over with."

"And Em, don't mind the flirting. Most of them aren't serious about it, anyway."

"Okay." Emily tried to remember Monica's advice as a wolf whistle greeted her entrance into the noisy, smoke-filled bar. Despite Monica's reassuring words, Emily realized that she was in for some culture shock. She wasn't used to bars; as a college student she'd been too intent on grades to go out drinking, even when she was of age. Her social life had been exactly as her father would have wanted it.

Nothing except television and stories told by her father and brother had prepared Emily for this waitress job. Nothing, perhaps, except her training as a scientific observer of human nature. That, she thought, squaring her shoulders, would have to get her through. Order pad clutched in one hand, pencil in the other, Emily approached her first booth filled with four grinning, grimy men.

"Must be our lucky day," said one, a burly, gray-haired man.

"I heard that, Smiley," Monica called over in the midst of taking orders from her booth.

"Aw, Monica, sweets, I didn't mean to hurt your feelings," the man called Smiley said. "I'll always love you best."

"Sure you will," Monica retorted with a laugh and continued taking orders.

Emily cleared her throat. "What will you gentlemen have this afternoon?"

"Oo-wee!" exclaimed a ruddy-faced man with blond hair and a mustache. "Did you hear that? She called us *gentlemen*."

Emily ignored him and faced a thin fellow on her left. Clockwise, she decided. "May I take your order, please?"

"Sweetheart, you can take anything of mine you want," the man replied with a wink at his friends.

"Hey, you know what we've got here, Mike?" questioned a redheaded fellow on her far right. "We've got us an educated gal. Listen to the way she talks. You're one of them coeds, right, babe?"

Emily thought she'd better answer such a direct question. If she antagonized these men they'd be useless as subjects for her study and she might lose her job. "Yes,

I am," she said, convincing herself it wasn't really a lie. She'd taken a course toward her doctorate last semester in addition to her teaching.

"See?" The red-haired man gazed at his cohorts and gloated over his correct assumption. "A college gal. So you guys can forget whatever schemes and dreams you had. The only one who can hold a conversation with this woman is Bookworm."

"Hey, yeah," the man with the mustache said. "Let's get Bookworm. He can interpret for us." He cupped his hands over his mouth and yelled in the direction of the pool tables. "Bookworm Tucker! Get your keester over here."

Bookworm Tucker, Emily thought. *Of course. Curt's older brother.* "Perhaps if I took your orders first," she said, trying to regain control of the situation. "I'm sure that the customers in the next booth would like to—"

"Did you catch that, guys?" Smiley asked. "We're gentlemen, but those punks in the next booth are only *customers.*" He glanced toward the men in question. "You *customers* over there don't mind waiting until we introduce this lovely young thing to Bookworm, do you?"

"Listen, Smiley," said a swarthy man in the corner of the booth. "You hold up our beer much longer and we'll introduce you to the Great Beyond."

"You see?" Emily appealed to Smiley for help. "I don't want to lose my job, so if you'll just tell me what you want to—"

"Here's Bookworm," said Smiley. "Bookworm, I'd be pleased to introduce you to an honest-to-goodness college gal by the name of—what did you say your name was, sweetheart?"

Emily barely heard the question. At Smiley's announcement she'd turned and found herself staring into the amused face of the man she'd noticed at the construction site. A quick glimmer in his hazel eyes, like the flash of sun on water, told her that he remembered, too.

He was dressed the same way he'd been when she'd observed him from across the street, except that his hard hat was gone and his unbuttoned long-sleeved shirt was a different color. The sleeves were rolled past his elbows now that he no longer had to protect his arms from the brutal summer sun.

His tousled hair, blending shades of brown like fine woodgrain, waved back from his forehead to reveal a well-defined widow's peak. Because Curt was of medium build and blond, Emily had expected his brother to be as well. Instead this man was hewn of stronger material, although there was a similarity about the nose, with its faint suggestion of a hook, and a firmness around the mouth that marked the two as brothers.

"My name is Emily," she said, dimly remembering that Smiley had asked the question. "Emily Johnson."

"Glad to know you, Emily," Curt's brother said, and the glimmer returned to his eyes for a moment.

"Bookworm, here," the man with the mustache explained, "always has something in his lunch box to read while the rest of us sit around and swap lies during breaks."

"Yeah," Smiley added. "And it's usually that garbage we had to read in school. Like one time he had *Tale of Two Cities*."

The redheaded man snickered. "And Smiley thought it was one of them porno books."

"Did not," Smiley said. "I was making a joke, monkey brains, and you'd best not bring up such things in front of a lady."

Emily flushed and wished she hadn't. She wanted to be one of them, prove she could take it. "Perhaps you'd all like to order?" she said brusquely.

"Aw, jeez," Smiley complained. "You jerk-heads have gone and embarrassed her."

"Hey!" the swarthy man called from the next booth. "Are we drinking tonight or having an ice-cream social?"

"I'll get that booth," Monica whispered as she whizzed behind Emily, "but you'll have to move a little faster, honey."

"I'm trying, but they—"

"I know, I know. Hi, Bookworm," Monica said, favoring him with a smile. "See if you can convince your friends to order so the lady can do her job, huh?"

"Sure thing, Monica." Curt's brother turned to the man with the mustache. "What'll you have, Al?"

"The usual. You know what I always have."

Emily panicked. Al was in the middle of the booth.

"Al wants Coors with a tequila chaser," Bookworm told Emily.

Emily started to protest but he threw another order at her, first for Smiley and then for the redheaded man, nicknamed Rooster. She scribbled furiously and tried to write an identifying trait next to each other. Bookworm apparently assumed that she'd done this before and he tossed orders at her quickly until all four were given.

"And you?" she asked when she finally finished writing.

"Bookworm will have his usual, one Bud to last all night," Smiley said. "When we first got to know this guy we had to decide whether to call him One-Drink or Bookworm, and Bookworm stuck."

Emily wrote down the order for Budweiser. "I'll be right back with your drinks," she said, and turned to go. "Thanks, uh, Bookworm," she added hesitantly.

Bookworm caught her elbow. "The name's Ned," he murmured.

She glanced into his eyes and swallowed. His hand gripped her bare elbow and the warmth of his skin against hers was pleasant. No, more than pleasant. "Is that what you'd prefer to be called?" she asked.

"By you, yes."

"I'll try to remember." She was aware of the interested audience for their interchange. As she walked away she heard laughter from the men in the booth and caught snatches of a few bawdy comments directed at Bookworm. At Ned. Ned Tucker. The literary ironworker and the man on the street were one. A current of anticipation surged through her.

CHAPTER TWO

EMILY FOUND MUCH TO LIKE about Ned Tucker. Her thoughts remained with him as she handed the drink order to Bailey, who tended bar until a relief man arrived at seven. While she waited for the order, Emily added up what she knew about Ned. First of all he was supporting his mother and helping his younger brother through school. In addition he seemed to be educating himself. In only a short time she'd sensed other qualities about him, as well—leadership, kindness, self-discipline.

"Snap out of it, Emily." Bailey pushed a tray loaded with drinks toward her. "I don't pay nobody for day-dreamin'."

"Right," she said hurriedly and hoisted the heavy tray in both hands. Monica balanced full trays with one hand, but Emily wasn't about to risk a trick like that yet.

The five men she'd left had become six by the time she returned. Ned remained standing by the table, leaning slightly on his cue stick, and another man, also holding a cue stick, had squeezed in on Rooster's left. He was Hispanic with dark, bushy eyebrows and a bandit's mustache. She'd have to take his order next, along with the others in the pool room. This fellow obviously had been in a pool game with Ned, a game interrupted when the man called Al had summoned Ned to the booth.

Balancing the heavy tray against her hip, Emily stared at her notepad and tried to interpret the hieroglyphics next to each drink order. She started to pass out the first drink, frowned and took it back.

"Here." Ned stepped closer and took the tray. "I'll give them out," he offered. "These turkeys always drink the same thing, so I have it memorized. In a few days you will, too."

"Thank you." Emily smiled and added "sensitive" to her growing list of Ned's good qualities. Then she glanced at his pool-playing friend with the imposing brows and mustache. "What can I get for you, sir?"

Ned handed her the empty tray. "Mean Mando will have a Miller Lite, on me."

Emily looked to the menacing, dark-eyed man for confirmation and he gave a slight nod. Briefly she wondered why Ned was buying a drink for a man nicknamed Mean Mando, a man who by the looks of him deserved the title. "I'll bring your Miller Lite as soon as I can take orders from the other three gentlemen in the pool room," she said, hoping he wouldn't take offense. Mean Mando merely nodded once more and she started to leave.

"Uh, Emily?" Ned touched her arm, and again she reacted with pleasure to the brief contact.

"Yes?"

"Haven't you forgotten something?"

"I don't think so." She inventoried drinks and men, and came out even except for Ned's friend, Mean Mando.

"The bill."

"Oh!" Emily couldn't disguise her embarrassment as she glanced in dismay at the single page of orders. "Did you want—" she gulped and looked around the table "—separate checks?"

"Nah," Smiley said, coming to her rescue and earning her unspoken gratitude. "I'm buying this round." He slapped a twenty on the table.

Emily picked up the bill and cast an endearing look at Smiley. "I'll be right back with your change."

"Take your time," Smiley said expansively, seeming to glory in his role as savior.

Emily hurried through the task anyway. Customers were waiting in the pool room and Monica had already assumed more than her share of the work, Emily thought. She wondered how soon the job would become routine enough to allow note taking for her sociology paper. She had much to document already, but she'd have to keep all of it in her head until she returned home tonight. Eventually, however, she hoped to make notes during the evening as things happened.

About an hour later while Emily was bustling back. and forth filling orders, Ned stopped her.

"Could I ask you something?" he asked, his voice low.

Her immediate thought was that he knew, somehow, that she was Curt's instructor at the University. She swallowed nervously. "Sure."

"I wondered if you, um, have a steady guy or anything."

Relief was followed quickly by anxiety. She wasn't ready for this sort of question, but here it was, hanging unanswered between them. "No, I don't," she said, unable to think of a better response as she looked into his eyes. The gray-green color reminded her of copper ore.

"Then I wondered if maybe we could go out for coffee sometime after you get off work."

"Well, I—"

"Not tonight," he said hastily, as if sensing a rejection. "But sometime."

He's an ironworker, she thought, and remembered her father's warning. But her father had also admitted that she was old enough to make her own decisions. "I don't get off until twelve each night and one o'clock on Saturdays."

"I know. That's fine."

"I'm not sure if Bailey has a rule about dating the customers."

"He doesn't. Besides, it's just for coffee. No big deal."

Emily gazed at him and knew it would be a very big deal, indeed. This was no minor decision on her part. "Maybe," she said slowly. "Maybe some night we could have coffee."

"Great." His smile appeared, brief yet brilliant in his tanned face. "Now you'd better get back to work before Bailey fires you."

"Yes." Emily jumped guiltily. "Yes, I'd better. I can't get fired."

"I know how that is." Ned touched her arm. "I'll be talking to you." Then he turned and walked out of the bar.

Emily hurried back to her work. The pressure of performing new tasks kept her thoughts from wandering very often to Ned. Sometimes, however, she'd remember the excitement that had leaped into his eyes when she'd replied "maybe," to his request. Then goose bumps would prickle her skin the way they used to when she'd buy a ticket for the roller coaster at the state fair. Perhaps, Emily thought, she'd just bought a ticket for the wildest ride of her life.

NED LEFT THE BAR and headed home to shower and fix a quick meal of hot dogs and beans. He was due at his mother's house tonight, and he didn't want to arrive much past eight-thirty. Curt would be up until all hours, but these days his mother was usually in bed by nine, and she'd be upset if Ned showed up so late that she didn't have a chance to say hello.

He had a pretty good idea why Curt had asked him to drop by tonight. Every summer it was the same old story. Ned wasn't planning to back down this time, either. In another year Curt would have his degree and could look for a decent job, one where he could use all that brain power. Ned didn't want anything messing up the schedule.

Then he chuckled and shook his head. *Yeah, right,* he thought. *Curt's not going to mess up the schedule, but you might if you let yourself get carried away with Emily Johnson, extraordinary waitress.* He shouldn't have asked her for a coffee date. She was far too close to his ideal image, and he couldn't afford to be interested in a woman for several months yet.

Of course, he reasoned, trying to justify his move, Emily Johnson would be gone by the end of the summer. She'd become a college girl again and he could easily lose track of her. At the moment she was on his turf, where a certain advantage belonged to him. If he could have met her a year from now . . . but he hadn't.

He'd also figured that if he hadn't acted, one of the other punks would have. Sure, they'd given him first dibs because they'd been awed by her education, but the awe would have worn off eventually. Somebody else would have asked her out, maybe Rooster, possibly even Mando. The idea of her involved with one of his buddies hadn't appealed to him in the least.

She was beautiful, even in the tacky outfit Bailey made her wear. He remembered what she'd looked like on the street that day in the classy red sundress with her hair hanging straight down her back. Funny, but he wouldn't have thought then that she was the type to interview for a job at Suds and Subs, but that was probably what she'd been doing.

He hoped that she'd take her hair down for their date. Ned pictured her that way, settled back and smiling as she rode beside him in the old Pontiac. He was glad he'd had the seats reupholstered. He'd had to choose between a paint job and new seat covers, and now he was pleased with his decision. It would be a good test of her character, to see if she agreed with him that the interior of something—or somebody, for that matter—took precedence over the exterior.

He thought he already knew the answer, which was one reason he'd asked her out so quickly. She hadn't looked at home on those three-inch heels. How Bailey must have licked his lips when she came through the door, Ned thought with a frown. Even though she didn't know the first thing about waitressing, the cagey manager had understood the value of Emily's considerable physical attributes.

Ned wasn't exactly immune to them himself, but he'd passed up sexy-looking women before who were all shine and no substance. This time, though, he'd recognized in Emily a combination of sensuality, vulnerability and intelligence that beckoned to him. He had no money to woo a woman, wouldn't have any for nearly a year, but he couldn't turn his back on this chance.

After parking in the driveway of his mother's small ranch-style house, Ned used his key to enter the carport door into the kitchen. "Anybody home?" he called, knowing full well they were both in the living room watching television, yet not wanting to scare his mother by suddenly appearing in case she hadn't heard his approach.

Ever since his dad's death she'd been nervous about intruders, especially after Ned had moved into his own apartment. She considered Curt, even at twenty, as the baby of the family and incapable of protecting her, much to Curt's annoyance. She ascribed only slightly more maturity to Ned, who had recently turned twenty-seven and had nine years of ironworking behind him, as well.

"Come on in," his mother called with the rising note of gladness she reserved for the arrival of her sons.

Ned walked into the living room and crossed quickly to his mother's recliner. "Don't get up," he urged as she reached for the handle to push the chair upright. "I can kiss you from here. Did you have your hair done today?"

"Curt took me," she said, hugging him as he bent down to kiss her cheek. "Got rid of those awful gray roots."

"Looks good." The years had taken their toll on his mother, but with her hair returned to its natural brunette and her blue eyes sparkling with pleasure at his visit, he thought she did indeed look good.

"If you're hungry," she said, "there are cupcakes on top of the refrigerator, or beer, if you want that."

"No thanks, Mom." He turned to Curt, who had left the couch to switch off the TV. "Don't do that on my account, bro."

"It's just reruns," Curt said, greeting him with a smile.

"If you say so. How're you doing, stud?" He punched Curt playfully on the shoulder.

Curt laughed and punched him back. "Ask me sometime when Mom's not around. How about you?"

"I'll tell you later," Ned said with a wink.

"Oh, you boys," their mother complained. "You're a lot of hot air. I wish you *would* find some nice girl-friends, both of you. Here I am past fifty and not a grandchild in sight."

"Give it time, Mom," Curt said. "Ned and I have to sow our wild oats, first."

"You can't fool me," she replied. "You're either studying or flipping hamburgers, and Ned is no better, either working iron, helping with chores around here or playing pool at that bar he goes to. When was the last time either of you had a real date?"

"As a matter of fact, I might have one soon," Ned told her, almost before he realized what he was saying. Funny, but he wanted his mother to know about Emily.

Curt grinned. "Yeah? Who's the lucky girl?"

"She's the new waitress at Suds and Subs. It's a sum-mer job, between semesters at college. She's...very nice."

"Oh, ho, a college woman, huh?" Curt waggled his eyebrows. "You should have told me that's what you wanted, and I could have lined up a whole contingent of—"

"I'll pick my own, thanks."

"Seems to me that didn't work out too well last time," Curt reminded him. "Or have you forgotten Cheryl?"

Mrs. Tucker shook her head. "I remember that poor girl. Ned felt sorry for her, that was all."

"Ned seemed to miss the fact that she had a screw loose," Curt added. "If I hadn't stepped in and handed you a few books on abnormal psychology, there's no telling what might have happened."

"Yeah." Ned smiled sheepishly. "That was kind of a mess, wasn't it?"

"I can understand how Ned was fooled," Mrs. Tucker said, defending her oldest son's judgment. "She was smart, and pretty, and—"

"Crazy as a bedbug," Curt finished. "Anyway, I hope your waitress is living in the real world and hasn't been hearing voices lately."

Ned shrugged. "Who knows. I'll find out when we go out. But somehow I don't think there are too many like Cheryl running around loose."

"Is she still at Palo Verde Hospital?" Curt asked.

"As of Christmas. Her parents sent me a Christmas card."

"Ned," Curt began, frowning, "you're not thinking that when she's discharged that you'll—"

"No."

"Good." Curt motioned to the couch. "Have a seat and relax. Sure you don't want a beer or something?"

"Nope," Ned replied, settling himself on the worn but comfortable cushions. "And don't try to butter me up, little brother."

"Me?" Curt sprawled on the opposite end of the couch. "Why would I do that?"

"You tell me."

"Aw, come on, Ned. It's my last summer before I graduate next June. I could make twice as much money working with you as cooking hamburgers for three months."

"No way."

Their mother tilted her chair forward and glared at Curt. "Is that why you invited Ned over, to pester him about an ironworking job? You know I don't approve of that."

"But, Mom," Curt protested, "what's the harm in one lousy summer? I'm sick of Ned carrying so much of the load around here, and if he'd put in a good word for me, I'd be sure to get on. Then next year he could ease off a little because I'd handle the tuition almost by myself. Besides," he added, pausing to flex his right arm, "I could build some muscle."

Ned shifted on the couch. "The answer is no," he said quietly, but firmly. "End of discussion."

"I should hope so," Mrs. Tucker added. "As if it's not enough that Ned goes out there every day. After what happened to your father, I'm a nervous wreck with one of my boys climbing around on that iron. Two of you would put me in my grave. On top of that I feel so helpless with this stupid back of mine."

"Hey." Ned gave her a scolding glance. "I don't want to hear any of that talk. You deserve a rest, after all the years of hard work you've put in."

"And I want to help give it to her," Curt complained.

"Next year," Ned promised him, "when you're a bigshot manager for some major company. Your day will come. Don't rush it."

Curt sat hunched over, staring at the carpet. "Damn," he mumbled.

"Sorry about that." Ned pushed himself up from the couch. "Well, if you two will excuse me, I have some grocery shopping to do at my favorite all-night supermarket and then I'm going to turn in."

"Yes," his mother said, patting his cheek as he leaned over to kiss her goodbye. "You get your rest. And be careful, you hear?"

"I always am, Mom."

"Hey, I'll walk you to the car," Curt said, standing.

"Okay." Ned feared that meant Curt wasn't through with his plea and he was right. The moment they were out the door Curt began again, this time saying they wouldn't have to tell their mother about it.

Ned leaned against the chipped fender of his Pontiac. "I won't do it, Curt. Especially not this summer, on this particular job for Johnson."

"Why not?"

"Because it's a bad job."

"You mean dangerous?"

"It could be," Ned replied, not wanting to worry his brother unnecessarily, yet hoping to end the question of Curt's working in construction with him. "I've got nine years of experience to help me around the rough spots, but a rookie like you . . ."

"I thought Johnson was a good boss?"

"He used to be, but he's turned most everything over to his son, who's letting all kinds of little things go. The chokers are frail, and he won't replace them. He keeps promising to put up safety railings as we go up, but somehow they're always late."

"Ned, you're not going to get hurt, are you?" Fear laced Curt's question.

"Absolutely not." Ned put a hand on his brother's shoulder. "I'm very careful. You know that."

"I know, but . . . so was Dad."

"Yeah, well, he was getting a little old for ironwork, Curt. His reactions weren't—hell, who knows exactly what happened? But his accident made a believer of me and I'm like an old lady up there."

Curt chuckled. "Sure, I bet."

"I *am*," Ned insisted, shaking Curt by the shoulder.

"Okay, but damn, I'd like to be working with you this summer."

"Nope. I'd be so busy checking up on you all the time that I really might get careless for myself."

"I wouldn't want that," Curt said with a sigh. "Well, guess I'd better let you go home and get your beauty rest."

"Yeah, and Curt, don't mention what I've said to Mom, will you?"

"I won't, but . . . shouldn't somebody report this guy or something?"

"Maybe, but the violations aren't real flagrant yet and I treasure my job." Ned clapped Curt on the shoulder and opened the car door. "Don't worry about it. A few more months and the job will be over, anyway. This is our family's crucial year. Once we get through this one, it's clear sailing for the Tuckers."

"You bet," Curt said as Ned got behind the wheel. "And by the way, I wish you some clear sailing with this new interest of yours."

Ned thought about Emily and grinned. "Thanks."

CHAPTER THREE

THE NEXT TWO EVENINGS at the bar, Ned was friendly to Emily but didn't mention taking her out. She began to wonder if he'd changed his mind, but on Thursday he asked her for the following night, Friday, because neither of them would have to get up early the next morning. Until the word came out of her mouth, Emily hadn't known if she'd say yes or no to his invitation. She said yes.

On Friday afternoon before leaving for work, Emily assembled a change of clothes to wear on her date with Ned. She wanted him to know Bailey's required outfit wasn't her style. After hanging a jungle-print blouse and khaki skirt in her monogrammed garment bag, she realized that she couldn't carry something that elegant into the bar. Instead she found a plastic bag from the cleaners and hung the skirt and blouse inside it. Then she worried that both items of clothing had expensive labels, and she took the bag off again and cut out the labels.

Emily wasn't used to this kind of deception, and she didn't like it. She comforted herself by thinking of people who had disguised themselves as blacks in order to investigate black culture. If the ironworkers knew that Emily had money and a teaching position instead of believing that she was a poor girl working her way through college, they would definitely "clam up," as her father had said.

Therefore, her Corvette, a graduation present from her parents, stayed in its parking space at her apartment complex and she drove an old Chevy station wagon she'd bought for eight hundred dollars. Emily hoped the rattling gas hog made it through the summer, or at least long enough for her to collect the information she needed.

The gas guzzler's air conditioner was broken, and each trip into town was a hot twenty miles. As she drove she considered what this date, "for coffee, no big deal," would be like. She had several romantic notions about going out with an ironworker, but she had to admit that they probably were pure fantasy.

In reality, she and Ned might have little to say to each other and after a few feeble attempts to bridge the gaps between them, they'd end the evening and both chalk it up to experience. Emily would have to acknowledge that her father had been right that she didn't belong in this crowd and she'd settle down to her scholarly paper.

Emily entered the bar through the back service entrance and found Monica in the hall enjoying a cigarette before she started work. Monica noticed Emily's clothes in the plastic bag and raised her penciled eyebrows.

"I, um, have a date with Ned, for coffee, after work tonight. I don't want to go in this." She gestured toward her shorts-and-blouse uniform.

"Ned Tucker? You mean Bookworm?"

Emily nodded.

"Well, that's nice." Monica punched out her cigarette in the tuna can that served as her ashtray. "I couldn't have picked a better one if I'd been match-making. Bookworm's the top of the line, honey."

"What do you mean?" Emily was eager for more in-formation about Ned. "Have you know him very long?"

"About three months, ever since I started working here, but I heard about him before from Jake. Of course Jake tried to find something wrong with Bookworm, because he was jealous of how good Bookworm was on the iron. Jake used to complain that the guy was *too* good and made everyone else look lazy, but I say there's no such thing as too good."

Emily hung her clothes on a nail outside the women's rest room. "Who's Jake, your boyfriend?"

"Husband." Monica looked away.

For the first time Emily noticed the narrow gold band on Monica's left hand. "Is he working this construction job?"

"Not anymore."

"Oh." Emily sensed that Jake's employment, or lack of it, might be a delicate subject and switched topics. "I should be able to carry my share of the load from now on, Monica. I've almost gotten the hang of taking or-ders."

"Sure," Monica said with a smile. "You're smart and I knew you'd catch on quick. It was logical for those guys to give you a rough time at first. I almost told you to pretend you were married, but considering this busi-ness with Bookworm, I'm glad I didn't."

"It's just for coffee," Emily said, echoing Ned's words. "No big deal."

Monica glanced at her. "You think not, huh? From what I hear, Bookworm doesn't date much. He's put-ting his kid brother through college and supporting his mother, so he doesn't have much spare cash. Bookworm asking you out for coffee is like some other guy springing for a steak dinner."

"Do you think I should offer to pay my share?"

Monica stared at her in amazement before starting to laugh.

"What's so funny?"

"Honey, when an ironworker asks you out, you'd better not offer to pay for so much as a stick of gum. They are a proud bunch." She paused. "Sometimes stupidly proud," she added, almost to herself. Then she glanced at her watch. "We'd better get out there before Bailey climbs on our case again. And don't worry about handling your share. You're doing just fine, and I enjoy having another woman around to talk to once in a while."

"Thanks. You've been a big help to me, Monica."

"My pleasure." She smiled and led the way into the kitchen.

Emily thought how pretty Monica was, considering she hadn't had the advantage of braces for her teeth or the attentions of a professional salon to make her choice of red hair look more natural.

In four nights of working side by side, Monica had earned Emily's respect for her generosity and diligence. Emily was glad Monica liked having her around, but she was only temporary and would quit at the end of the summer. Chances were Bailey would then dump the whole load back on Monica, who couldn't afford to complain because she had two mouths to feed if her husband was, as Emily guessed, out of work. Emily thought Monica deserved a better deal from life than that.

Emily took her order pad and pencil from the drawer in the kitchen and adjusted the waistband of her shorts.

Going into the bar tonight should have been easier than her first night, yet she felt more nervous than ever because of her date with Ned. From the first day on the street, her reaction to him had never been neutral.

She started out the swinging doors with a smile but quickly composed her expression so as not to look like the Cheshire cat. Calm interest, not gleeful anticipation, was the emotion she wanted to convey. She tried to achieve that look as she approached the booth where Smiley and his friends sat.

Everyone except the pool players always choose the same booths, Emily had realized after the second night, which made the memorization of drink orders easier. Ned, Mando and a few others usually headed for the pool room, where Ned often won enough in side bets to pay for his games and a beer. He might join his friends in the first booth now and then, but he seemed to prefer the challenge of pool to idle conversation.

Emily felt like a seasoned waitress as she took orders from Smiley, Rooster, Mike and Al. She accepted their cheerful banter in stride and moved on to the next booth while thinking the entire time that Ned was in the pool room, possibly watching her between shots. She walked a little straighter and smiled more often than she might otherwise have done as she imagined his gaze on her. But when she turned at last in the direction of the pool room, Ned wasn't there.

Mean Mando was, and Emily wanted in the worst way to ask about Ned, but Mean Mando scared her a little, and she didn't know if the other three men were particular friends of Ned's. She quickly took the orders and hurried over to the bar, where Monica was waiting for Bailey to mix her second tray of drinks. Emily noticed that she still wasn't up to Monica's speed.

"Monica, he's not here!" she whispered urgently.

"You mean Bookworm?"

"Yes. I expected, since we have a date tonight, that he'd be over there playing pool, but he's not. Could something be wrong?"

"I doubt if anything serious has happened or the whole bar would be buzzing with it." Monica picked up her loaded tray. "Did you ask someone? Mean Mando should know where he is."

"That guy scares me, and no, I didn't ask."

Monica chuckled. "I'll ask around and find out where Bookworm disappeared to. I can understand that you wouldn't want to do it yourself, considering your date and all."

"Thanks, Monica." Emily wondered what she would have done if someone less understanding had been the other waitress at Suds and Subs. Silently Emily vowed that when the summer ended she'd find a way to repay Monica for all her kindness.

By the time Emily and Monica were filling orders at the same time again, Monica had information on Emily's date for the night.

"It's perfectly logical," Monica said with a grin. "He went home to clean up. He'll be here later, the guys said. In fact, every ironworker in the place knows about this date tonight, even though Bookworm tried to keep it quiet. Rumor travels fast around here, and when a guy goes home to clean up instead of coming in for his beer after work, everyone figures out the reason."

Emily blushed. "I feel as if I'm back in high school where everyone knew who everyone else was dating on a Friday night."

"High school's about as far as most of these guys ever got," Monica commented. "Bookworm, too, probably, except he always seemed different because of his reading. I imagine if the money had been there, he could have gone to college, too, like his brother."

"Probably. His brother is very—" Emily caught herself before she said "smart" and revealed her true identity to Monica. "Lucky," she finished.

"He sure is. Bookworm would do anything for that kid." Monica glanced at the full tray that Bailey pushed toward her. "Guess I'd better deliver these beers where they belong. Don't fret about Bookworm. He'll be along before the night's over."

"Thank you, Monica, again." Emily wondered how many times she'd end up saying that to Monica during the summer. Yes, the redheaded waitress definitely would get some sort of repayment after this crazy experiment was over.

At about ten o'clock, the front door of the bar opened and Emily knew, even before he stepped inside, that Ned had arrived. A premonition had caused her to glance toward the door seconds before he came through it, and when he appeared, her heart began to hammer and she nearly spilled the pitcher of beer she was carrying.

His gaze swept the room and settled on her. Then he gave her the same grin she remembered from that afternoon on the street. Once again he'd caught her staring at him, no doubt with the soulful look of an adoring puppy. She smiled briefly in return and glanced away. So much for calm interest instead of gleeful anticipation.

Doggone it, but he looked wonderful! She'd thought that he couldn't appear sexier than in his work clothes. She hadn't counted on the effect of his muscles bulging under a white knit polo shirt. His slacks, too, were white. *My white knight,* she thought, and the idea didn't seem entirely silly.

Ned stood out like a searchlight among his grubby pals, who were all making a night of it to honor the end of the week. They saluted him with wolf whistles and razzing as he wound his way over to the pool tables. Emily thought of the extra gas he'd had to squander to drive home and back again, just for this coffee date with her. Monica was probably right, that this effort for Ned was the equivalent of a steak dinner from anyone else.

She waited for what she considered a reasonable amount of time before walking to the pool room to take his order. The trip was unnecessary, because she remembered what he'd ordered each time and she'd learned that the ironworkers were creatures of habit. Still, the idea of bringing him his favorite beer, unasked, seemed too familiar an act.

He was leaning over the pool table to line up a shot when she arrived. He glanced up, smiled his greeting and focused on the cue ball again. Emily stood and watched, her tray propped against her hip, as he cradled the narrow end of the stick in the crevice between his thumb and forefinger. His fingernails, unlike most of the other men's, were clean.

He stroked the cue stick back and forth and determined the exact spot where the felt tip had to strike the white ball for a successful shot. Emily had watched men play pool many times; she'd played herself in her parents' large rec room. Still, she gazed with fascination at Ned's hand poised on the green table cover, the flex of muscles in his forearm, the intensity in his hazel eyes as he brought the stick back and drove the tip against the cue ball.

With a crack the white ball hit the purple one he was after and sent it zipping into the corner pocket. His opponent, Mean Mando, shook his head sadly.

Before lining up his next shot, Ned straightened and his gaze softened as he turned toward Emily. "Could you please bring me a Bud?"

"Right away." His request and her answer were ordinary words, and yet her heart warmed as if they'd exchanged endearments. She spun around and left the pool room, and from behind her she heard someone remind Ned that he had another shot. He must have remained standing there staring after her, she thought with satisfaction. When she returned with his beer, Ned was still playing and from the number of balls left hadn't missed a shot while she'd been gone.

One of the men from the other table wandered over during a break in his game and whistled under his breath. "Too bad the guy can't play pool, Mando. If you want a real challenge sometime, look me up."

Mando's brows drew together in a fierce expression. "Think I should break his arm, Duke? Maybe he needs a handicap, this gringo."

Emily gasped. Who was this terrible man that Ned treated with such friendliness?

The man named Duke glanced at her, apparently hearing her gasp of fear, and turned to grin at Mando. "Whatever you think best, man. I always thought the guy was too big for his britches. You can get another connecting partner, right?"

"Right," Mando growled, watching Ned clear the table. "One who doesn't play pool so good."

Throughout the exchange Ned had pretended absorption in the game, but when he'd sent the eight ball into the side pocket to end the game, he gazed at Mando. "You want to meet me out back, fella?" His lips twitched, and Emily couldn't decide if he was about to laugh or explode in anger.

"Nah." Mando shook his head and his dark eyes glittered. "I'll catch you sometime when you're not lookin', gringo."

"Where you're concerned, Mando, I've got eyes in the back of my head," Ned shot back.

Emily shuddered. If they weren't teasing each other, and she couldn't tell if they were, her father had been right there these men had a roughness she'd find hard to accept. She walked over to Ned with the beer on a tray.

"Thank you," he said softly, placing the money for the beer plus a generous tip on the tray.

"No," she protested, handing back a dollar. "That's too much."

He closed her hand around the bill with gentle pressure and smiled at her. "I have a thing about helping struggling college students."

"But I'm—" Emily stopped before she blurted out the truth, although her conscience pricked her painfully for her deception. She took the extra dollar and thanked him, all the while vowing that she'd find a way to straighten this out between them. If she could trust him to keep her secret, she could tell him part of the truth, about being a college instructor working on a research paper. Spending time alone with him after work would give her a chance to decide whether to divulge that much of her plan. She couldn't, however, reveal that she was also the boss's daughter.

She retreated to the kitchen, afraid if she stayed in Ned's company any longer she'd tell him about her project in front of the other men, which would ruin her entire mission here this summer. Allowing herself to become involved with Ned Tucker wasn't wise; she could see that now. Unfortunately something besides wisdom was directing her behavior regarding Ned. She felt an uncontrollable urge to be with him, and although to-night's date should, by all rights, be canceled, Emily knew that she wouldn't consider it.

The kitchen was deserted, and Emily decided that the cook was taking a break. Emily had discovered that when the sandwich orders were slow the cook retreated to the storeroom and read the evening paper. Emily thought she might join him for a minute and rest her feet, which weren't used to teetering on three-inch heels for several hours at a time.

As she walked into the storeroom she discovered that the cook was there, reading the paper as usual, but he wasn't alone. Sitting across from him at the small card table was Monica, stuffing already prepared submarine sandwiches into her large purse. She glanced up, and a sick feeling washed over Emily. She knew without a doubt that Monica was stealing the sandwiches.

CHAPTER FOUR

MONICA'S GAZE locked with Emily's. Neither of them spoke, but Emily's mind raced. Monica was stealing the sandwiches, she thought, and the cook was allowing it. No doubt the practice had been going on for some time, from the nonchalant way they'd both been acting before Emily walked in.

Slowly the cook lowered his newspaper and studied the two women. Then he hid behind it again.

"So," Monica said at last, "are you going to report me to Bailey?"

"It's not right, Monica, taking this stuff."

Monica's expression changed from apprehension to anger. "If you want to report me, then do it, but spare me the moral lectures, okay?"

Disillusionment left a bitter taste in Emily's mouth. All week she'd pictured this world she'd entered as lacking in polish, but honest and friendly, nonetheless. Tonight she'd witnessed strong words between Ned and his connecting partner, and now she'd discovered Monica, the good-natured woman who'd helped her so much, in the act of stealing food from the management.

Vaguely she remembered Monica's comment that perhaps Emily could "do her a favor sometime." Maybe this was the favor. Not the one she'd have chosen, she thought, but then, who was she to act as judge and jury in a situation she knew nothing about? "No, I won't report you to Bailey," Emily said, "but if you're really short on money for food, I could let you have some."

"Oh? A few days ago you were out of work, and now you have so much extra you can loan me some, even before your first paycheck? Did somebody die or what?"

"No." Emily fumbled for the right words. "I have a little put by... for emergencies, and I hate to see you taking—"

"Look, before you came, Bailey had me working my tail off, all by my lonesome, and he wouldn't give me a raise. Sure, I got more tips, but I spent some of that extra on antacids for a nervous stomach and corn plasters for my feet. I figure Bailey owes me."

"Why didn't you quit, find a better job? You're a good waitress. I'm sure you could get something else right away."

"Oh, I could find something else, but no guarantee it would be any better. Except for Bailey being so tight with the money, this job isn't so bad. It's close to where I live, the customers are nice and in the summer like this my days are free for the kids."

"You have children?" Emily hadn't imagined Monica with kids. She'd seemed too young, too—what? Unmotherlike?

"Yeah, children." Monica looked away, as if to dismiss that topic.

Emily couldn't condone Monica's taking of the food, but she began to understand the reasons behind it. Monica's husband was out of work, and her waitress job was all they had to keep the family afloat. Monica had decided that Bailey should have paid her more, but he had the power to deny her a raise, so she'd given herself one with a few sandwiches here and there.

"Look, I'll just forget I came in here," Emily said. "You don't have to worry about me."

Monica gazed at her, as if trying to decide if Emily would be her friend or foe. "Okay."

"And I'd better get back to work, before Bailey shows up." She left the storeroom and returned to the noisy atmosphere of the bar. Slowly she was beginning to realize how sheltered her life had been until now. She'd imagined the ease of writing a paper about ironworkers and their environment because she "knew" about it. In fact, she knew nothing. Perhaps by watching and listening very carefully, by refusing to judge and trying to understand, she might learn.

Shortly before midnight Emily served her last drink and collected the money before going back to the women's bathroom to change clothes. She should be exhausted, she thought as she closed the door of the small room and untied her blouse. Instead she was churning with excitement.

For the past two hours she'd been aware nearly every minute of Ned's presence. She'd watched him play pool and laugh with his buddies, and had felt an unreasoning pride in his obvious popularity with them. It occurred to her that she'd never had much chance to observe the academic types she'd dated in a male atmosphere of comradery.

Through watching Ned, she discovered that he was neither a braggart nor a bully, although he possessed the accomplishments and the size to be both. She learned to pick his laugh from all the others and found it always good-humored, never malicious as some of the men occasionally were. By the end of the night Emily knew pretty well how Ned reacted with men. How he reacted with women remained to be seen.

Emily buttoned her blouse and reached for her skirt. As she was zipping it, someone tapped at the bathroom door.

"Em?" called Monica. "Can I talk to you before you leave with Ned?"

"Sure. Just a sec." She adjusted the skirt and unlocked the door. "I was changing clothes," she said, glancing into the hallway to see if Bailey was around. The hall was empty except for Monica.

"I figured you were in here," Monica said, twisting her ring and looking at her hands. The two women hadn't spoken except when necessary after the incident with the sandwiches. "I needed to, uh, that is, I wanted to say that I . . . well . . . thanks for not ratting on me to Bailey," she finished in a rush and peeked warily into Emily's face.

"I have no right to." Emily gazed at Monica. The bare bulb in the hall emphasized the shadows under her eyes and exposed the dark roots of her red hair. Emily wondered how she'd ever categorized Monica as perky and fun.

"I know what I'm doing isn't right," Monica said, "but if I don't, the boys will eat junk for supper, candy and stuff. These sandwiches are all fixed, so they can grab one and eat in front of the TV, like they always do."

"But it shouldn't be your responsibility," Emily said, as anger gripped her. "Your husband should—"

"He's not there."

"He works nights, too?"

"No." Monica's gaze shifted away from Emily again. "He left," she said matter-of-factly. "I don't know where he is."

"That's terrible! He can't leave like that, Monica."

Monica laughed bitterly. "Tell him that. He does it all the time."

"But—but why do you stay married to him, then?"

"Because I don't know if I could manage alone. Jake's smarter than I am. He finished high school and he has a trade. Besides, the boys need a father."

Not this kind, Emily wanted to say, but she restrained herself. Only hours ago she'd promised herself not to make judgments and to observe and learn. "How old are your boys?" she asked gently.

"Four, six and seven."

Emily's heart squeezed. Such young boys, and they were left alone each night. "I'll bet you worry about them."

"God, do I worry." Monica massaged her forehead. "Before when he'd leave my sister was in town and could help out, but she moved to Texas. This time I got a big old dog from the Humane Society. Rambo eats a ton but at least he's some protection for the boys, and the locks are good, but those kids could still have some terrible accident, you know?" Her brown eyes gazed fearfully at Emily.

"Yeah," Emily agreed, knowing that she couldn't possibly begin to understand Monica's torment, but wanting to try.

"I call whenever I can, but Bailey has this rule about two personal phone calls a night, so I have to sneak the extra ones and hope he doesn't catch me. Even though he leaves every night when Henry relieves him as bartender you notice he drops in, unexpected, and of course he's always around to close the place up."

"That's true." Emily remembered being startled a few times by the sudden appearance of Bailey, who was undoubtedly hoping to catch his employees at something.

Emily hadn't thought much about the telephone rule, because she had no one she needed to call on a regular basis. "Listen, I have an idea," she said. "I don't use my two phone calls anyway. What if you give me your number, and we alternate calls? Tell your kids who I am, so they won't be afraid to talk to me. I can give you two reports a night, and you can make two calls on your own. Would that help?"

Monica's expression was guarded. "You don't have to do that, Em."

"I'd like to. You've been good to me, Monica, and I'd like to help. Please."

"You're sure it wouldn't be too much trouble?"

"Absolutely sure."

"Then . . . thanks." Monica touched her arm briefly. "Thanks a lot. Now I'd better let you go. Ned is waiting out back."

"I know. He told me he would."

Monica glanced at Emily's outfit. "You look real nice. Are you going to take your hair down?"

"Think I should?" Emily smiled.

"Yeah." Monica smiled back. "I'm glad we talked. I didn't want any hard feelings between us, Em."

"Don't worry. There aren't. And tell your kids about me, okay? We'll start tomorrow night with the phone program."

"They already know about you," Monica said. "I've told them that you're real nice. Maybe sometime—" Monica stopped and fingered the point of her collar.

"What?" Emily prompted.

"Oh, maybe sometime you could come over and meet them, but then again, you might not want—"

"Sure, I would."

"Yeah?"

"Yeah."

"Okay!" Monica backed away down the hall, smiling. "We'll do it, then. Have fun tonight."

"Thanks. I hope I will."

Monica glanced toward the back door. "You will," she pronounced. "I'll tell him you'll be right out."

"Thanks." Emily turned her attention to her wavy image in the cracked mirror over the sink. The shabby condition of the women's bathroom didn't matter much to Bailey, she knew, because Suds and Subs was primarily a men's bar. In the five days she'd been working there she'd only seen a couple of female customers.

She pulled the pins from her hair and ran a comb through it. Then she changed out of her three-inch heels, reapplied lipstick and blusher and turned off the bathroom light. Bundling her work clothes together with the hangers and plastic bag she'd brought that afternoon, she picked up her purse and walked down the hall. "I'm leaving, Bailey," she called, knowing he was still in the kitchen, counting the night's take.

"Yeah," he called back, sounding as if his mouth was full. "See you tomorrow."

So Bailey probably ate up some of the profits, too, Emily thought as she approached the back door. For all she knew, the bar's owners, whoever they were, expected it. Still, she hated seeing her new friend Monica put in a position where stealing was one of her few options. Emily didn't know exactly how she could help, but she decided to look for a way, something more concrete than the twice-nightly telephone calls to Monica's kids.

Ned was leaning against the back wall of the bar when she came out. He pushed himself away from the wall and shoved his hands into his pockets. "There you are," he said, his smile faintly seen in the dim light of the alley.

"I'm parked around the corner. Will your car be okay for a while if we leave it?"

Emily laughed. "If someone stole that junk pile, they'd probably be doing me a favor. Let me stash this stuff in it, though."

"That's the advantage of having old cars." Ned followed her over to the station wagon and waited while she put her work clothes inside. "I keep telling myself that I'm lucky that way, not to have the worry of a new Porshe or a BMW."

"I guess so." Relocking the wagon and walking beside Ned down the alley, Emily thought of her red Corvette sitting at the apartment complex. Ned assumed that she and he were in the same economic situation, and knowing that they weren't made her feel guilty.

"I like your hair that way."

She glanced at him. "I guess I'm trying to avoid looking like a cocktail waitress. Bailey's uniform isn't exactly my style."

"That's what I thought. Well, here we are." He unlocked the door of a car that was part tank, part sexy convertible. She recognized it vaguely as a Pontiac, a very old Pontiac, one that looked from its faded and scratched paint job and worn convertible top as if it had seen action on the battlefield. "This used to be my dad's," Ned explained as he helped her into the roomy interior.

She prepared herself for ripped upholstery or at least terry-cloth covers to hide the damage. In amazement she slid onto crushed velour and rested her feet on cushioned carpet. The inside of the car was as luxurious as the outside was battered.

"This is very nice," she commented after Ned unlocked his door and settled himself behind the wheel. "Obviously you've done some restoration."

"You like it?" He grinned at her. "Me, too. Constant reminders of poverty are depressing, don't you think? When I discovered that Mando's brother had an upholstery shop and needed the work, I needed to have this done. It was that or a paint job, and I spend a heck of a lot more time on the inside of this car than staring at the outside."

"Good point." Emily wondered how long she could keep up this deception. She, after all, had a car that looked good inside and out. She wondered how much difference knowing that would make to a man like Ned.

"Is Coco's okay?"

"Fine."

"So," Ned began as they drove toward the restaurant, "how do you like working at Suds and Subs? You seem to feel more comfortable with it now that you've had a few more nights' experience."

Emily leaned back against the soft upholstery. "Was it so obvious on Monday that I'd never had a waitress job before?"

"Pretty obvious, but so what? Once you get your degree, you probably won't ever have to be a waitress again."

Emily didn't respond, afraid that she'd blurt out the wrong thing.

"You picked kind of a rough crowd to begin with, though," Ned continued. "You looked a little scared that first night."

Emily realized that he'd interpreted her silence as shyness and was trying to draw her out. "I was a little scared," she said, remembering the first moment she'd stepped into the noisy bar in her brief outfit and high heels.

"But you seem to have conquered that." Ned pulled into the parking lot of the restaurant and switched off the ignition. As he opened his car door, Emily reached to open hers. "Hey, I'll get it," he said.

She sat in the car and waited for him to open the door for her. Maybe, she thought, after they knew each other better, she'd discuss the idea that he didn't have to open doors for her. Now wasn't the time.

As they entered the country-kitchen atmosphere of the restaurant, Emily smelled pies baking and decided maybe she'd have a piece with her coffee. Then she thought of Ned's financial situation and wondered if she should stick with coffee. He solved her dilemma by suggesting they both have pie, if she'd like some. It almost seemed as if he could read her mind, and she hoped that he couldn't read all of it.

"The only person who comes into the bar who really scared me, and still does, is Mando," Emily said, picking up the conversation where they'd left off.

Ned chuckled. "I'll be sure to tell him. He'll like that."

"Don't you dare tell him!"

"Okay, if you say so, but it would do the poor guy a world of good to know that his disguise is working."

"His what?"

Ned sipped the coffee the waitress had poured for each of them. "He's trying to live down a reputation for being a soft-hearted slob and not doing a good job of it. Ever since he risked his life to save a kitten, the guys haven't let him rest."

"A kitten?" Emily doctored her coffee with plenty of cream and sugar.

"Yeah, one night this pathetic little orange kitten somehow made its way to the third floor of the job we were working. We found it the next morning crying its head off and hanging on the end of a beam. It wouldn't budge, sort of like ironworkers who freeze with fear and can't move, I guess. So Mando went out and got it. Damn near killed himself, too. That's why they call him Mean Mando, to tease him about it."

"My goodness." Emily shook her head. "I thought Mando was one rough character. I have a lot to learn about ironworkers, I guess."

"If you stick out the summer, you'll learn more than you ever wanted to know. And by the way, Mando has saved more lives than just a kitten's. He's also saved mine."

A thrill of fear shot through Emily. She'd heard stories like this before, from her father and her brother, and she didn't like hearing them. Yet not knowing the details allowed her active imagination to run wild, so she asked, as she always had with her father and brother, "How?"

"I stepped on what I thought was a solid beam, and it turned."

"On this job?" Emily prayed that it hadn't been.

"No. A couple of years ago. Anyway, we were twelve stories up, and if Mando hadn't been there to grab me, you wouldn't be talking to me tonight."

Emily swallowed a mouthful of coffee too fast and coughed.

"You okay?"

She nodded, but kept coughing, and finally Ned reached over and rubbed her back until she stopped.

"Okay now?" he asked, keeping his hand resting lightly against her back.

"Yes," she said, enjoying the comforting pressure of his touch. "Those stories always—any story about people in danger always bothers me," she amended quickly.

"I didn't mean to upset you."

"No, it's okay. I asked for the details."

The waitress arrived with their pie, cherry for Ned and apple for Emily, and each piece topped with a melting scoop of vanilla ice cream.

Ned took his hand away and pulled the napkin out from under his silverware. "Anyway, needless to say I'd do just about anything for Mando."

"And he for you, I'll bet," Emily said, knowing the deep friendships that developed between partners in this business.

"I like to think so. He's a good man. Most of the guys are. Of course, there are always the bad apples."

"Like Jake Spangler," Emily said without thinking.

Ned swallowed the pie he'd been chewing and glanced up in surprise. "You know Jake?"

"Not really," she said, instantly regretting her impulsive remark. "And I shouldn't have said that."

"Maybe not, but you hit the nail on the head. All the guys think Monica's got a bum deal. A few wish she'd leave the jerk and consider them, instead, but Jake is the father of her boys, and she has strong feelings about breaking up the family."

"So I gathered," Emily said. "And I really don't know Jake. I've never met him. Still, Monica seems like a quality person, and I hate to see her struggling the way she is."

"So do I. I've offered to help out with the boys, but she thinks that might look funny, as if she and I had something going. She doesn't want Jake to have any ammunition against her, if you know what I mean."

Emily glanced at him as a thought struck her. "You said some of the guys would like Monica to dump Jake so they could date her. Was that sort of a personal comment?"

He smiled into her eyes. "No. Monica's sweet, but she's not my type."

"You know, I always wonder what men mean when they say that."

He pushed away his empty plate and leaned his forearms on the table. "The same thing women mean when they say it. Don't you have a type of man you like more than others?"

Emily thought about that. "I'm not sure, to tell the truth. You see, my parents have always had strong ideas about what sort of man I should date, and at this point I'm not sure if my choices reflect my tastes or theirs."

"How old are you, Emily Johnson?"

His use of her last name, coupled with her remark about her parents, made her shiver. "Twenty-five."

"Don't you think, then, that it's time you found out for yourself what sort of man you like?"

"Yes, I suppose so." She gazed at him and thought how familiar his question sounded. Subconsciously she'd been asking it herself recently. She suspected that her abrupt shift in life-style this summer had something to do with that question.

"Finished with your pie?" he asked.

"Yes, thanks. It was delicious."

"Good. Are you ready to call it a night, or would you like to take a drive? I'll see if I can get the ancient top down on my car."

"You're not too tired?" She knew from experience that ironworkers rose at dawn, and in the summertime that was very early, indeed.

"I can sleep tomorrow," he said. "Besides, I've always thought that in the desert we should stay up all night and sleep all day, especially during the summer."

"Then let's go for a drive," Emily said, not wanting to leave his company.

In the parking lot Ned unhooked the convertible top and then fiddled with the balky mechanism that collapsed the top into the well behind the back seat. Finally, with much laughing and pushing at the canvas-covered frame, they managed the job and Ned opened the passenger door with a flourish.

"Your chariot awaits," he said, bowing low.

"Thank you." She dropped him a curtsy before getting into the car.

"I don't imagine you've ever worked so hard for a simple drive in the summer air," Ned said as he rested his arm across the seat and looked behind them while he backed out of their parking spot.

"I like challenges," Emily replied, aware of his arm near her shoulders.

"Your hair's going to blow like crazy. I didn't think of that."

"You're right, and despite ads and movies to the contrary, hair blows forward, not back, in a convertible."

"Ah, so this isn't your first ride in one," Ned said, sounding a little disappointed.

"I'm afraid not. Anyway, I still have the big barrette I use to hold my hair up for work." She rummaged through her purse. "This will help," she said, clasping the barrette at her nape. "All set," she said, turning to him with a smile.

"Then let's go."

They rolled down all the windows, and Emily rested her bare arm against the cool metal of the car door and leaned back. The night air, iced down by several hours of darkness, swirled around her, tugging at her hair and billowing her skirt. She tucked it under her knees and saw Ned glance at the motion.

She didn't ask where they were going; perhaps Ned didn't even know. For now they were gliding through the nearly empty streets, past car dealerships, video stores and fast-food restaurants, all closed. The neon reflection from the signs slid along the hood of the car and up the windshield. Against the silky darkness of the night, Emily felt caressed by color.

She couldn't remember the last time she'd driven through the city at one-thirty in the morning. Unlike cities she'd visited on the East and West Coast, Tucson didn't bustle with nightlife, even on the weekend. Yet Ned was right, Emily thought. Now was the perfect time to be awake, instead of during the day, when temperatures topped one hundred degrees by the first week in June.

They were heading, she realized, in the general direction of her apartment, but of course Ned couldn't know that. He was probably aiming for Skyline Drive, which stretched across the foothills and presented a breathtaking view of the city lights.

As the Pontiac picked up speed the wind rushed past them, discouraging Emily from making conversation. She didn't really want to talk, anyway. Riding through the darkness with the stars overhead and this interesting man beside her was stimulation enough to give her tingling pleasure.

They reached Skyline and sailed east. Emily was familiar with this view of the city at night; it glistened from the huge picture window of her parents' home not far away. Still, the carpet of lights held a magic quality tonight. For a brief moment she wished that she could be exactly the person Ned thought she was—a struggling college student forced to wait tables to pay her tuition.

Ned slowed the car and found a shallow turnoff beside the road. After growing up in Tucson, Emily was familiar with this maneuver. Every high-school girl knew what happened next. She tensed, expecting Ned to casually drape his arm across her shoulders.

Instead he leaned back against the car door and smiled at her. "I know this isn't original, but the view's pretty," he said.

Emily laughed. "Yes, on both counts."

"Where are you from? I never thought to ask."

"Tucson."

"No kidding?" He paused, as if to piece this new bit of information in with his other knowledge about her. "Went to high school here and everything?"

"Yes. Amphitheater." Emily was glad that the school she named wouldn't reveal her parents' wealth. Amphitheater drew from a wide area that included foothills kids, as she had been, and children from more modest homes in the valley. "How about you?"

"Palo Verde," he answered absently before returning the conversation immediately to her. "Do your parents, the ones who want to pick out your guy for you, still live here?"

"Yes." Emily knew that eventually she'd have to tell him a few of the true facts about herself, but she longed to postpone the moment. "Speaking of that, you never answered my question when I asked you why Monica wasn't your type."

He studied her for a while. "Stupid as this sounds coming from an ironworker, I like educated women," he said. "I think Monica's intelligent, but she's not using her brain. Or rather, Jake won't let her, and she listens to Jake. And really, that's the main reason Monica's not my type. She thinks she can't talk back to her husband."

"She has three kids," Emily said. "That kind of responsibility can curb a woman's tongue."

"Maybe, but she doesn't even think she has the right to cross him, you know? She doesn't think enough of herself to do it, kids or no kids."

"I guess that's true, but neither of us knows the real circumstances."

"Let's put it this way." Ned leaned forward. "Would you put up with someone like Jake?"

"Not for one minute."

"That's what I thought." He smiled again. "In case you haven't gotten the message, Emily Johnson, my type is a lot like you."

CHAPTER FIVE

NED'S WELCOMING EXPRESSION urged Emily toward him as if pulled by an invisible velvet rope. He hadn't tried to dazzle her, as men often had, with abstract ideas and philosophies. Instead he'd revealed his ability to care about others, a trait she found far more seductive than cleverness. She wanted him to care about her, too.

He met her halfway, and only their lips touched. His kiss was soft, gentle, fleeting. Slowly she opened her eyes to find him watching her, his expression bemused.

"What is it?" she murmured.

"You're so perfect you scare me," he said softly. "You're my dream come true, and I can't figure out what you're doing working in that bar. It doesn't fit."

Her heart lurched. He sensed the secrets that she'd withheld from him, and a man like Ned deserved at least some of the truth. "All right," she said, resting her head against the seat and closing her eyes. "I'll tell you why I'm working at Suds and Subs, but if you repeat this, my project will be ruined."

"Project?" He sounded puzzled.

Emily knew their conversation would destroy the mood between them, but she hoped that it wouldn't end the possibility of a friendship. She took a deep breath. "I'm not a student at the University of Arizona. I'm a first-year instructor in sociology." She waited while Ned absorbed that information and made the obvious conclusion that her "project" in sociology involved the bar.

"You're studying us, aren't you?" he asked in a neutral tone.

"Yes. In fact, your brother Curt inadvertently gave me the idea."

Ned sat up straighter. "You know Curt?"

"He was one of my students this year. We became friends."

"God, now that you mention it, I vaguely remember he mentioned a teacher named Johnson, but of course I thought that Johnson—"

"Was a man," Emily finished with a sigh.

"Right."

"Well, I'm not."

"Nope."

Emily glanced at him and noticed his faint smile. "I hope you're not angry, Ned, but if I announced to the ironworkers that I wanted to study their social structure at the watering hole, I'd be thrown out on my ear."

His smile faded. *"Their social structure at the watering hole,"* he repeated. "Sure sounds like you're researching a bunch of animals."

"No," she protested, touching his shoulder. "Sociologists study people because they respect them, not because they feel superior. I'm interested in the structure that these men create in the process of making an obvious one of steel. Sometimes your lives are literally in each others' hands, right?"

"Yes." He continued to eye her suspiciously.

"The work must build a lot of tension, which most of the men find ways to release in the comradery of the bar."

"I suppose. Does Curt know about this?" Ned asked, not commenting on her assessment of the bar environment.

"No." She removed her hand from his shoulder and clasped both hands in her lap.

"That's a relief. I was beginning to wonder if my own little brother had set me up."

"Set you up?"

"Sure." Ned shifted in the seat and draped his arm over the steering wheel. "Apparently he talked to you about me, which gave you the idea to study ironworkers. Or are you paying special attention to me, the weirdo who reads classics on his lunch hour?" he asked, glancing in her direction.

"I'll admit I was curious about you, but the study is about everyone, Ned."

He looked away again. "Curt and his big mouth."

"Please don't be so hard on him." Emily thought of the enthusiastic way Curt had talked about his big brother. "He idolizes you. He thinks you're smarter then he is and probably should be the one going to college instead."

"That's hogwash. I hated school."

"Hated it?" Emily was aghast. "Then why all the reading? Why the love of books?"

"Mrs. Pembroke, when I was a sophomore. She was the kind of English teacher who comes along once in a blue moon. She made reading an adventure, not a grind. We could bring any kind of books to class, even comics."

"Did you read comics?"

"No." He grinned. "I looked for the sexiest novels I could find, to test her, but she never batted an eye. Eventually, after she got me hooked on the fun of reading, she nudged me toward literature, some of which is sexy, too, I discovered.''

"I'll just bet you did."

"Anyway, since then I've been devouring all the poetry, fiction, and even essays, I could get my hands on. My English grades improved, but I never liked being told what to read, or being cooped up inside some classroom. Curt's different. He's the scholar, not me. I didn't realize he was also the town crier."

"Maybe I shouldn't have told you," Emily said.

He glanced at her. "That wouldn't have been very nice. No telling what sort of fool I might have made of myself, thinking that you were a poor college girl, thinking that you were interested in me, other than as a subject to study, that is."

"I am interested in you," she protested. "All that I told you about my parents, and the men they've pushed me toward, was true. I've enjoyed this evening with you more than any I've spent with a man in a long time."

"I'm glad you've had fun, but it's getting late." Ned reached for the ignition. "We'd better go."

She put her hand over his. "Don't do this."

Slowly he turned and gazed into her face, which was only inches from his. "What do you want me to do, Emily?"

She smelled the tang of his after-shave, felt the warmth of his breath. "Be my friend."

"So I'll be your friend. Is that all?"

"No." She took his face in her hands. "No, it isn't." She enjoyed the solid strength of his jaw under her fingers as she brought her lips against his. She began the kiss, moving her lips persuasively until she felt his mouth soften and heard his surrendering sigh.

Ned finished it, wrapping his arms around her and raising the stakes with a teasing flick of his tongue. In answer she drew his questing tongue inside. Then her world began to spin in ever faster circles as he laid claim to her mouth with heart-shattering thoroughness. Passion fizzed within her, intoxicating her more completely than a million bubbles of champagne.

At last he let her go. "Is this what you wanted?" he asked, breathing hard. "To find out how an ironworker kisses a woman?"

She touched her tongue to her throbbing lips. "Not an ironworker," she managed to say. "You. Can't we just be two people, Emily and Ned?"

"I don't think so."

"Why not?"

"Because I'm not just an ironworker," he said, struggling to breathe normally. "I'm a broke ironworker. I have no business dating anyone seriously, but you were so..." He shook his head. "Anyway, I thought you were in the same boat, broke like me. Hell, I'll bet that old station wagon you drive is part of the disguise."

"You're right," Emily admitted.

"What's your regular car?"

She hesitated. "A Corvette."

He frowned in disbelief. "I didn't realize first-year teachers made such good money."

"The car was—" She stopped herself before she confessed who had bought the car. Ned already knew that her parents lived in town. If he also discovered that they were wealthy, he might begin to suspect whose daughter she was. "The car was an extravagance," she said.

"An extravagance." Ned looked at her. "You know what was an extravagance for me? These seat covers."

"None of that matters."

"Easy for you to say. Do you think I'm going to feel good, driving you around in this old Pontiac, when you have a Vette sitting in the garage? Not this boy."

"Ned, that's stupid! I thought you were the one who didn't care about the outside of things?"

"This is different."

"No, it's not!"

"Emily—" Ned sighed and reached for the ignition again. "You've thrown a lot at me tonight, and you're going to have to let me think about this."

"You're making a fuss about nothing, is what you're doing."

"Maybe." He started the big V-8 engine. "But from where I stand the situation doesn't look good for us. So I'll take you back to your station wagon, and then I'll think about all of this."

"All right," she agreed, not having much choice.

They rode back the way they'd come, in silence, but this time Emily found no magic in it. Perhaps Ned would change his mind about her, and perhaps not. She didn't know him well enough to predict the outcome of his thoughts concerning her. Monica had said that iron-workers were a proud bunch, and Emily was observing some of that pride firsthand. Foolish pride, in her estimation.

At last they reached the alley where her car was parked. He walked her over to it and waited until she'd unlocked the door and slid behind the wheel.

"Thank you for the evening," she said, gazing up at him and wishing he'd smile.

"It was memorable, all right."

"Ned, you won't....tell anybody about me, will you?"

"No."

"Although I guess it doesn't matter if Curt knows. You can . . . ask him about me, if you want to."

"Thank you." He gazed steadily at her. "I'll think about that, too."

She tried a small smile. "I think you'd like me, once you got to know me."

He rested both hands on the open window and leaned down closer to her. The security light behind the bar threw a mantle of light around his shoulders. "That is exactly what I'm afraid of," he said. They gazed into each other's eyes for a long moment before he pushed himself away from the car. She backed out of her parking space and drove down the alley with a lump in her throat.

ON SATURDAY NIGHT a completely different atmosphere pervaded the bar. Because it wasn't a workday, most of the ironworkers were absent, including Ned. Only a few, those who lived near the downtown area, wandered in. Otherwise the faces were unfamiliar to Emily, although Monica seemed to know many of the Saturday-night customers.

More women came, a few without dates. Emily wondered if they might be prostitutes but decided not to ask. Her project centered on ironworkers, not general patrons of the bar. On Saturday nights she'd discard the role of sociologist and simply be a barmaid.

A barmaid and a friend to Monica, she reminded herself. On Saturday they traded off telephone calls to Monica's boys. Before her first call of the night, Emily memorized their names. The oldest was J.J., short for Jake Junior, and the middle boy was Louis. The four-year-old, the one who gave the two older ones fits according to Monica, was Freddy.

On her first call, Emily got Louis. She knew because he answered the telephone with a formal, "Spanglers' residence, Louis speaking." Emily imagined Monica drilling them on telephone manners and was touched by the little boy's earnest effort to do it right.

"Hi, Louis," she said. "I'm Emily, the lady who works with your mom. I think she told you I'd be calling tonight to find out if everything's okay there."

"Yes," Louis said, obviously shy.

"And is everything okay?"

"Except for Freddy spilling Kool-Aid on the bed."

"Oh, dear." Emily winced. "What color?"

"Red."

Emily searched her scant knowledge of spills and decided red Kool-Aid was about the worst for staining. Vaguely she remembered something about club soda, or was it white wine? At any rate, she doubted the wisdom of having the boys try to get the stain out. "Did you blot it up with paper towels or something?" she asked.

"We wiped it up the best we could, J.J. and me."

"Well, then, that's about all you can do. Whose bed is it?"

"Ours."

"Yours and J.J.'s, you mean?"

"No, Freddy's, too."

"Oh." Emily began to understand just how tight finances were for Monica, if all the boys slept in one bed. Trying to deal with the spilled Kool-Aid problem also gave Emily a helpless feeling, one that Monica probably had each time she tried to be a mother to the boys over the telephone, Emily thought. "Tell you what," she said, rejecting the possibility of the boys changing the sheets. "Why don't you pull up all the blankets and sleep on top of the bed until your mom gets home?"

"We don't have blankets. It's too hot. We could lie on the floor with our pillows," Louis added helpfully.

"Well, okay. Maybe that's the best idea for now. You can pretend you're camping out."

"Hey, yeah, we could," Louis said with growing enthusiasm. "'Cept we don't have a camp fire."

Emily panicked. "You don't need one!" she said, far too sharply and absorbed the hurt silence on the other end of the line. "I mean, not a real one, Louis. How about a flashlight?"

"We got a flashlight."

"You could put it on the floor and crumple some newspaper over the top of it, maybe the comics. That should work."

"Okay. Don't worry," he said, sounding very adult for his six years. "We wouldn't really start a fire. Mom taught us that."

Emily's shoulders sagged with relief. "Good. Now I have to go back to work. Is there anything else I should tell your mom?"

"Nope."

"Then I'll say goodbye. Your mom will call in about two hours, but you call here if you have any problems, okay?"

"Okay. Bye."

Emily reluctantly hooked the receiver into the pay phone on the wall. If she hated to hang up and break the connection with these kids, she wondered what it was like for Monica night after night. Emily's anger against Jake moved up a notch.

She reported to Monica and learned that the boys slept on a hide-a-bed in the living room. The arrangement worked well because they could fall asleep in front of the television and not have to be transferred to another bed. Monica believed that the sound of the television kept them from feeling alone, and Emily thought she was probably right.

What Emily really wanted was to provide a baby-sitter for the boys, but she had no idea how to pay for something like that without offending Monica. As much as Emily already disliked Jake, she wished that he would come back so the boys wouldn't have to stay alone.

The night dragged for Emily without the prospect of seeing Ned, and she was grateful that she had the next day off. The new job was more exhausting than she cared to admit. Her mother had planned a big family dinner for noon on Sunday, and Emily looked forward to one of her mother's lavish meals and a chance to relax.

At least she hoped to relax. Danny and Gwen would be there with their two children. Emily's relationship with Gwen was uneasy at best, and Emily's niece and nephew showed signs, even at the age of four and six, of being willful and spoiled.

Yet it had been several weeks since the family had gathered around the table, and Emily believed in principle that families should enjoy each other. The fact that hers didn't achieve that ideal hadn't destroyed her belief. Each time her mother planned one of these occasions, Emily approached the opportunity with fresh optimism that this time they'd all get along as well as the Waltons or the Cosbys.

Therefore, on Sunday at eleven in the morning, she was in an expansive mood as she left her apartment. She experienced guilty joy in driving her air-conditioned Corvette again after the baking misery of the station wagon. On the way to her parents' house she counted her blessings, blessings that she'd taken pretty much for granted until this past week.

Her father could have been like Jake, a man who never held a job for long. Had Dan Johnson been that sort of man, his family wouldn't have fared much better than Jake's, because Emily's mother had no particular work skills and would have been forced to work at some minimum-wage job, just like Monica had been. Emily felt a rush of love for her father, whose drive and ambition had resulted in the formation of his own company and a host of advantages for his entire family.

She parked in the circular driveway behind Danny and Gwen's BMW. As she stepped out of the car, she heard shouting and splashing from the patio behind the house. Jeremy and Lynette were already in swimming.

Emily deliberately had left her suit behind, although a dip in the pool appealed to her on this hot summer day. She'd learned, however, that the minute she went in Jeremy and Lynette would follow, and they played rough. Once Jeremy had dislocated her shoulder by jumping on her from the diving board. Because Emily wasn't allowed to discipline them, she found it easier to avoid the swimming pool when they were around.

She walked through the open wrought-iron gates of the front entryway and down the curving path lined with marigolds and asparagus fern. To one side of the heavy carved door a fountain gurgled a welcome. Her parents had spared no expense in building this house that perched on a knoll and commanded a view of the valley on the living-room side and the Santa Catalina Mountains from the patio.

Emily was glad for her parents that they'd achieved so much—the house, the maid, the gardener, the elaborate "cabin" on Mount Lemmon, and the yearly trips to the Bahamas. Her mother and father had worked hard. They deserved to enjoy their money, and they'd certainly been generous with her and Danny, as well.

Yet after this week, Emily couldn't help contrasting the abundance of her parents' life-style with the poverty of Monica's. The amount her mother and father spent on a gala party for their friends would provide a month of baby-sitting for Monica's kids.

The house was empty except for Carmen, the maid, who was setting the table for the midday dinner. After the meal she would clean up, but Emily's mother had retained all the cooking chores for herself. She'd always been an excellent cook and, although her husband had offered to hire someone for that job, too, she'd asked him not to. Emily often thought that her mother needed food preparation in order to feel like a contributing human being now that her children were grown.

"Hi, Carmen," Emily said as she passed the dining room on her way out to the patio. "I guess everyone's outside."

"Yes," Carmen replied in her soft Spanish accent. "I don't understand it. Air conditioning in here and everyone is out there sweating."

"Oh, you know Mom and Dad. They like to watch the grandchildren having a good time."

"Oh, those grandchildren have a good time, all right," Carmen said, raising her eyebrows.

"Yeah, I'll bet." Emily grinned at Carmen, who shared her opinion about the uncontrolled behavior of Jeremy and Lynette. "I'd better get out there. I'm late as it is."

She opened the French doors and stepped onto the shaded portion of the patio, where she found her mother and Gwen sitting on cushioned lawn chairs, each with a gin and tonic in her hand. Both her father and Danny were in the pool with the kids.

"Hi, there," she said, bending down to give each of them a hug. Gwen's return hug was, as usual, perfunctory, but Emily's mother kissed her daughter enthusiastically on the cheek.

"Cute outfit," her mother said with an approving glance at Emily's tan shorts and white halter top. "I wish I still had the figure to wear something like that."

"Oh, Mom, you know you're a sexy grandma, so stop it."

Her mother laughed. "Thanks. Want a drink? The stuff's on the cart."

"Maybe just some tonic and lime."

"Emily's probably had enough of mixing and serving drinks the past week," Gwen said. "What a grind! I can't imagine doing such a thing, scholarly or not."

Emily glanced at her sister-in-law, her blond hair permed at a high-priced salon, her slacks and blouse bought at an expensive boutique, her shoes imported from Italy and her jewelry insured for hundreds of dollars. A stint at Suds and Subs might do Gwen a world of good. "The job isn't so bad," she said, not wanting to admit the agony of hours on three-inch heels or the fatigue of carrying heavy trays all evening.

"I don't see how it could be so good, either," Gwen said, wrinkling her nose. "All those sweaty men. God! I make Danny head straight for the shower the minute he gets in the door, and he doesn't even do any of the heavy labor anymore."

"Oh, I don't know." Emily dropped some ice cubes into a glass with silver tongs. "Being around those men brings back some nice memories, when Dad used to come home from work, and we'd all run to meet him. Remember, Mom?''

"My goodness, yes. I didn't care how smelly he was, as long as he hadn't broken any bones.'' She glanced toward the pool, where the men were playing water volleyball, with each of them holding one of the kids and letting them handle the ball. "I never got used to the danger, and I wish Danny hadn't decided to follow in his father's footsteps. Now I still have to worry.''

"Oh, Danny's careful,'' Gwen said.

Gwen's casual tone made Emily frown. One of the things about Gwen that bothered Emily, she realized, was her sister-in-law's apparent lack of concern for Danny's safety when he risked his life all the time climbing around on multistoried buildings. Of course, Gwen kept herself as separate from the business as possible and had never, as far as Emily knew, visited a construction site. Emily tried to be charitable and imagine that Gwen was denying the risks because they frightened her so much.

Emily dropped a wedge of lime in her glass of tonic and took a chair next to her mother's. "Something smelled mighty good when I walked through the house,'' she said.

"Oh, it's just a little piece of beef I found, and I, you know, added a few spices, a little of this and that. I hope it's good.''

"It'll be good,'' Emily said, glancing with pride at her mother. Her hair was prematurely white and she'd left it that way because her face was still youthful, despite her fifty-one years. She complained about the extra ten pounds she'd put on in the last decade, but Emily thought she looked wonderful, blooming with health.

And she should, Emily thought. Other than her son's safety as an ironworker, she had few worries.

"So how is your job?" her mother asked, patting Emily's bare knee. "Your father hates to even talk about it, so maybe you'd better fill me in before he comes out of the pool."

"It's an education, Mom. I've been racing home each night to document the interaction among the ironworkers. They each seem to have a certain role to play, like one's the clown, and one's the ditzy guy that everyone puts up with, and another's the caretaker, the problem-solver. It's amazing. And of course, there's the leader, the one they all go to for final decisions about things."

"You mean Danny, of course," Gwen said.

"No, Danny doesn't go in the bar," Emily said.

Gwen looked annoyed. "Well, of course I know he doesn't go *in there*, but he's the one in charge of the men, so naturally he would be considered the decision-maker."

Emily strove for patience. Gwen's expression when she said *in there* with such disdain angered Emily. Gwen had no right to pass judgment on a place that created a warm haven for the men who worked for Johnson Construction. "I'm documenting the social structure of the men in the bar only," Emily explained. "So if Danny never goes there, he can't be part of that particular social structure."

Emily's mother frowned. "Danny never has a drink with the men? His father made a practice of doing that every so often when he was the supervisor. He thought it was good for morale."

"Well, times have changed, Mother Johnson," Gwen said.

Emily glanced at her mother and looked away again so that neither of the women could see her smile of amusement. Her mother hated to be called Mother Johnson, and she'd tried in vain to persuade Gwen to call her by her first name of Maria.

"From what Emily says about the bar they don't seem to have changed much," Emily's mother said stiffly.

"Oh, the men still go to the bar for a drink after work, if that's what you mean," Gwen said. "But according to Danny all they want to do is complain about working conditions. Danny says they're all a bunch of wimps."

Emily blinked. First her father had warned her about this with the men, and now Gwen was saying it, but in the week Emily had worked at Suds and Subs, she hadn't noticed the men complaining. Of course she'd been busy and had noticed conversational tones and gestures more than actual words. Body language had given her most of her conclusions so far about how the men viewed each other.

Beginning Monday she hoped to be proficient enough to keep a notebook while she was on the job. Maybe she'd also catch more word-for-word conversations then and find out if what her father and Gwen said was true.

"Well, I don't know the business like I used to, of course," Emily's mother conceded, "but I always thought Dan was doing the right thing by staying friendly with his men."

"All they care about these days is getting paid on time," Gwen said, swallowing the last of her drink and getting up to fix another.

"Mom, do you need a refill?" Emily asked when she realized Gwen wasn't going to offer.

"No, thanks. I'm fine."

Gwen finished putting together her gin and tonic and strolled toward the edge of the pool to say something to Danny.

When she was safely out of earshot, Emily's mother turned and gazed assessingly at her daughter. "So who is this leader person in the bar, now that we've established that he's not your brother?"

Emily flushed. Her mother had caught something in the way she'd described Ned, even though she hadn't named him. "They call him Bookworm," she said, "because he reads all the time."

"Hmm." Her mother sipped her drink and continued to scrutinize Emily. "You know the main thing your father was worried about with this project is that you'd take a shine to some ironworker. I told him that was silly, that you'd find nothing in common with any of those men after all the education you've had."

"That's probably true, Mom."

"Your father's an exception, you know, Emily. Most ironworkers don't end up living like this." She gestured around the patio.

"I know."

"Not to mention the problems that could come up if you're smarter than the man you marry."

"Mom, smart and educated aren't the same things. There are people in that bar who are very smart, but they just haven't had lots of formal education."

"Emily, you worry me with that talk. I saw your face when you talked about this leader, this Bookworm person. Your father would never forgive you if you settled for an ironworker. You know that."

"Mmm," Emily mumbled.

"Of course, if this is just a fling, something to get out of your system . . ."

"I don't know what it is, Mom." She thought of Ned's remark Friday night that she was old enough to choose for herself. She met her mother's gaze. "But it is, after all, my life."

"Yes," her mother said quietly, "I suppose it is. But your father has such hopes for you, Emily. I hope you won't let him down."

Emily gazed at her mother, unable to promise that she wouldn't do anything to distress her father. By going out with Ned on Friday night, she already had.

CHAPTER SIX

CURT HUNKERED DOWN beside Ned on the roof of their mother's house and glared at the rusty evaporative cooler. "What we need is a new one of those blasted things, or better yet, an air conditioner."

"Next year." Ned wiped sweat from his eyes with the back of his hand before unlatching one of four louvered panels. Then he laid it, damp pad side up, on the roof beside them. "Look at the bright side of this job. You can work on your tan and enjoy the view."

"You mean the mountains, or Suzanne next door lying out in her bikini?"

"Both, my boy, both." Ned grinned at him. "And don't think Suzanne doesn't notice that you're up here, showing off your manly chest and great legs."

"Hah. I don't stand a chance against your muscles. You could do me a favor and wear a shirt next time."

"You shouldn't worry about an old man like me. Why, I'm old enough to be Suzanne's—"

"Next-door neighbor," Curt finished, laughing. "Come off it, Romeo. You've still got them swooning over you. And speaking of that, you haven't said one word about your date Friday night."

Ned still hadn't made up his mind whether to discuss Emily with Curt. "It was just a date," he said, pretending great interest in the tropical-smelling interior of the cooler. "As I thought, we'll have to replace the fan belt," he remarked. "That's what all the racket was about. If you'll take off that side next to you, we can get at it better."

"Okay."

"Just a date, honest," Ned repeated, smiling to take the sting out of his refusal to confide in Curt. He didn't like to shut out his brother, but Emily was a touchy subject with him at the moment. He'd spent far more time thinking about her in the past twenty-four hours than he should have.

Logic warned him to steer clear of a lady college teacher who drove a Corvette and was studying ironworkers like so many bugs in a jar. Then he'd remember the light in her blue eyes, the warmth of her lips, the luxurious abundance of her dark hair, and his priorities would become jumbled again.

After loosening the tension on the fan belt, Ned took the cracked circle of rubber off and tossed it aside. "I sure hope this baby can make it through one more summer," he said, testing the conversational waters to find out if Curt was angry.

"It probably will," Curt said without animosity. Then he handed Ned the new belt. "But I worry about Mom. She doesn't tolerate the heat the way she used to, and once the rain starts in July, this swamp monster doesn't make much difference in the temperature of the house."

"Yeah." Ned shook his head. "Damn. Maybe I ought to buy her a window air conditioner for her bedroom, at least."

"I know what that means. You won't have your car painted, after all."

"So what?" Ned worked the belt on. "Who am I trying to impress?"

"You tell me. Here, let me brace that while you tighten the bolt."

Ned worked silently beside his brother. Sweat stung in his eyes and trickled down his chest as he tightened the nut. It would be a long, hot summer in Tucson, as always. He didn't know if Emily could be a refreshing oasis in the middle of it, or a brushfire that would wipe out any hope of respite. At last the belt was tight and he sat back on his haunches and looked at Curt. "As it turns out, my date Friday night was with your sociology instructor, Emily Johnson."

Curt's mouth dropped open.

"My reaction exactly."

"But you said she was the new waitress at Suds and Subs," Curt said in confusion. "Miss Johnson wouldn't have any reason to—"

"Ah, but she does." Ned took a bandanna from the pocket of his cutoffs and mopped his face before handing the red patterned cloth to his brother. "She's got a summer project, a report on the social habits of ironworkers."

Curt stopped wiping his face and stared at Ned. "The hell you say."

"It seems she got the idea from you."

"Now wait a minute, Ned. She did no such thing."

"But you did mention me, right?"

"Sure, I mentioned you!" Curt scowled defensively. "Once in class we were discussing blue-collar workers and white-collar workers, and she and I ended up correcting the upper-class prejudices of a few snobs. Afterward I stayed to tell her why I'd said some of the things I did, and I told her about Dad, and you. I sure never thought that she'd do something like this!"

Ned reached for a panel and shoved it back into place. "Well, it seems she has, and I asked her out, thinking that she was a student, which is what she wants everybody at the bar to think, of course. During our date, she finally confessed what she's up to."

"Are you saying that she went out with you because of the project?"

Ned sighed. "I hope to God not. She says no. She says the project is just about how the ironworkers interact at the bar, the social patterns they establish there. Her relationship with me is separate."

"Humph." Curt pushed his panel back on with a clang and turned the clamps holding it in place. "On the other hand, maybe she means it. How do I know?"

"I was sort of hoping you might. After all, you've been around her longer than I have."

"She's a good teacher, I'll give her that. She made sociology come alive for me last semester." He glanced at Ned. "I know that sociologists study human behavior, but somehow I always imagined them studying other people, not someone I knew. It seems weird."

"No kidding. And you're not even the one under the microscope," Ned commented.

"Listen, if I'd known what she'd do with the information, I never would have told her about you."

"I know." Ned put his hands on his thighs and pushed himself upright.

"What now?" Curt asked, standing to face him. "I suppose that ends any ideas you had of dating her, huh?"

"If I had any sense, it would. Did you know she drives a Vette?"

"Yeah, I've seen it. Late model. Red."

Ned winced. "There goes my hope that it was some old clunker that she bought for peanuts."

"You know, this might not be all bad." Curt handed back Ned's bandanna and crossed his arms over his bare chest. "I don't blame you for not liking this study she's doing, but forgetting the study for now, what's so wrong with a matchup between you and Miss Johnson?"

"She's out of my league, Curt."

"Hey, don't talk like that. You always liked brainy women, and she qualifies. Not to mention that she's also a fox. So what's a little Corvette gonna hurt? I should do so well myself."

"There's more to it than that. I've gone over everything she said Friday night, and she hinted that her parents have been pushing her toward a certain type of man. I'll bet good money that an ironworker isn't what they had in mind."

"So?"

"So what if she's dating me as some sort of rebellion against them?"

Curt shook his head. "Maybe, but I'd give her more credit than that. If all she wanted was a summer romp, she wouldn't have told you about the study. Instead she risked her project in order to be honest with you. Why did she do that?"

"I don't know. I guess for some crazy reason she trusts me."

"She trusts you, knucklehead, because she realized that you're a quality guy, the kind of person who attracts her, and she doesn't want to start out with a lie between you. That seems like a simple enough explanation, without all this rebellion business you're putting on her. Why not just sit back and enjoy the ride? Literally?"

"In a red Corvette?"

Curt's eyes twinkled. "Why not?"

BY THE TIME Emily arrived at work on Monday she'd decided that no matter what else she accomplished that night, she'd find time to talk with Ned. He might be ready to call a halt to their relationship, but she wasn't.

Something special happened when she was with Ned, something beyond the obvious sensual attraction. She liked herself better, liked the world around her better. Ned was warm and energizing for her and she didn't want to lose him before she'd had a chance to find out if the feeling was mutual.

She'd also decided to take her notebook to work on Monday. The job had become routine enough that she felt able to jot down the conversations of the ironworkers. She and Monica had a special cupboard in the kitchen where they kept their purses, and Emily tucked the notebook under her purse. Monica would probably assume it had something to do with school, Emily thought. In a way, it did.

Over the weekend Emily had been brainstorming about Monica's problems, too, and she was anxious for her new friend to arrive. Emily's suggestion was a simple one, once she thought of it, and everyone could wind up winners, except perhaps Jake. Emily didn't care much about Jake.

Monica walked into the kitchen with a warm smile for Emily. "The boys are driving me crazy, wondering what you look like and all. Any chance you could drop by Sunday afternoon?"

"I'd love to," Emily said.

Monica's smile grew wider. "Great. Well, it's quittin' time, as Bailey will soon remind us if we don't get out there."

"I know. Can you take just a minute first, though? I have this idea."

"Oh? What's that?" Monica picked up her order pad and stuck a pencil behind her ear.

"I know how worried you are about the boys staying alone, and I thought if you advertised for another woman to live with you, someone who worked during the day and was tight on finances, like you are . . ." Emily's voice trailed off as Monica shook her head.

"If I had another woman living there, what would happen when Jake came back?" Monica asked.

"I don't know. Something could be worked out, maybe." Emily also didn't think Monica should put her children in danger because Jake might show up again someday, but she was reluctant to risk being so blunt.

"Like what?"

"Well, if you're worried about having to kick the woman out on short notice, I'd let her stay with me until she found another place," Emily heard herself say. She hoped she wouldn't regret the impulsive suggestion.

"Oh, I couldn't ask that of you," Monica said.

"Sure you could. I have the space." Emily realized that her involvement in Monica's problems could eventually blow her cover with Monica, too. Keeping her disguise in place was becoming more difficult every day, but she couldn't ignore the welfare of those kids.

"I still don't think it would work," Monica said. "If Jake came home and found some woman living there, no telling what he'd do, but he wouldn't like it."

To hell with Jake, Emily wanted to say, but she didn't. "Think about it, anyway, will you?" she asked, hoping that Monica's good sense would prevail over her loyalty to Jake.

"Okay, I'll think about it," Monica promised. "And Em, thanks for even caring about those boys." She gave Emily a hug. "Now we'd better hustle before Bailey catches us talking again."

"Right." Emily followed Monica out of the kitchen just as the first wave of ironworkers came through the front door of the bar. She hurried to clean the glasses and plates from a booth recently vacated by a couple of old men who stopped in the bar each day for lunch, according to Bailey. They never stayed past three-thirty, as if sensing that by four the bar belonged to the ironworkers.

As she wiped the table clean and picked up the tray of dishes, Ned walked in with Mando. Mando was intently describing the incredible pool shot he'd made over the weekend at another bar. It was the kind of shot he could never make when Ned was playing against him, he complained.

"I tell you, man, I was better than Minnesota Fats on Saturday night," Mando bragged. "If you'da been there, I woulda whipped your butt."

"Lucky for me I wasn't," Ned replied, and glanced in Emily's direction.

She held her breath and couldn't move. The next few seconds counted for so much. If he turned away without acknowledging her gaze, she'd know that he'd decided to reject the relationship. She could still try to talk him out of it, but she doubted that he'd listen.

"You're the luckiest SOB I've ever known," Mando continued, heading for the pool tables.

"I must be," Ned answered, and winked at Emily before following Mando for their nightly battle.

She let out her breath and smiled. She wanted to do more than smile. She wanted to shout and spin around the room, but the booths were filling up with ironworkers, and she had a job to do.

"Hey, Emily!" called Rooster in a loud voice as he swaggered into the bar in his usual fashion. "How was your weekend, babe?"

"Wonderful!" she called back, loud enough for Ned to hear.

"Couldn't have been," Rooster said, sliding into the booth where he always sat. "You weren't out with me."

"Rooster, I'm gonna tell your girlfriend on you," Smiley said as he waited for Al to move into the booth and then with a sigh dropped his thick body onto the plastic cushion.

Emily laughed and took the dishes to the kitchen. By the time she returned Mike was there, finishing off the foursome. The men always sat in the same order in the semicircular booth, with Mike on the left, then Smiley, then Al, and Rooster on the far right. Whenever Mando and Ned came over, they made room or someone pulled up a couple of chairs, but that was the only variation to the pattern.

"Did you all know each other before you worked together on this job?" she asked, much braver about questioning them than she'd been a week ago.

"I knew this mug on the last job." Smiley jerked a thumb toward Al. "Much to my dismay, he showed up again on this one."

Emily chuckled. One of the ways the men showed affection was by insulting each other. She mentally noted the exchange so that she could jot it down later in the kitchen. In her paper the identities of the men would be disguised, as well as the bar and even the city. She had no wish to invade anyone's privacy.

"I worked with you before, Smiley," Rooster said. "It's been a few years, though. I moved back East for a while, but my first jobs were in Tucson."

Smiley studied the redheaded man. "Is that so? Now that you mention it, I remember some pimply-faced punk who wasn't worth a bucket of bolts. Was that you?"

"Seems to me I remember a gray-haired old guy who was jealous of me 'cause I could do the job twice as fast as he could," Rooster shot back.

"Yeah, but could you do it *right*?" Smiley asked with a jaunty grin.

Emily listened carefully. By now she realized that beneath this bantering lay a deep affection or these men wouldn't be sitting here together night after night. "Will you gentlemen have the usual?" she asked, as she did every time. Calling them "gentlemen" had become a joke they all enjoyed.

Mike cleared his throat and adjusted an imaginary tie around his thin neck. "I considered champagne," he said in his imitation of a wealthy businessman, "but I wouldn't want to show you gentlemen up, so—" he was greeted with a round of boos, and over the chorus he finished his sentence "—so I'll have my customary rye whiskey, straight up, so's not to stand out from the crowd."

Eventually the ritual was completed and Emily moved to the next booth, where a similar scene took place. She hadn't become quite as attached to the men in the second booth, however; they hadn't been her first customers and they weren't as close to Ned. At last she approached the four men playing pool.

She took Mando's order first with a new sense of understanding about the rough-looking man. Here was a person who had risked his life to save a kitten, not to mention the time he'd kept Ned from plunging twelve stories to his death. Next Emily took orders from Bill and Tony, the others who habitually played pool. Deliberately she left Ned for last.

"A Bud?" she asked, her heart racing as she looked into his face and remembered the pressure of his lips on hers.

"Please."

She gazed at him and longed to rub the smudge of dirt from his cheek. "I'll be back in a jiffy." She returned quickly to the bar and handed Bailey the list of drinks. Within ten minutes she'd served the booths and was on her way back to the pool tables, back to Ned. She collected his money last, and with everyone served, decided she had time for a quick conversation. "Could I talk with you for a second?" she asked, angling her head away from the others.

"Sure." He turned back to Mando. "Excuse me for a minute, okay?"

"Is she your good-luck charm?" Mando asked. He almost smiled, but seemed to catch himself just before that happened and returned to his habitual scowl. "We don't allow no good-luck charms," he muttered. "Especially for punks who don't need 'em."

Ned walked with Emily over to the corner of the pool area. "What is it?"

"I don't think we did a very good job of communicating on Friday night," she said, glancing into his hazel eyes.

Amusement flashed there. "I wouldn't say that, not entirely."

Emily flushed. "About my work, I mean, and...other things, like money, and cars... I'm not saying this well, but I'd like to see you again, and try to straighten this mess out."

"Good. So would I."

She felt like hugging him, so she hugged the tray to her chest instead. "That's nice."

"I think so." He paused. "I talked to Curt."

"I'm glad. Curt's a great kid. Good student, too." She felt the warmth of Ned's personality surrounding her again.

Ned kept his voice low. "He claims you're a great teacher."

"That's good to hear." From the corner of her eye Emily noticed Bailey watching her. "The boss is on alert," she said, wishing that Bailey and the rest of the bar would melt away so she and Ned could be alone. "I'd better go."

"I know. And you work until midnight, and I have to be up at four-thirty. How about the lunch hour? Is there a chance you could come into town early tomorrow? I'm off from noon to twelve-thirty."

"You'll miss your reading time," she said, teasing him.

"So I'll be with an educational woman instead of an educational book," he said, grinning at her. "I'll meet you by the fence at noon. I'll even pack an extra sandwich for you."

Emily laughed softly. This would be fun. "Okay."

"If you like bologna, that is."

"Sure. I—" She paused as his expression hardened and his gaze went past her to the door of the bar. Someone had come in, someone who caused the boisterous talk among the men to cease. Emily turned around and found herself staring across the smoky room at her brother, Danny.

CHAPTER SEVEN

DANNY'S GAZE flickered when he saw Emily, but without any other sign of recognition he turned and walked toward the booth where Smiley and his crowd sat. "Whatcha say, guys? How's it going?" he asked, standing in front of the booth with his thumbs hooked in his belt loops.

Emily was glad there wasn't much family resemblance between them. He'd long complained that Emily got the height while he, the male child, had been unfairly cheated of it. His hair was light brown, his eyes a paler blue than hers. Danny's decision to become an ironworker had been prompted, Emily suspected, by his longing to be identified with his father in some way, because physical similarities had been denied him and given to his sister.

"Hi, there, boss," Smiley said, and the others murmured some sort of greeting. Nobody moved. Nobody offered Danny a chair, the way they always did when Ned and Mando came over.

Emily knew in that moment that the men disliked Danny. She wondered if by some wild chance he was here because of the comments her mother had made on Sunday. Maybe her father had agreed that more socializing was needed, and Danny had been told to put in an appearance at the bar this afternoon.

Emily watched Danny try to build a conversational bridge with the men in the booth, but the process wasn't going well. For the first time in her life she saw vulnerability in her older brother, and was touched by it. She'd never noticed that Danny was putting on weight and had a slight roll of flab bulging over the waistband of his jeans, or that his posture had begun to sag. He was the same age as Ned, and yet looked several years older.

Danny's wife was still as trim as ever, Emily thought, remembering how slim and well cared for her sister-in-law had looked on Sunday. But Gwen had a membership at an expensive spa. Danny didn't have time for exercise, except what he got on the job, and now that he didn't do any heavy work, that exercise was limited.

Finally, unable to tolerate the scene taking place, Emily walked over to the booth. "Would you care for a drink, sir?" she asked.

To Danny's credit, he played his part well. "Yeah, I'll have a Miller," he said, displaying no emotion.

With that, Mike apparently decided that some gesture was necessary. "Let me get you a chair, boss," he offered, unfolding himself from the booth.

"Thanks, Mike."

Emily left to get Danny's beer, and by the time she returned, the men had loosened up some and were engaging in small talk with her brother. Emily recognized the difference between this stilted dialogue and what usually took place in the bar, but maybe Danny wouldn't notice, she thought. After all, he hardly ever came in here.

He paid her and left a tip on the tray. She bit back a smile. The whole episode had a farcical quality and she felt a little giddy with the increased awareness of her contrasting double life. Danny, who had always called her the spoiled brat kid sister who always got everything, now had to give her a tip. She wondered if the next time she saw him he'd ask for it back.

Danny drank his beer quickly and didn't order another. Watching him with the men, Emily wished that they liked him better. She wished that Ned's eyes hadn't revealed such bitterness when he'd first caught sight of Danny. Would Ned include her in that kind of look if he knew that she was Danny's sister?

That thought brought her to another. Although her father rarely visited the construction site anymore, Danny was there every day. If she met Ned for lunch tomorrow, Danny would probably see her. If she didn't talk to him first, he might relay to her parents that she'd shared a lunch-bucket meal with one of the ironworkers. That wouldn't be so good. Emily thought about canceling the lunch, but couldn't bring herself to do it. She'd just have to call Danny tonight from work.

Emily's head began to ache as she remembered that she'd promised her two personal phone calls to Monica, to check on the boys. Besides that, if anyone overhead her conversation with Danny, she'd be in deep trouble.

Once this project of hers had seemed so simple. For one summer, she'd become another person in order to research a paper. Yet her two identities refused to stay far enough apart, and the resulting tangle might be impossible to unravel when the time came, when the summer ended.

Finally she decided to set her alarm for five in the morning and call Danny then. Gwen, a late sleeper, would hate it. Danny always tried to dress and leave the house without waking her, and a telephone call would definitely wake her. *To heck with Gwen,* Emily thought.

She'd worked so hard to like her sister-in-law, but Gwen made friendship difficult. From the moment they'd met, the year Emily had started college, Gwen had acted jealous of Emily's educational opportunities and the favoritism Emily's father showed her. After that Gwen had kept Danny busy providing her with luxuries to take away the sting of that jealousy.

After Danny left the bar, the men relaxed and ordered another round. As Emily served them, she heard comments that made her cringe.

"Whatcha suppose Danny-boy was doin' in here?" Rooster asked.

"Slummin'," Mike replied.

"Maybe he thinks bending an elbow with us will make up for those frail chokers and the safety goggles we have to buy ourselves," Al said.

"If he wants us to forget that, why didn't he stand us a round?" Smiley proposed, and was greeted with loud laughter.

"Him?" Rooster snorted. "He's so tight he squeaks. The other day, I thought somethin' was loose on the iron, 'cause I heard this squeaking, but sure enough, it was Danny-boy walkin' by." Rooster's comment was followed by more laughter.

It wasn't good-humored, either, Emily thought. Their merriment had an edge to it that was missing when they joked about one another. And what was this about frail chokers and not supplying goggles? Her father had warned her that the men would whine about small things, but Emily didn't consider safety measures small.

A faint suspicion glimmered in her mind. She pushed it away but it kept returning. She hated to consider the possibility that Danny, unknown to her father, was cutting corners at the cost of safety to make a bigger profit. Emily decided to postpone that thought.

If the right moment came, she'd ask Danny, but she wouldn't bring the matter up on the telephone tomorrow. Or maybe she'd ask Ned. Ironworkers risked enough, even with all precautions in place. The possibility that Danny might be running an unsafe job site made Emily slightly ill, but she reminded herself that she had no real evidence yet.

Before Ned left the bar, he caught Emily's arm as she walked by him to deliver a drink. She felt the individual impression of each finger on her skin. "Tomorrow, then?" he asked softly.

"I'll be there," she said, glancing into his eyes.

He smiled, and Emily knew that tomorrow at noon would be a long time in coming. "Good. See you then," he said. Then he left, and the warmth in the room left with him.

At first when the alarm rang at five in the morning, Emily couldn't remember why she'd set it. Once she did remember, she crawled out of her queen-size bed and stumbled into the bathroom to splash cold water on her face. She wanted to be alert for this call. She knew that Danny had been up for half an hour and had probably consumed at least two cups of coffee by now. Even with her face tingling from the cold water, she'd be at a disadvantage. She sat on the rumpled bed and punched in the numbers slowly while she yawned into the receiver.

The phone rang three times and Emily cringed each time. She willed Danny to pick it up before Gwen did. Finally she heard his curt "Hello" and sighed with relief.

"Danny, it's me, Emily," she said.

"Emily? Anything wrong?"

"Nothing, Danny, nothing. I have to talk to you, that's all."

"At five-fifteen in the morning? The last time you climbed out of the sack this early was the Christmas you were seven. What gives?"

Emily stifled another yawn. "I have a big favor to ask. Where are you?"

"At home. Are you sure you're awake?"

"No, I mean, which *room* are you in? Did I wake Gwen?"

"I don't think so. I'm in the kitchen."

"Good. I don't want her to know that I called, if you can help it. And by the way, thanks for not giving me away yesterday at Suds and Subs."

Danny laughed. "It was tough. I wanted like heck to kid you about that outfit. Let's hope Dad never decides to pay you a visit. He'd go crazy if he saw you running around like that, in a roomful of ironworkers."

"That's what I called about, Danny. I'm meeting one of those guys for lunch today, at the site."

"For lunch? Is that part of your project?"

"No. It's ... private business. The point is, you'll probably see me there, but I don't want Mom and Dad to know about this—not yet, anyway. Not until I have a better idea where it's heading."

"What are you up to, girl?"

"Danny, listen. Ned's a really nice guy, and I want to get to know him."

"Ned? Ned Tucker?"

Emily clutched the phone tighter. "Yes."

"The guy's a troublemaker, Emily. Stay away from him."

"What do you mean, a troublemaker?" An uneasy feeling settled in the pit of her stomach.

"He expects management to roll out the red carpet for the workers. The guys who hang around him have developed a real bad attitude, and Tucker's the reason."

"Is that why you were in the bar yesterday, to smooth things over?"

"Yeah. I had a talk with Dad, and he said to try it. You notice that Tucker wasn't particularly friendly with me while I was there? He's antimanagement, Emily. If he knew who you were, he wouldn't give you the time of day."

Emily swallowed. "I hate to think that."

"You can hate thinking it all you want, but it's true. I have to leave now, sis, but I advise you to forget this lunch date and forget Tucker. He's bad news."

"I promised I'd be there, and I will. If what you say is true, I'll find out soon enough. Just don't mention it to Mom and Dad, okay?"

Danny sighed. "Okay. It's your funeral, but don't say I didn't warn you."

"I won't, and Danny?"

"What?"

"Thanks for the tip yesterday."

He chuckled. "Yeah. Tipping my rich little sister. What a joke. Take care, Emily."

"You, too." Emily hung up the phone and stared at it while she thought about what Danny had said. He considered Ned a troublemaker, antimanagement. Something about the tone Danny had used bothered Emily. Her brother hadn't always sounded so superior, as if he were on a level above the common workers like Ned.

After all, Danny had once worked alongside the other men. The only reason he didn't now was that he was Dan Johnson's kid, and Emily's father had turned most of the operation over to him. He had no justification for placing himself above anyone, as if his efforts had earned him his position. The only man with the right to a superior attitude was her father, and she'd never seen him take it.

Not until the other day at lunch, whispered a voice inside her head. That was what was bothering her, she thought. This morning Danny had talked the same way her father had when he'd warned her about listening to the complaints of the workers. On Sunday Gwen had said the same thing basically.

Emily might have believed their evaluation if she hadn't been working at Suds and Subs for the past week, but she'd become fond of the very men who were supposed to be causing problems, and she didn't see them as malcontents. She especially didn't view Ned that way.

Thoughts of Ned made her snuggle back into bed and relive the moments she'd spent with him. She lingered over the memory of his fiery kiss and the haven of his arms. Instinct told her that Ned was a good man, a man she could trust. She wasn't sure why her brother had misjudged him, but she felt certain that he had.

At least Danny had agreed to keep her secret, she thought later that morning as she hunted for a parking space near the construction site. She'd decided not to park in the alley behind Suds and Subs. No point in advertising her activities to Bailey, she concluded.

Despite the blistering heat she'd worn slacks instead of shorts, a blouse instead of a cool halter top. She realized that she might be foolishly hoping to alter the image she presented every night in the bar by dressing differently away from it, but she felt the need to try.

The noise assaulting her as she walked toward the site made her think of war movies on television. Members of the various building trades—electricians, plumbers and carpenters—swarmed the area like troop divisions, with the ironworkers in the vanguard of the attack. Fifty-pound rattle guns driving bolts into the iron sounded like automatic weapons and lumber cracked against cement floors as sharply as rifle fire. Even the constant growl of engines might have been tanks advancing.

She paused and glanced up at the top girders. It wasn't yet noon, and as part of the raising gang Ned was among the men up there, but she doubted that she'd be able to pinpoint him. Then someone moved to the end of a beam and she recognized the man's shirt.

Shielding her eyes, she stopped in the middle of the sidewalk and ignored the jostling of people around her. Silently she stared upward while her heartbeat pounded in time with the noisy rattle guns. One misstep, one piece of iron not as steady as he thought, and Ned would plummet to his death.

Emily slowly understood the difference between admiration and terror. She could admire strangers who risked their lives on this job. Ned was no longer a stranger, and she was paralyzed with fear for him.

The figure she'd identified as Ned walked away from the edge and disappeared. Released from her trance, Emily hurried down the sidewalk so that he wouldn't arrive at the gate before she did and think that she hadn't kept her promise to be there.

She recognized Smiley and Mike as they came through the gate. They grinned and waved with no show of surprise that she was there. Ned had told them she would be, she realized, and was glad he'd smoothed the way. No one in the bar had a second thought about an alliance between her and Bookworm Tucker. Emily wished their relationship could be that simple.

Ned appeared, confirming by the color of his shirt that he had been the man she'd seen on the top floor. The brown-and-green plaid was the same one he'd worn the first day she'd noticed him. A white hard hat shaded his face and made his grin seem even more brilliant when he spied her.

"I wondered if you'd really be here," he said as he came through the gate carrying a battered black lunch box and a large bottle of Gatorade.

"I'm really here," she said, subdued by her fearful reaction to seeing him on the iron.

"Then let's head for the park and find a shade tree." As they walked, Ned took off his hat and wiped his face with his sleeve. "Good thing you're used to grimy construction workers, or I'd be embarrassed to have lunch with someone as clean and sweet-smelling as you."

Emily glanced at his sweat-soaked hair and dirt-smudged face, and thought that she'd dated men in tuxedos who didn't appeal to her half as much. "Working hard isn't anything to be ashamed of," she said.

"Yeah, but only an idiot would work construction in Tucson in the summer, don't you think?" They reached the city park and Ned gestured to a grassy spot under a California pepper tree that provided a thick umbrella of shade. After they sat down he took off his long-sleeved shirt and folded it on the grass next to him. "If I had any sense, I'd be up north somewhere instead," he said, opening his metal lunch box.

"You have plenty of sense," Emily said, trying not to stare at the abundance of muscle covered only scantily by his green tank top. "You're here because your family needs you to be. You can't disguise your generosity by pretending to be stupid. I know better."

He laughed. "Then if I'm so noble, you must be my reward. Thanks for coming to have lunch with me." He handed her a carefully wrapped sandwich.

"You're welcome." She looked into his hazel eyes as she accepted the sandwich and thought that he had it backward. She was the one who felt rewarded, being here with him.

"Milk or Gatorade? I have both."

"Milk, please. You're a terrific host, Ned."

"Thanks." He poured milk from the thermos and handed it to her. "I figured I'd better be, dragging you down here hours before you have to work. Are you going to stay downtown or go back home after lunch?"

"I'll stay. I can do some research at the main library. I've been meaning to, anyway."

"Hey, that's great. Maybe we could make this a regular event." He took a bite of his sandwich.

She remembered the paralyzing moment on the sidewalk and shook her head. "I don't think so."

"Why not?" He gazed at her with a troubled expression.

"I saw you on top of the building just now. It scares me to death."

He frowned. "I shouldn't have told you about that time with Mando."

"No, I'm glad you did. That story changed my whole concept of him, which was obviously all wrong."

"Yes, but now you're spooked about guys falling off. It doesn't happen all that often, Emily."

"I know, and after being around all of you every night at the bar, I didn't think I'd be so bothered by watching you up there. But knowing what you do each day before you come through the door of Suds and Subs is one thing. Actually seeing you do it is something else.''

He gazed at her steadily and finally smiled. "Maybe I should feel complimented that you're concerned.''

She flushed and looked away. "Maybe.'' Self-consciously she unwrapped the sandwich and took a bite. "It's very good,'' she said, glancing back at him.

"Thanks.'' He unscrewed the top of the Gatorade bottle and lifted the bottle to his lips. His tanned throat rippled as he drank nearly half the contents. When he put the bottle down again, he turned to her. "I'm curious about something.''

"What's that?'' She wished her pulse wouldn't jump every time he indicated curiosity about her. She wished that she didn't have so much to hide.

"On Sunday when I told Curt about you, he pointed out that you took a chance in talking about your study. Why did you tell me? I probably never would have found out. At least not until the study was over and you quit your job at the bar.''

Emily was relieved. This question she could answer. "I didn't like the way we were starting out, with this big deception on my side. It didn't seem fair to you.''

He nodded slowly. "That's what Curt said, but it's nice to hear it from you.''

"I also want to clear up something about that study. It will be completely anonymous. I hope to publish it in a sociology journal when I'm finished, but all the names will be changed and even the town and state won't be mentioned. No one will be able to recognize where I got my material.''

Ned chewed on his sandwich. "That's good,'' he said, swallowing. "I wondered about that. Not that any of the guys would read that kind of journal, but I still didn't like to think of some stuffed shirt professor—'' He paused and grinned at her. ''Sorry.''

''It's okay,'' she said quietly.

''Anyway, I didn't want Mando and Smiley and Rooster being made fun of or anything by some over-educated guy who thinks he's better than they are.''

''That won't happen.''

He nodded again. ''Good. Now, as for us, I keep asking myself why you'd be interested in me. I have very little money and only a high-school education. I work with my hands at a job that you've just admitted frightens you out of your skull. What's the attraction?''

She smiled at the question. Was it possible that he didn't know how rare a man he was, how warm and caring? When she coupled that with the picture he made sprawled on the grass in his tank top and hip-molding jeans, she couldn't believe that he'd wonder at her interest.

''You're different from most of the men I've known,'' she began.

''That's what worries me. You're a social scientist. I don't want to be some sort of experiment. More than I already am as part of your study, that is. In other words, I don't want to be some personal testing ground for you to find out how the other half lives.'' He gave her a piercing look. ''Or loves.''

Emily felt as if someone had trickled warm water all over her. He held her gaze and her throat went dry. She gulped some milk. ''You're not an experiment,'' she managed to say.

''On Friday night you mentioned that your parents kept trying to pick out the type of men they wanted for you. I'm not that type, am I?''

"No, you're not," she said softly. "But this isn't about proving a point to my parents."

His tone grew gentle. "Then what is it about?"

She chose her words carefully. "When I said you were different, I didn't mean different because of money or education. I meant . . . more human, somehow. You're dedicated to helping Curt and your mother. You're liked and respected by the men you work with, and I think it's because they know you care about them, too. You're involved with people, Ned—not with a career, or making money, or proving yourself with women—"

His eyes twinkled. "I'm not sure you know me well enough to make that last assessment."

"I know how you are with me."

"No, you don't. We had half a date. For the other half I was backpedaling like crazy. You don't know how I'd be if I felt sure of myself."

"Maybe I don't." She paused and decided to go for broke. "But I'd like to find out."

CHAPTER EIGHT

"ALL RIGHT," Ned said quietly. "When are you free this weekend?"

Her skin tingled. Just like that. Just like that her world could be changed forever. "I promised Monica I'd come over to her place on Sunday afternoon, and of course I work Saturday night," she said.

"Let's drive up to Kitt Peak Saturday morning and have lunch there." He smiled. "This time you can bring the sandwiches."

"Okay. Fine." Even in the heat of summer, she was trembling with a nervous chill, and she wrapped her arms around her body.

"For now, you'll have to put up with things like picnics, dates that don't cost much."

"I don't care. Money doesn't matter to me, Ned. I told you that."

He rubbed his chin and looked at her thoughtfully. "Your car or mine?"

"I don't think you'd like that station wagon," she said, chuckling. "It really—"

"I meant the Corvette."

"Oh. You...you would consider riding in it?"

He looked at her sideways. "I thought perhaps I'd force myself."

She saw the twitch of his lips that soon became a grin and she began to laugh. "Oh, Ned, this will be all right, believe me. We're just two people. The other stuff doesn't matter."

"Let's hope not because I'm really starting to like you, Emily Johnson."

"I'm glad. Shall I pick you up on Saturday morning, then?"

"I'll have to do a lot of talking to myself between now and then, but sure, you can pick me up in your red Corvette, Madam Instructor." He shook his head. "Whew. I can't believe I'm doing this. Curt would be proud of me."

"I'm proud of you, too."

Ned glanced quickly at his watch. "The pusher isn't going to be very proud of me, though, if I'm not back on the job in five minutes."

"Then you'd better hurry," she said, getting to her feet as he did. "That's one person you don't want to make angry."

"You know who a pusher is?" He looked surprised.

Emily blanched. "Well, I thought—isn't he sort of a foreman?"

"Yeah. Good guess." Ned continued to gaze at her with curiosity.

"Anyway, you'd better go," she said, cursing her loose tongue.

"Right. Look, I'll have to run to make it. Why don't you stay here with the rest of the food, and I'll pick up the lunch box from you after work?"

"Be glad to," she said quickly, relieved that he'd dropped the subject of her ironworking knowledge.

"Goodbye, Emily. Have fun at the library. Read some books for me." Without warning he leaned over and kissed her lightly on the lips. Then, before she could react, he grabbed his yellow hard hat and shirt from the grass and sprinted toward the construction site.

Emily watched him until he was out of sight. She hoped that he wouldn't be late and most of all that Danny wouldn't be the one to catch him. Ned thought that he knew what he was up against, dating a university instructor who owned a red Corvette. He thought that all he had to overcome was her education and her income. He didn't know that she was also the owner's daughter.

Emily sat back down and plucked blades of grass from the green expanse beside her while she thought about Ned. She could tell him everything, of course. Perhaps he'd accept the last bit of information the way he'd finally seemed to accept the news of her research project at the bar.

Yet instinct told her that he wouldn't react well to her final secret. Apparently he didn't like the way Dan Johnson and his son were running this job. If Emily revealed her connection to them, it might create a barrier that Ned would be unwilling to cross.

She chafed at the obstacles in the path of friendship between her and Ned. She hated the veils she had to draw across parts of her life, but total honesty might end their relationship before it began, and she very much wanted it to begin.

Glancing at the half-eaten sandwich in her hand, she imagined Ned at five in the morning spreading mayonnaise on bread and peeling bologna from the package. She pictured him wrapping the sandwiches, pouring the milk into the thermos, remembering napkins and a small bag of potato chips. Even though she wasn't hungry, she finished every bite of the sandwich.

As he ran to the construction site, Ned crammed his hard hat on his head and hoped that people he jostled on the sidewalk would figure out that he was late for work instead of fleeing a bank holdup. Those were the only two logical reasons he could imagine for sprinting through Tucson's midday summer heat.

But oh, being late was worth it, he thought, ducking through the gate in the fence and hopping aboard the self-operated construction elevator. Curt was right; only a fool would let his pride get in the way of spending time with a woman like Emily.

Despite the sweat plastering his tank top to his body, he put on his shirt as the elevator cranked upward. Some of the guys didn't bother, but he'd seen too many lacerated arms and cases of skin cancer. Maybe the men figured those concerns were petty compared with taking a dive several stories to the pavement, but Ned didn't plan for that to happen, either.

He gazed across a skyline etched against a brilliant blue summer sky and thought of her eyes, so startling when set off by her dark lashes and midnight-colored hair. He was entranced with that hair, whether she wore it streaming loose as she had Friday night or pulled back from her delicate face with combs, as she had today.

Of course, her glorious hair was a bonus, and he could do without it if necessary, just like the man whose wife cut hers in "Gift of the Magi," he thought. The elevator came to a halt and he stepped out, then climbed the stairs to the floor where Mando and the others were shaking out a load of iron.

"Well, if it isn't lover boy, come to pay us a visit," Mando said with a grin when Ned arrived and strapped on the tool belt he'd left hanging on a bolt. "Think you could be bothered to pick up the end of that beam?"

Ned pulled on his work gloves. "Has the pusher been looking for me?" he asked, hoisting the beam and helping Mando carry it to a spot designated by a number painted on the iron.

"Nobody's been lookin' for you yet, so I guess you're safe."

Mike called over. "You guys wanna quit jawin' and work faster?"

"Keep your pants on, gringo," Mando called back.

"Why?" Mike asked, "when life's so full of beautiful women?" He wiggled his hips suggestively and everyone within earshot laughed.

Mando turned back to Ned. "While you were fooling around with your waitress lady we got most of this iron shook out," he said, gesturing to the beams laid out along the plank floor. "Mike's gettin' on all of us to work faster and finish this job quick. He don't like it much."

"Neither do I." Ned moved to pick up the end of another beam Mando indicated.

"One of the chokers holding this load here looked real bad," Mando said as they carried the beam. "Mike thought it would break and spit iron everywhere, but it held."

Ned's pleasant mood evaporated as anger tightened the muscles of his jaw. "Did anybody mention that to our Danny-boy?"

"Yeah, Rooster made a special trip down to the construction shack. We all figured the pusher never does nothin' when we tell him, so Rooster went straight to Danny-boy with the complaint. He's not back yet."

Over Mando's shoulder, Ned saw Rooster top the stairs. "He's back now. Hey, Rooster, what happened?" he called.

"What the hell d'ya think?" Rooster made a face. "He asked if the choker held. I told him by only a few strands, and he said that was all that mattered and to get back to work."

"Damn!" Ned exchanged a look with Mando. "Something'll have to be done about that son of a bitch."

"If a load ever gives way, I hope he's the one under it," Rooster said as he walked back to his position on the floor.

"Him or his ugly mama," Mando growled.

Ned stared after Rooster and shook his head. "God, I wish this job was union. Danny-boy isn't worth soiled spit, and he thinks he can get away with anything, since the union's not around to keep him honest."

"Ain't that the truth," Mando agreed.

"I wonder if I should make a written complaint to old man Johnson."

"I don't know, Ned. You're gettin' a reputation, and I know you need this job." Mando winked. "Especially if you're goin' courtin'."

Ned sighed and picked up a wrench. "Yeah. Well, I'll think on it. In the meantime let's put this erector set together, buddy."

Two DAYS LATER, Monica came to work late. As Emily hurried from booth to booth, covering her area and Monica's, she heard Bailey chewing Monica out in the kitchen, but she was too busy to go back and try to defend her. Soon Monica appeared, looking more harried than usual, and reclaimed her regular side of the bar.

Another hour passed before business settled down enough for Monica to take a break in the storeroom.

Making a cursory inspection and deciding her customers were fine for the moment, Emily slipped back to find out what was wrong in Monica's life.

"You were right, Em," she said, nervously puffing on a cigarette as she paced around the storeroom carrying her tuna-can ashtray. "I can't leave those boys alone anymore."

"What happened?" Emily started with fear. Although she hadn't met them except by telephone, she felt attached to Monica's kids.

"Freddy talked the other two into building him a high dive with the kitchen chairs. He was all set to jump from the top into this beanbag chair we have, when I walked into the room. What if I hadn't been there?"

"Good Lord." Emily sat down and rested her elbows on the card table where she'd once found Monica hiding sandwiches in her purse. "Will they be okay tonight, or will they try something like that again?"

"They most certainly won't try anything tonight, if they know what's good for them. I told those kids that if they got into any trouble between now and Sunday, you wouldn't come over to see them."

Emily burst out laughing. "Oh, you did?"

"I certainly did. I said that you wouldn't have any interest in visiting naughty boys." Monica smiled. "Pretty good thinking, huh?"

"Sure is, except I get to be the ogre around here, the one who won't tolerate naughtiness."

"Nah. Think of it like Santa Claus. They do."

"I hope I can live up to this image. Monica, I meant to ask you before, but would it be okay if I brought them each a little present on Sunday?"

Monica looked wary.

"A small something," Emily added.

"As long as you don't spend much," she said. "I didn't invite you over so you could spend money on us."

"I know that, but I don't have any kids of my own, and I love toys. I'd have fun shopping for them."

"Just don't spend much," Monica insisted.

"I won't. So what are you going to do about finding someone to stay with them nights?"

"What you said. The reason I was late is that I made up the notice and tacked it on the bulletin board at the laundromat where I do our clothes. I said 'Single woman who works days needed to share apartment with single mother who works nights. Rent in exchange for watching three small boys.' How's that?"

"Sounds perfect to me," Emily said, pleased that Monica had decided to solve her problem.

"Did you, uh, really mean what you said that time? About being willing to let the woman stay at your place if Jake suddenly shows up?"

"Yes, I really did."

Monica looked relieved. "Then if someone answers my notice, I'll tell them straight out about Jake. Otherwise he could scare them to death, coming in sometime with his own key. I'll tell them that if Jake should come back, I have another place for them to stay until they work something out."

"That's fine." Emily wondered if anyone would accept Monica's offer, considering the strings attached. But lots of people were broke in Tucson, she was discovering, and surely someone could use a free roof over her head in exchange for keeping an eye on Monica's boys. Then, if Jake came back, Emily would simply have a roommate for a little while. But Emily couldn't help thinking that with Monica's new plan, everyone would be far better off if Jake never returned.

"Guess we'd better get to work," Monica said, stubbing out her cigarette and leaving the can on the table. "Sounds like the natives are gettin' restless out there."

"They are kind of noisy tonight," Emily agreed as she followed Monica through the kitchen and out into the bar area. She noticed quite a crowd gathered around Smiley's booth, and the men were talking in loud voices. In the middle of the crowd, she noticed as she drew nearer, was Ned, leaning on his cue stick, listening.

"It's just a matter of time before someone gets hurt," Mike said. "I say we report them to OSHA."

OSHA, Emily thought with dismay. *The Occupational Safety and Health Administration. They were talking about safety on the job. Again.*

"Yeah, and you know what happens to whistle-blowers," Smiley said. "You want to be the one to do it?"

"Well, I would, but I have the wife and kid to think of, and they love living in Tucson," Mike replied. "I can't afford to get blackballed."

"Most of us have families and need regular paychecks," Al said. "Except maybe Mando and Rooster, and of course Bookworm."

Rooster sat up straight. "Don't go askin' me to be no whistle-blower. I took a big enough chance the other day. I've got bills, like all the rest of you guys. I like eatin', too."

Emily heard the comments with growing alarm. The men were talking about her father's company as if it were some evil monster and they needed a knight to ride forth and slay it. For one horrible moment she imagined Ned leaning on his lance instead of the pool cue. *Please,* she prayed, *don't let this turn into a battle between Ned and my father.*

Ned glanced at her, as he usually did when she came into the room. Since their lunch together they'd developed small signals to acknowledge each other: a lift of the eyebrows, a slight wink, an angling of the head. This time, however, he held her gaze as if drawing strength from it. She could see that he was troubled from the tense lines around his mouth.

"You guys can't ask Ned, either," Mando said, and everyone looked at him in surprise, including Emily. She'd never heard any of the men address Ned by his first name, especially not Mando.

"But he knows more about these things than any of us," Rooster said. "He reads a lot, and not just those classics, either."

"I don't care," Mando growled. "He's got a mother who depends on him, and a kid brother in college. Leave him alone."

Ned smiled at Mando. "Thanks, buddy." Then he turned to the others. "Listen, you guys, I know you're hot about the way things have been going. We've seen a few frail chokers. We have to buy our own goggles, and the railings aren't always up when we think they should be. But we've only talked about stuff—we haven't written anything down."

"And when are we supposed to write it down?" Smiley asked. "While we're standing under a load of iron, looking up at a choker about to snap? I don't know about you, but I'm too busy trying to save my ass to jot down notes about it."

Everybody laughed, including Ned. "Okay, good point. Tell me when you can, and I'll write everything I can remember at lunch and after work."

"Hey, we got us a secretary," Al said with a grin. "Tell me, sweetheart, will you sit on my lap while you take that there—what's it called?—dictation?"

"Why, Al, I didn't know you cared," Ned replied, smiling broadly as more laughter roared through the group.

The tension had largely disappeared, Emily noted with relief, but the matter of safety on the job hadn't been forgotten. Gradually the men who had gathered from other parts of the room wandered back to their tables, but each assured Ned before they left that they'd keep him informed about any violations they saw.

Ned had taken their complaints and created a plan for documenting them, Emily realized. The men looked to him for this sort of guidance, as she had suspected they would after she'd observed the hierarchy in the bar for nearly two weeks. He was a sort of hero to the men, although Danny and her father might apply a different term. They'd probably call Ned Tucker a ringleader.

EMILY MADE fried chicken and potato salad for Saturday's picnic with Ned. This wasn't the occasion to dazzle him with gourmet foods, she decided. Getting past the shock of her shiny Corvette would be progress enough for one day.

The buff-colored complex where Ned lived on the east side of town was fairly new but plain, and lacked the tennis courts, weight room, whirlpool and sauna that hers included. It did have a small swimming pool, she noted as she pushed her Ray-Bans to the top of her head and climbed the open stairway to his second-floor apartment. He could offer her a swim sometime without putting out extra money. She wondered how soon she'd be able to invite him to her place without risking the delicate balance of their relationship.

As she walked along the balcony searching for the right apartment number on the second floor, she tried to calm her rapidly beating heart. After all, she'd been on picnics with men before, lots of times. She'd even, she reminded herself, been inside single men's apartments. Nervousness looked silly on a twenty-five-year-old woman who worked every night in a bar full of construction workers.

Nevertheless she was nervous. She walked quickly past double-paned windows, some with curtains drawn, others open. She didn't look into the windows, not wanting to come unexpectedly face-to-face with Ned. From somewhere a stereo thumped out a persistent rhythm. Finally she located the correct brass numerals on one of the doors. Taking a deep breath, she rapped on the brown painted surface.

He opened the door almost immediately, his smile telling her how much he enjoyed seeing her there. "Right on time," he said.

She shrugged. "It's a habit of mine."

"And I'm usually late."

"You look ready to me." *Did he ever,* she thought, not quite prepared for cutoffs and a muscle shirt, although they were the perfect outfit for a picnic on a hot summer day.

"I am, just about." He glanced down at his bare feet. "Come on in while I find some shoes and socks."

"I wore sandals," Emily said, following him into the small living room. "So I hope you weren't planning to hike around up there."

He glanced at her, his gaze sweeping over her bare legs, white shorts and blue halter top. "Nope." Then he turned and walked into the bedroom, where she glimpsed part of an unmade bed. "Be back in a second."

She couldn't have explained to anyone why his single "Nope" had sent a delicious tremor up her spine. Something about the tone, perhaps, or the look in his eyes. With his single-syllable answer and one glance he'd conveyed that he had a definite idea of what they'd do on the mountain, and it wouldn't involve hiking.

She listened to him opening and closing closets and drawers, and smiled. *Typical disorganized bachelor,* she thought. The living room could have belonged to a graduate student instead of a construction worker, considering the number of books, magazines and newspapers scattered around. A cement-block-and-board bookcase similar to hundreds she'd seen in dorm rooms and student apartments lined one wall.

A paperback lay facedown on the coffee table, and Emily wandered over to read the cover, expecting perhaps an adventure novel. Instead she found a collection of Robert Browning's poetry.

"He's a sexy writer," Ned commented from the doorway of his bedroom. He walked toward her, his sunglasses in one hand. "I discovered him last year."

Emily glanced again at the book. Its cover wasn't the least bit dusty. He might have discovered Robert Browning last year, but he'd been rereading him last night. She longed to pick up the book and find out what poem was on the open page. "I like Browning myself," she said instead.

"We could take it if you want," he said, studying her. "I think Browning goes pretty well with picnics."

"Sure, why not?" She picked up the book and glanced at the page. From her brief look she discovered that the poem dealt with lovers sitting on the grass, just as she and Ned had done earlier this week. "Do you want to keep your place?"

"Sure. Just turn down the corner of the page."

She went against her training and did as he asked. She'd never dog-eared a page in her life. Books, even paperbacks, had been presented to her as temples not to be defiled. She even had trouble underlining material in her own research texts, although she'd taught herself to do it.

Ned seemed to view books and their contents without trepidation. Emily wondered if her careful handling of the printed page had prevented her from having the kind of intimacy with it that Ned seemed to possess. She remembered his admonition to "have fun" at the library after their lunch together this past week. He'd said that because he would have had fun. Perhaps she, the woman with two degrees, had something to learn from this "uneducated" ironworker.

"Did you bring a blanket?" he asked.

"There's one in the trunk," she said, and felt silly for blushing. Blankets went with picnics, and just because people took them didn't mean that they ended up in each other's arms. But wasn't that what she was hoping would happen today?

"Then I guess we're ready."

"I guess so."

As he ushered her out the door he put his hand lightly against her bare back. Her intake of breath caused him to give her a quick glance. "Cold hands?" he asked.

"No, I just . . ." She couldn't finish the sentence because she didn't know how it ended. She just what? Felt like one of those lamps that flashed on every time someone touched its base? She decided no explanation was better than any that might tumble uncensored out of her mouth.

"Funny," he said as they walked side by side down the stairs. "I was the one who started out afraid of you, and now I wonder if the tables are turned."

"Maybe," she ventured, "I've never met anyone like you before, I guess. You make your living in a very rough-and-ready job and then come home and read Browning. That makes me feel a little off balance."

"Strange," he said with a grin. "That's how I stay balanced. I have a physically demanding job but it doesn't exactly strain my brain. You know what they say—all an ironworker needs is a size eighteen shirt and a size three hat."

Emily laughed. "I've—" She stopped herself before she made the mistake of admitting that she'd heard that comment from her father. "I'll bet you get tired of dumb ironworker jokes," she said.

"I just let them pass. It doesn't matter. They aren't much different from absentminded professor jokes. Hey, is this your mean red machine?"

"Yep." Emily pulled her Ray-Bans down to shade her eyes.

"Get many tickets in this baby?"

"Not a one."

"I would." Ned surveyed the car appreciatively.

"I'm beginning to believe you," Emily said, unlocking the car. "You dive into life headfirst, don't you?"

"Whenever I can."

"Would you like to drive, then?"

"Yes."

She liked the unequivocal way he answered her question. She was tempted to follow with a couple more. *Would you like to kiss me? Would you like to wrap those brawny arms around me?* Instead she handed him the keys.

"I was kidding about the tickets," he said, opening the passenger door for her. "I wouldn't take chances like that with your car."

"I figured as much. But remember, it's only a car."

He gazed at her for a moment before closing the door and walking around to the driver's side. "Usually the people who say things like that can afford to replace the item they're saying it about," he said as he slid behind the wheel. "I don't want to make a big deal about money differences, but I have the feeling I'm dealing with more than a beginning instructor's salary."

"My... family is very generous with me," she said.

"Ah." He glanced at her. "And now you're repaying that generosity by dating a construction worker instead of a rocket scientist. Are you sure this is such a good idea?"

"Do you think my family's generosity gives them the right to dictate that sort of thing?" she asked, feeling brave.

"Maybe you should tell them what you're up to," he said, gazing at her intently, "and find out if the generosity continues after that."

"Perhaps." Her bravery faded in the face of his challenge. "Although I don't see any point in riling them just yet."

His gaze flickered. "I see."

"I didn't say I wouldn't tell them," she said, fearing that he thought her weak.

"No, that's true."

"When the situation warrants it, I will. After all, it isn't as if we've....I mean, we haven't..."

"Made love?" he suggested softly.

Emily grew limp and fluid as she gazed into the gray-green depths of his eyes. "Not....necessarily."

He simply smiled. "Let's go," he murmured, and put the key into the ignition.

CHAPTER NINE

NED DROVE the car up the winding road to Kitt Peak with care and confidence, which pleased Emily. Even though she'd referred to the Corvette as "just a car," she'd never before handed the keys to anyone.

The Corvette responded differently under his guidance than under hers, and that pleased her, too. He asked more of it going up the hills than she would have. Her brother, Danny, often teased her about driving too conservatively and told her she'd be better off with an economy car. Danny would approve of the way Ned drove a Corvette. Too bad he wouldn't approve of Ned driving *her* Corvette.

Emily held the copy of Browning's poetry on her lap. Watching Ned at the wheel, she tried to get a fix on this poetry-reading man with arm muscles that rippled every time he took a corner. His workmen friends knew that he read books they didn't care to understand; did they suspect he read love poems as well?

Caressing the spine of the book with one finger, Emily glanced at Ned to savor the enigma that fascinated her so, the potent combination of brawn and intellect. He was fast becoming an obsession with her. Just looking at him kicked her heart into overdrive.

To distract herself, Emily turned and gazed out the window. The valley spread below them, revealing more of itself with every upward curve in the road. The distinct outlines of palo verdes and mesquites, desert washes and rocky outcroppings gradually blended into swaths of sepia and pistachio-green laced with ivory and lemonade. Mountain ranges trimmed the horizon like rickrack. Their brown-green color, softened by distance, reminded Emily of Ned's eyes, and her thoughts boomeranged back to him once again.

"Nice day for a picnic," he said, breaking the silence.

"Yes. I don't do this enough," Emily said, keeping her attention on the landscape, though her mind was on him.

"Do what?"

She glanced at him and caught his half smile. Could he have somehow sensed her erotic imaginings? "Well, all of this, probably," she hedged. "Spend a day with someone who doesn't teach for a living, have a picnic outdoors, let someone else drive this mean machine."

"The car's a treat," he said. "I appreciate the chance to drive it."

"I appreciate the chance to enjoy a spectacular view," Emily said, thinking not only about the landscape but about the man beside her. "There's something liberating about traveling up a mountain," she added. "Petty problems seem to stay down there, in the valley."

"And now you know why I love being up on the iron, danger or no danger. The view puts everything into perspective."

"I never considered that." Emily remembered the paralyzing effect of glimpsing Ned moving around high above her on the day she'd met him for lunch. "I'll take this drive over scrambling around on open girders, though. I can't understand how you go up there, day after day."

"Practice." Ned slowed the car as they came up behind a sedan with an out-of-state license plate. "It's just like driving, or any other unfamiliar activity. Take this poor guy in front of us. He's never been on a road like this and he's driving the way I walked the first time I went up on the iron." A straightaway opened up with no oncoming traffic, and Ned gunned the Corvette to pass the older couple in the sedan.

Ned's aggressive handling of the car stirred Emily to a depth she hadn't expected. Macho behavior usually didn't affect her, but perhaps that was because it was seldom paired with sensitivity. "You were afraid when you started working on the iron?" she asked when they were safely around the other car.

"Damn right. That iron's poison."

"Poison?"

"Sure." He flashed her a grin. "One drop'll kill you."

Emily groaned.

"Maybe you have to be twenty stories up before my jokes are funny," he said, laughing.

"No, thanks." She liked hearing him laugh. "How old were you when you first went up?"

"Seventeen. Dad got me a summer job between my junior and senior year. Then, when he died, I knew the best money was in construction, and I'd made some friends there. I was hired and put on a raising gang the day after graduation." He shrugged. "So there you have it, the story of my life."

"Your father was an ironworker?"

"All his life."

"Ned . . ." She hesitated, wondering if it was none of her business. "What happened to him?" she finally asked.

"He fell from ten stories up."

"Oh, God."

"Pride did it, at least that's what I think. His eyesight was going and he refused to get glasses. I think he misjudged the edge of a beam."

Emily thought of her own father, also a proud man who didn't want to admit to any weaknesses. "That's rough," she said softly.

"Yeah, and it's been especially hard on Mom. She can't let herself think that she lost him over a stupid pair of glasses, so she imagines that someone else's carelessness caused it. So does Curt. That's okay. I understand why they have to think that way. But after nine years up there I know how crucial eyesight is and I'll damned sure buy glasses when I need them."

"You'll stay in the trade until you retire?" Emily couldn't imagine such a thing. Her father said once that it was a young man's game, and only fools stayed on past their prime.

"I'm not sure what I'll do," Ned replied.

"You could go into management, maybe start your own company someday."

"I suppose." He took one hand off the wheel and rubbed the back of his neck. "You know what I'd really like to do?" He paused. "This will sound crazy."

"Try me."

"I'd like to write a book about the experiences I've had. Maybe more than one book. I've already got piles of notes." He glanced at her. "I've never told anybody that, and here I'm announcing it to someone who'll probably think I'm nuts. You have an idea of what it takes to publish something and I don't."

"I have some idea, that's true," Emily said, touched that he'd confide in her. "But I wouldn't call writing a book crazy, either."

He leaned back and stretched his arms against the wheel. "It is for now, anyway. Besides, the longer I work, the more material I'll collect."

"And the more often you'll risk your safety."

He shook his head. "Lots of things in life are potentially lethal. You can die on a mountain road if you're not alert, or you don't have enough experience to drive it well."

"Maybe," Emily said, admiring just how well he drove the mountain road. "But all this metal surrounding us makes me feel safe. Up on the iron you're completely unprotected."

"I could teach you to walk along a beam. You start one floor up and then move to the next level, and the next. Gradually you lose your fear."

Emily shuddered. "I doubt it."

"Maybe I shouldn't have told you about my dad."

"No, I'm glad you did."

"What you should realize is that what happened to him makes me even more careful. And the guys I work with are more like little grandmothers than daredevils, believe me, although I'll deny saying that if you ever repeat it to them."

The scene in the bar, when Ned had agreed to write down the other men's complaints, had been working its persistent way forward from the back of her mind. "They seem a little worried lately," she began uncertainly. "Worried about the company they're working for, I mean."

He took his eyes from the road and gave her a penetrating look. "I figured you'd pick up on that."

"I couldn't help it. Ned, is there any danger?"

He sighed. "Some, and yes, I'm uneasy about it. I hate to tell you that, after spending so much time convincing you that we're perfectly safe up there."

A numbness crept through Emily. *No. Don't tell me. I thought I wanted to hear this, but I really don't.*

"It's sad," Ned added. "Johnson used to be one of the best companies to hang iron for, but I've been hearing stories. This is the first time I've worked for him in a couple of years, but it's not the same operation. I don't know if his son is the problem or what, but they're getting sloppy about stuff."

Fortunately for Emily the winding road commanded all of Ned's attention. She wouldn't want him to look at her and notice her stricken expression. Somehow she managed to maintain her end of the conversation. "Have you talked with anyone about it?"

"Yeah, I've tried talking to Danny, but the guy doesn't like me. For the past few weeks I've been back and forth on what to do, because I need the work and I don't want to permanently tick him off. If I can stay on, the money from this job will guarantee that Curt can finish school. After that I can afford to be more independent."

"But you've agreed to keep a record of everything for the other men."

"Yes. If Danny-boy found that out, I'd be out on my rear in no time. But the guys are getting upset, and if we're going to build a case, we have to document what's been happening."

"So you might still risk your job?"

Ned was silent for a while. "If I have to."

Emily swallowed and gazed out the window again. Her first thought was to talk with Danny and find out exactly what was going on. But of course Danny knew that she had a connection with Ned and probably would decide that she was influenced by her new romantic interest. Her brother might fire Ned just because of her interference, and Ned wouldn't thank her for that.

"But I vote that we don't ruin a beautiful day with talk about job problems," Ned said more brightly. "We're almost there. Lunch first, or did you want to go to the observatory and look around?"

The Kitt Peak Observatory ordinarily fascinated Emily, but not today. She wondered if Ned wanted to take the tour and hoped that he didn't. "I've been through the observatory," she said, "but I'm willing to go again."

"Willing to and wanting to are very different. What do you want?"

He shouldn't have asked, she thought as her body responded with a rush of warmth. "Lunch first," she said.

"You've got it."

A short time later he parked the Corvette beside a secluded picnic table. Emily noticed that he angled the low-slung car so that it blocked the picnic area from the road and gave them a measure of privacy.

Ned lifted the ice chest from the trunk while Emily carried the blanket and the Browning. The blanket was something she'd appropriated when she'd left home—an old quilted bedspread covered with a blue flower pattern that she'd loved as a child. Too worn now to decorate a bed, the quilt had seemed to her like a perfect picnic blanket, but she'd had no reason to use it until today.

"Just smell that fresh air," she said, sounding more casual than she felt.

"Yeah," Ned replied, setting the chest on the cement table and taking a deep breath. "I love it in the mountains."

"You just like anything tall," she teased, remembering Bailey's comment about ironworkers.

Ned laughed and turned to face her. "You bet," he said, his gaze sweeping from her head to her sandaled feet. "Especially when she has blue eyes and—let me see—raven hair. That's it, raven hair that flows over your shoulders like ebony silk."

"My goodness, how you talk." Her cheeks grew warm.

"Pretty corny, huh? And I'm talking about becoming an author."

"No, not corny," she said, bending her head to hide her flush as she put the folded blanket and the book on the table's cement bench. "Just extravagant. You're embarrassing me."

His tone was quiet. "You must know how beautiful you are."

She glanced into his unsmiling face. "In my teaching, pretty can be a detriment," she said, "so I guess I've trained myself not to think about it." *But she had thought about it today,* she admitted to herself. *She'd allowed her hair to hang loose because she'd wanted Ned to look at her the way he was looking at her now.*

"I don't think 'pretty' covers it, Emily. When I opened my apartment door this morning and saw you standing there, with your hair down and that sexy little halter top on, 'pretty' wasn't the word that came to mind." He let out a shaky sigh. "You have a powerful impact on me, lady. You may as well know it."

She swallowed. "I'm not exactly immune to you, either."

His slow smile gathered her in. "I think," he said, gazing at her, "that we have some wonderful moments in store for us, Emily Johnson."

"So do I," she said, completely captured by the way he looked at her.

He allowed the silence to lengthen and her imagination to paint vivid pictures of the moments in store for them. At last he spoke. "Let's have that lunch you packed," he said softly.

She cleared her throat. "All right." Acutely aware of his presence, she laid out containers of fried chicken and potato salad. "Are we eating on the table or the blanket?"

"Table. The blanket's for later, and I for one don't want food spilled on it. Spoils the mood."

"Oh." Emily's pulse quickened at his implication. This was a man who knew how to organize picnics. "Then I guess we're ready," she said, handing him a paper plate, napkin, fork and can of soda.

He chose to sit across the cement table from her, which she found more exciting than if he'd been right beside her. Rather than touching her physically, he touched her with his glance, and she tingled from the force of it.

"Good food, Emily," he said, finishing off a piece of chicken. "You put my bologna sandwiches to shame."

"I don't cook very often. It was fun to have an excuse." She ate mechanically, without tasting any of it, and wondered at his appetite.

He noticed her appraisal and smiled. "Something wrong?"

"No. I'm . . . glad you're hungry."

"Well, you took the trouble to make this and I wouldn't dream of letting it go to waste." He smiled again. "No matter what else is on my mind."

"Oh," Emily said again and flushed. Embarrassed by her intense reaction to him, she searched for something to say that wouldn't be charged with emotion. "I heard some good news last night at the bar," she said finally, picking up her fork and poking at the potato salad.

"About what?"

"Monica thinks she's found a woman to share the apartment with her and watch the kids at night. Monica's conducting the interview this morning."

"No kidding? That's great. Who thought of that solution?"

"Well, um, I did." She loved the way he looked at her then and wished that she could bottle this feeling and sprinkle it around whenever she needed to feel wonderful.

"You're terrific, you know that?"

"It seemed like a logical thing to do," she said with a shrug. Still, she was enormously pleased that he approved of the help she'd given Monica.

"It may have seemed logical to you, but I'll bet Monica had to be convinced. She wants to hold Jake's place for him. I've heard her say it. What happens if he comes back?"

"I guess the woman will move in with me until she can find a new apartment."

He nodded. "I'm impressed, Emily, really impressed."

"Thank you. Your praise means a lot to me."

"I don't know why it should, but you certainly have it."

"Don't you?" She pushed her plate aside. "I admire so much what you're doing, sending Curt through school and helping your mother. Then there's your bravery on the job and the way you've educated yourself, and your dreams of writing a book. You amaze me, Ned."

The surprise reflected in the gray-green depths of his eyes gave way to concern. "Don't put me on some sort of pedestal, Emily. I'm just an ordinary guy."

"Not in my opinion. I'm a little awed by you, to tell the truth."

"God, I hope not." He picked up his plate and left the table. "I think it's time for a little Browning," he said, taking her plate and throwing both in a trash barrel nearby. "There's something I want you to hear."

Intrigued, she stood up and took the blanket from the bench beside her. Ned had made reading one of Browning's poems sound like an object lesson, not a soft seduction. Together they shook out the quilt. It billowed between them and floated to the bed of pine needles at their feet.

Ned picked up the book and began nudging off his sneakers. "My mother taught me not to walk on a blanket with shoes on," he said, stretching out amid the quilt's blue flowers.

"Mine, too." Emily reached down and pulled off her sandals one at a time before stepping barefoot onto the quilt. She had the unsettling sensation of getting into bed next to this man who was lying on his stomach, leafing through the book of poetry. She eased herself down beside him. Following his example she turned on her stomach and propped her face in her hands.

"Here it is," he said, finding the page he wanted. "Something he wrote for Elizabeth Barrett."

As Ned began to read, Emily rolled to her back and listened to the verses that another man had written for the woman he'd loved. Browning's words became Ned's, somehow, as if he were creating them anew for her. Above her the pines sighed. Shade from their boughs dappled the ground and sunlight coaxed the aroma of cedar from the carpet of needles. Turning her head, she studied Ned's high, intelligent forehead, his strong nose, his lips moving over the poem with easy familiarity.

Ironic, she thought, that of all the scholarly men she'd known, none had read poetry to her. She listened to the words and slowly understood the message Ned was sending. The poem described the lovers as seen by the world, and as seen by each other. And the side they turned to each other was different, perhaps flawed, and more precious because only they shared it.

The sun and the gently spoken words warmed her, relaxed her into a lazy acquiescence. If this was a lesson, she wanted Ned to teach her everything he knew. She closed her eyes and allowed his voice to sweeten her like honey.

When the poem was finished, she opened her eyes. He'd laid the book aside and was watching her. She knew that he was waiting for a movement, a sign from her that she'd understood. Slowly she raised her hand and brushed the back of it against his cheek. The contact made her tremble.

He caught her hand and pressed his lips against the throbbing pulse at the inside of her wrist. The pressure of his mouth brought remembered pleasure, and the memory traveled through her body, slowly building a familiar ache deep within her.

He lifted his head and looked into her eyes. "So many people in my life expect me to be strong, to take charge of the situation. I can't let my guard down with anyone else in my life. I was hoping that maybe, just maybe, I could do that with you." Above his head, the tall pines seemed to whisper the words of the poem.

She combed his tousled hair with her fingers and watched his expression soften with her caress.

"Let me be an ordinary man, Emily, not some hero to be worshiped. Just a man, as Browning was for his Elizabeth."

In answer she cradled his face and guided him down to her parted lips. Bracing one elbow beside her head, he sipped at the offering she made. His shirt brushed tantalizingly against her bare midriff.

Her breathing grew ragged as his kisses teased the corners of her mouth and nibbled at her bottom lip. At last, wanting more, she locked her fingers behind his neck and arched upward, meeting his forays with an intensity he couldn't ignore.

With a groan he thrust his tongue fully into her mouth and pressed her down against the quilt. She gloried in the weight of his chest and the firm purpose of his kiss. Sliding his hand beneath the small of her back, he rolled to his side and brought her with him in a rustle of pine needles. The scent of musky desire mingled with that of the forest floor as they lay entwined and absorbed each other's heat.

His hand went to the catch at the back of her halter. Then he paused, his fingers on the hook, and drew away from her a fraction. Breathing hard, she gazed into his eyes. "The answer is yes," she whispered.

"Don't be afraid," he said in a voice rough with passion as he worked the catch loose. "We're shielded from the road, but I won't . . . when we make love, it won't be here."

"I know." Her heart pounded as he reached under the loosened halter and cupped her breast. His callused thumb stroked her nipple and she moaned.

"I had to touch you," he murmured. "Sometimes I almost think . . . you're not real."

"I'm real," she gasped as waves of desire traveled from the tip of her breast to the apex of her thighs. "I'm human. I ache just like you."

"You're so soft," he said, bending his head and pushing the material up just enough to kiss the underside of her breast. "A man could go crazy from wanting you," he whispered against her skin.

"Women....can go crazy, too," she said, tangling her fingers in his hair. "Please, love me just a little."

He lifted his head and his eyes smoldered as he slipped the strap from her shoulder and the top fell away, baring her breasts. His chest heaved and he gently urged her to her back. Silently he gazed at her.

"I'll never forget the way you look, lying there in the sunlight, your hair falling around your shoulders," he said softly. "Poor sun." He traced the outline of her bikini top. "Never to see you like this until now." He leaned down and kissed her throat, dipping his tongue into the hollow as he rubbed his palm with gentle friction across the tip of one breast until it rose pouting and eager for his mouth.

As he placed his lips there and his moist warmth surrounded the aching nub, Emily clutched his shoulders and arched her back. He reached beneath her, supporting her with one arm while his gentle suction created a swirling passion.

"Ned," she moaned, grabbing the back of his shirt.

He lifted his head and gazed down at her, his eyes brilliant with passion. "There are no words for this," he whispered, covering her mouth with his.

She held him tight and submerged herself in his kiss, blotted out everything but his lips, his tongue, his caressing hands. Life became condensed to the sensation of touch.

Then slowly, with nibbling kisses to stave off the inevitable parting of their lips, he pulled away. "We can't stay here," he murmured. "I'm losing track of where I am."

"Me, too." She sighed.

"I can tell, and that's liable to drive me over the edge. This isn't the place, or the time." He combed her hair back with his fingers and gazed into her eyes. "However, I could pick you up after work tonight," he suggested softly.

Her heartbeat thundered in her ears. "At one in the morning? Won't you be fast asleep?"

"Not with the thought of you to keep me awake, I won't be." He adjusted her halter top with warm fingers and smiled at her tiny gasp. "But if you need to go home and rest, say so."

"You know the answer."

"I hope so."

"Do you..." She paused, still shy. "Would you rather go to your place? I'm warning you that mine is sort of, um—"

"Upscale?"

She nodded.

"I figured as much." He guided her to a sitting position and hooked her top again. "Your folks treat you pretty well, don't they?"

"I guess they do." She realized the implication of his question. Earlier today when they'd discussed whether she planned to tell her parents about him, she'd implied that she and Ned weren't involved enough to make that necessary. From the sound of this discussion, they were about to become very involved. "I will tell them, Ned. I promise."

"Good. I don't like deception."

She smiled and glanced away. Didn't he? Then what would he think if he knew that the woman he had so sweetly loved moments ago was Dan Johnson's daughter? Emily felt the guilt of not telling him, but revealing the truth would take more courage than she had at the moment.

Although powerful, their relationship was still new, she reminded herself. It would not take the strain of such a revelation easily. Maybe later, when Ned cared more deeply, she could risk explaining why she hadn't been completely honest with him from the beginning. Maybe then he could forgive her.

"Well, since you've seen my apartment, I may as well find out what sort of palace you live in," Ned commented with a chuckle. "I said I'd pick you up after work, but maybe the best idea is for me to follow you home. That is, if you allow beat-up Pontiacs in your section of town."

She studied his expression. "Was that a crack?"

"No, not really." He rubbed her cheek with his knuckles. "Don't mind me. But remember about the poem. I'm not perfect, and sometimes I may act stupid about the fact that you're better off financially. I'll work on it, but pride is a stubborn flaw." He grimaced. "Sometimes I'm more like my father than I think."

"Pride may very well be the only flaw you have," she said, enjoying the play of light in his hazel eyes.

"There you go again. I warn you, if you keep shoving me up on that pedestal I'm liable to fall someday and break something."

"Like what?"

He traced her lips with his finger. "Two very important, very fragile hearts," he said, holding her gaze.

CHAPTER TEN

MONICA GREETED Emily at the bar that night with a beautiful smile. "I have a roommate," she announced with quiet jubilation as she stood in the hall with her tuna-can ashtray, smoking her before-work cigarette.

"Monica, that's fantastic." Emily leaned against the wall. "We've got five minutes before Bailey gets on our case. Tell me the details."

"Her name is Carrie Simmons. Wait'll you meet her tomorrow afternoon. You're still comin', right?"

"I sure am. Two o'clock?"

"Two o'clock," Monica said with a nod. "Carrie gets off work at three, so you'll meet the boys first, and then her. She's the sweetest person. Broke, though." Monica rolled her eyes. "And I thought I had problems. She has the saddest story. The court gave her kids to her ex-husband because he has a better job. He convinced her it would be better for the kids to go along with it, the jerk." Monica stubbed out her cigarette with extra energy. "He's got to be a real creep."

Emily listened eagerly. Maybe Carrie's plight would awaken Monica to the hazards of her own. "Is Carrie with the boys tonight, then?"

"Yep. She loves being around them, since she can't be around her own. Today was her day off, so she took care of moving right away. Poor thing, she didn't have much to pack. She was staying at the Y. Luckily she waitresses in the daytime. Otherwise the whole thing wouldn't have worked.''

"Did you warn her that Jake might come back?''

Monica evaded Emily's gaze. "Well, not exactly.''

"What do you mean?''

"I told her that Jake had gone off somewheres, and I didn't know where he was, but I didn't say he might be back.'' Monica looked at Emily with a pleading expression. "I didn't want to scare her off, Em. She's so perfect, and besides, she needs a place really bad.''

Emily pushed herself away from the wall. "But you have to tell her. You said yourself that Jake has a key and could come walking in anytime. Poor Carrie would be scared out of her wits.''

"Yeah, you're right.'' Monica brightened. "Could we tell her tomorrow, you and me together, when you come over? That way she'd be able to see who she'd be rooming with, if it's not me.''

"Well, I guess so.''

"Thanks, Em.'' Monica hugged her with one arm while she held the tuna can away from her with the other. "That'll be much better.''

"I hope so. I hope she likes me.''

Monica laughed. "Are you kiddin'? If she doesn't, I'll throw her out, no matter how perfect she is. If she can't recognize quality when she sees it, too bad for her.''

"Why thank you. What a nice thing to say.''

"I mean it. By the way, didn't you have a picnic with Bookworm today? How was it?''

Emily was glad the light was dim in the hallway. "We, um, had a wonderful time.'' The statement sounded pale compared to the reality of her day with Ned. Her entire life had been altered in the space of a few hours by the force of his personality and the tenderness of his loving.

"Did you, now?" Monica cocked her head and regarded Emily with amusement. "Uh-*huh*."

"He's a wonderful person, Monica."

"You don't have to tell me, but I'm glad you think so. Gonna see him again tonight?"

"As a matter of fact, he's coming by at closing time. We'll... get some coffee somewhere, or something." Emily hugged herself to control a tremor of excitement. When she'd left Ned at his doorstep less than two hours ago, he'd promised that tonight he'd hold her until dawn.

"You can spend time drinkin' coffee if you want, honey," Monica said with a wink, "but if I had a man like Bookworm interested in me, I'd find something more thrilling to do than pour caffeine down my throat."

Emily grinned. "Maybe I will."

"Thataway, kiddo." Monica made a circle of her thumb and forefinger. Then she frowned. "I'm not cuttin' in on your time with Bookworm, askin' you over tomorrow, am I? Because we could make it another—"

"Don't be silly," Emily interrupted. "I'm dying to meet those boys of yours, and now I'm curious about Carrie, too."

"Yeah, but Sunday's your only day off, and if you have a romance cookin', I don't want to interfere."

"Monica, the way I feel now, nothing could interfere with Ned and me."

"I sure hope not. You two would be great together. And now we'd better get to work, or neither of us will be around here at closing time to greet Bookworm."

"Right," Emily agreed, following her redheaded friend into the kitchen. She thought about what she'd just proclaimed so loudly to Monica, that nothing would interfere with her relationship with Ned. Strange as it seemed, considering her circumstances, she felt that way, although she hadn't put it into words before.

True, Ned might be upset when he learned her identity, but that obstacle seemed insignificant compared to the strong feelings generated whenever they were together. She'd never believed in destiny before, or the concept of one man for one woman, but the longer she knew Ned Tucker, the more she began to believe that fate had placed him in her path.

AT TWELVE-THIRTY Ned came through the door of the bar and Emily felt as if someone had suddenly increased the wattage of the lights in the room. He smiled at her and wandered over to the pool tables to watch the games in progress.

After serving the drinks that she carried on her tray, Emily walked over to where he leaned against the wall, his hands in his pockets. "Would the gentleman care for a drink?" she asked. He was wearing a pale green short-sleeved shirt and tan slacks. All he needed was a tie to fit right into the business world, she thought, and wondered if he'd dressed up because he was traveling to her side of town tonight.

"The gentleman would not care for a drink," he said, gazing at her fondly. "The gentleman has other things on his mind and wouldn't want to cloud his concentration with alcohol."

"I see." She savored the intensity in his eyes. "It's been a long night."

"Tell me about it." He glanced around the room. "Not much of a crowd, though. You shouldn't have any trouble winding up this party and getting out of here."

"I'll sure try. Monica knows I'm seeing you after work, so she might handle the last few orders if I ask her."

"Ask her."

Emily gazed into his eyes and her heart raced with anticipation. "All right. She has a roommate, by the way. The woman's name is Carrie, and she's with the boys tonight."

Ned's eyebrows rose in surprised approval. "Yeah? That's great, Emily. You should be proud of that one." He paused and looked over her shoulder. "Bailey's giving you the eagle eye."

"Then I'd better go. If you're not a paying customer tonight, I don't have much excuse to stand here talking to you."

"Want me to buy a beer? I don't have to drink it."

She smiled. "Don't be silly," she said, starting to move away from him. "I'll be through in twenty minutes or so, and then I'll change and—"

"Don't bother with that."

Emily lowered her voice. "But these clothes smell like cigarette smoke."

"Lady, I wouldn't care if they smelled like formaldehyde. Don't waste time on that junk. Now go, before you get fired because of me."

She left with a secret smile that made Ned's heart turn over. He watched her pause at one of the booths to ask if anyone needed anything before the bar closed, and he heard her laugh at something one of the men said. Jealousy rippled through his gut.

The trouble was, he knew how most of the guys acted toward the waitresses that worked in here. That was why Bailey picked reasonably good-looking women and put them in shorts and high heels. Ned would bet that Emily outclassed all the others that had ever worked here, though. No wonder Bailey had hired her, even without experience.

Ned was glad that Bailey had done him that favor and brought Emily into his life, but now he had to stand by without saying a word while other men eyed her suggestively or made crude remarks. He had no doubt that Emily could take it; she was pretty nonjudgmental. He was the one having problems with some of the animals that wandered into the bar.

"Hey, buddy, want a game?" One of the men playing pool twisted the tip of his cue stick in the square of blue chalk and pointed to his opponent. "Jerry's goin' home."

"No, thanks. I'm just watching tonight."

The man grinned. "Got a date with that waitress, don'tcha? She looks like pretty nice stuff."

Ned felt his expression grow tight. The guy was only being friendly, but Ned bristled at his casual attitude and his implication that Emily's chief attribute was her body. Not that Ned hadn't spent a lot of time in the past few hours fantasizing about Emily's body. Maybe he just couldn't deal with the idea of someone else doing the same thing.

He didn't respond to the man's remark, fearing that he'd start a fight if he did. Instead he left the pool area and walked over to the bar. "I'll take a 7-Up, Henry," he said to the relief bartender.

"Sure." Henry plunked ice into a glass and squirted 7-Up into it from the hose attached to a canister under the counter. "You're all dolled up tonight, Book-worm," he commented, handing him the glass. "Going out with Emily?"

"Yeah, and I think next time I'll take out a billboard ad and save everyone the trouble of asking."

Henry glanced at him. "Didn't mean to pry, Book-worm."

"Hey, I'm sorry, Henry. Don't mind me."

"Yeah, well, I understand. You're not like the other guys. You're a more private fella."

Ned took a gulp of his soft drink. "That's pretty tough to be when you're dating the most beautiful wait-ress the Suds and Subs has ever seen."

"That Emily's a looker, all right."

"And every guy in here wants her," Ned added, ges-turing toward the rest of the room with his glass. "But they haven't the foggiest notion what's really wonderful about her, like her intelligence, and her kindness. She's got a depth that most of these monkeys aren't notic-ing."

Henry studied him from across the bar. "Pardon my sayin' so, but you sound like you've got a case on her."

Ned stared into his glass and turned it around several times on the polished surface of the bar. Finally he glanced up at Henry. "Can you blame me? She's a really special woman."

"I'm not blamin' nobody. I'm a bartender. My job is to listen, not blame people."

Ned chuckled. "And you're doing a good job of lis-tening to me. Thanks."

"I like you, Bookworm. I've seen lots of guys come in here, and I don't say much, but I have my opinions. You may be the lucky fella who's caught Emily's eye, but she's lucky, too."

"I appreciate that. I just hope she's willing to stick around until I'm in a position to offer her something."

"Why wouldn't she? Where's she goin'?"

"With a woman like Emily, that's not an easy question," Ned replied, protecting her secret.

"I wouldn't worry about it, Bookworm. Here she comes, and she's lookin' at you like you was the à la mode on top of the pie."

Ned swiveled his stool and watched Emily approach. She had her purse over her shoulder and her change of clothes in a plastic cleaning bag. She'd honored his request not to waste time, and his heart pounded at the look in her blue eyes. "Hi," he said softly. "All set?"

"All set. Monica's finishing up for me."

"Then let's go."

A short time later he was behind the wheel of his Pontiac following her battered station wagon as she headed toward the northwest area of town. He wished they could have driven together, but it hadn't been practical. Practical. He was beginning to hate the word. It seemed to have no place in the explosive emotions he felt whenever he thought about Emily.

Yet he couldn't lose his head in this matter. A year from now Curt would graduate, and nothing, not even this relationship with Emily, could be allowed to interfere with that. Ned already had troubles enough with problems on the job, without adding problems in his personal life. But maybe Emily didn't have to be a problem. Maybe she would be pure pleasure. At the moment, thinking of a night in her arms, Ned believed in that prospect.

Her apartment complex was as he'd expected—red Spanish tiled roofs, balconies offering both mountain and city views, arched windows with custom wooden shutters, tennis courts—yuppie heaven. Warning himself not to be a reverse snob, he parked beside her station wagon. The Corvette was two spaces down.

"Is this okay?" he asked, getting out of the car.

"Fine," she called across the dented roof of the old wagon. "The parking spaces never fill up in the summer."

"Ah, a snowbird nest. I thought the residents would all be yuppies, but I guess you've got your share of winter visitors, too."

"And dinks," she said, rounding the car holding her cleaning bag of clothes over one shoulder.

"Dinks?"

"Double income, no kids. They stay here while their houses are being built."

He gazed at her and shook his head. "Do the folks who live in this complex know that you wait tables every night at a bar downtown, a bar frequented by brawling, nasty construction workers?"

She laughed softly. "No. I'm not that intimate with any of them."

"How about the construction workers?" he asked, sliding an arm around her waist. "Are you intimate with any of them?"

She snuggled against him, and he was astounded by how her curves meshed so perfectly with his body as they walked. "I'm working on that," she said.

"I think you're about to succeed," he said as desire for her rose in him, hot and hard.

She had a ground-floor apartment, which told him that she wasn't paying the highest rates in the complex. The tenants with the balcony views would definitely have to shell out the bucks for them.

"This is it," she said, fitting her key into the lock and swinging the door open.

He liked what he saw. The sofa and love seat were covered in an off-white, nubby material that went well with the bleached gray color of the coffee and end tables. He recognized the southwestern look in the accent colors of pillows and throw rugs in sea-green and peach. He'd seen arrangements like this in more expensive furniture stores and had a rough idea what it might have cost her...or her parents.

"Very nice," he said, turning to her.

"I've been lucky, Ned." Her blue eyes searched his face. He could tell that she was worried about his reaction.

"So have I," he said, taking the cleaning bag and purse from her and laying them on the couch. "By a wild throw of the dice, I met you." He cupped her soft face in his hands. The texture of her skin drove him crazy every time he touched her. He wanted to press his lips against every silken inch of her, and he would...soon.

"It wasn't a wild throw of the dice." She slipped her hands behind his neck and he closed his eyes to better enjoy the sensation of her fingers caressing him beneath the collar of his shirt. "Your generosity sent Curt to school, your dedication to that goal caused him to tell me about you. Everything happened because of the wonderful person you are, Ned."

He gazed down into her eyes, as blue as sapphires against a fringe of dark lashes and finely etched brows. He might never be able to afford sapphires, but he didn't care anymore, as long as he could look into Emily's eyes.

"I must have done something to deserve this, to deserve you," he said. Her lips waited, pink and moist. He held himself back, knowing that once he abandoned himself to that sweet mouth, he might ravish her right there in the middle of her decorator living room.

"There must be more to this apartment," he said.

"Did you want to see the kitchen?" Her eyes sparkled with the same reined-in passion that surged through him.

"No."

"The bathroom, then?"

"No."

Her saucy smile gradually faded and her expression grew serious. "You were the first man I ever let drive my car, and you'll be the first man I've invited to my bedroom. I thought you should know that."

His heart thudded in his chest. "Emily, maybe we should talk about this. If I'm the first man you've ever made love with..."

"That's not what I meant," she said gently. "There was a man, one of my teachers at Stanford. But since I moved back to Tucson, I've... well, I haven't found anyone that I cared to issue an invitation to, I guess." She gazed up at him. "Until now." She swallowed. "It seemed important for you to know. Maybe it doesn't matter much, but—"

"It matters." He looked into her eyes, trying to let her understand how much. He rejoiced in knowing that she valued herself as highly as he did.

"And now would you like to see the bedroom?" she asked with a shy smile.

"Yes."

"Then I'll show you." She caught his hand and led him toward a door that connected to the living room.

He noticed fewer details of the bedroom. His mind was beginning to fuzz with the strain of wanting her, but he took in the bed, most significant to him at the moment. It was covered with a sea-green spread and a mass of pillows in various shades of green and peach.

"I told you about my celibate habits," she said, leading him to the bed and opening a drawer of the table beside it, "because this room comes equipped with birth control, but only as of this week."

He looked at the box of condoms and had to smile when he thought of what he'd carefully tucked into the pocket of his slacks. "This week, huh?" he said, drawing her close. "When this week?"

"After the bologna sandwich," she replied, her color high. "Before I went to the library, I went to the drugstore."

"I see." He enjoyed the prospect that she'd planned for this all along. She flushed a deeper pink, and her coy glance made the blood pound through him and settle persistently in his groin. "Please take your hair down."

"I hope you don't think me too forward," she said, backing away and reaching for the pins that held her hair. "Or that I assumed too much."

"You assumed just the right amount." He watched hungrily as she shook her hair free. "Beautiful," he whispered.

"It feels good to take those pins out," she said.

He guessed that she was nervous and needed to talk her way through it.

"And the other thing I love getting rid of are these shoes," she continued, sitting on the bed and reaching for the ankle strap on her high heels.

"Here, let me do that." Kneeling in front of her, he took her foot in his hand. "I'll bet you hate these things," he said, unbuckling the thin strap. "But Bailey's right, they're sexy."

"Maybe so, but they sometimes give me wicked leg cramps." Her voice sounded breathy to him and he wondered if her heart was pounding the way his was.

"Here?" He massaged her nylon-covered calf.

"Mmm." She closed her eyes and leaned back on her outstretched arms. "Yes, there."

"Lie back. Let me work the kinks out," he said, taking off the other shoe and wishing she'd never have to wear them again. Gently he kneaded her calf muscles, but touching her there wasn't enough, and his body was letting him know it. At last he slid both hands up to her hips and leaned over to kiss the bare strip of skin beneath the tied ends of her blouse.

She drew in her breath as he worked the knot loose. Slowly he edged his way upward, easing onto the bed next to her as he unbuttoned her blouse and placed his lips against the warm skin he gradually uncovered. At last the blouse lay open, revealing a confection of white satin and lace cupping her generous breasts. Unsnapping the front clasp, he pushed the material aside. She gasped as he took one pebbled nipple in his mouth.

Rolling the pouting tip against his tongue, he felt her body arch under him and her fingers press against his scalp. God, how he loved loving her. One breast filled his mouth, the other his cupped hand, and as he relinquished the sweetness of one nipple, she rolled to her side and offered him the other.

She fumbled with the buttons of his shirt and he helped her part the material so he could feel her caressing him at last. He trembled as she ran her hands over his chest. He wanted so much from her tonight. His body cried out for her loving.

He took his mouth from her breast and gazed into her smoky eyes. He had no idea how wise she might be in the ways of men. "I want you to touch me," he said, knowing that she was already touching him, knowing that he wanted more.

A blue flame burned in her eyes. "Take off your shoes," she urged, "and lie back."

He nudged off his loafers and swung his legs onto the bed. As he let his head sink to the pillow, she smiled down at him, her hair a shining curtain on either side of her face. Kneeling on the bed beside him, she shrugged out of her blouse and bra, but the cascade of her hair partially concealed her breasts.

"Like Lady Godiva," he murmured, combing the dark strands aside to rub his thumb across the still-moist nipples. "Have I mentioned how beautiful you are?"

"You have," she said, capturing his hand and bringing it to her lips. "And now it's my turn to tell you."

"Men aren't beautiful." His body tightened with desire as she ran her tongue over his fingers.

"That's what you say." She took his little finger into her mouth and watched his face while she sucked gently.

He couldn't believe the effect such a simple action was having on him. He began to quiver as she swirled her tongue around the tip of his finger. The bow of her upper lip pursed and the fullness of her bottom lip dented with the impression of his finger—her mouth was driving him crazy.

He heard the rasp of his own breathing and saw her secret smile. Slowly she reached for the fastening of his slacks, and he groaned as she pulled the zipper down. When she slid her hand beneath the elastic of his briefs to caress him, he thought he would go out of his mind.

Then she withdrew her hand and lovingly undressed him, planting kisses and murmuring endearments until he closed his eyes and prayed for control. He'd asked for this, he reminded himself as he clenched his jaw against the delicious torture. Gradually her kisses became more explicit until at last she dared the ultimate intimacy and he moaned aloud and clutched a handful of her hair.

"Emily," he gasped, nearly helpless from the assault of her sweet mouth, "that's...all I can...take..."

"Then it's time," he heard her say through a haze of desire.

Breathing hard, he forced himself to pause and reach for one of the cellophane packages on the bedside table. Finally he urged her to her back and plundered the lips that had brought him such pleasure. Impatiently he tore at her remaining clothes and he heard a button snap from its moorings.

When the shorts and panty hose were gone she opened to him and offered the warm sanctuary of her body and relief from the throbbing ache that pulsed beyond his control. He should wait, he thought briefly. She might not be ready for him, might not be able to fully enjoy their first union.

But he couldn't wait. He needed her more than he ever remembered needing a woman before. Moving between her thighs, he gazed into her flushed face. Her eyes were feverish; her hands on his hips urged him forward. Watching her eyes all the way, he slid between the moist folds, pushing gently forward until he was locked within her.

He used whatever scrap of restraint he had left to keep from climaxing right then, so inviting was the silken welcome she gave him. She tightened around him and he closed his eyes, fighting for a few moments longer, just a few. "Easy," he whispered, opening his eyes again.

Her lips parted; her breath came in ragged spurts. "Just love me," she said, pressing upward against him. "Love me, Ned."

He started the rhythm slowly, but she wouldn't let him keep it that way. Miraculously she was as aroused as he. With each thrust her shudders grew, and he abandoned himself to the shared frenzy of their movements, the shared ecstasy of their cries. Her first convulsion triggered his and they spun through the maelstrom they'd created together, gasping out each other's name.

Sometime later, lying side by side, knowing they would love again that night, and maybe again after that, he held her hand and gazed into her eyes with the smile of one who has found, after years of searching, a treasure he'd thought might not exist. "I think," he said, tracing a line across the curve of her shoulder, "that you'd better tell your parents about me very soon."

"I couldn't *not* tell them," she said.

"Do you want me to come with you?"

A shadow crossed her expression. "Not yet." Then she smiled again, banishing the shadow. "But soon," she said. "I promise."

CHAPTER ELEVEN

OVER BREAKFAST the next morning Emily and Ned decided that she should stop by her parents' house on her way to Monica's apartment and casually mention that she was dating him.

"And you're right, I shouldn't show up this first time," Ned commented. "That would put way too much importance on everything." He took her hand and kissed her fingertips. "Not that there isn't a lot of importance there."

Emily was relieved that Ned wanted her to downplay this announcement to her parents. She tried not to think about what would happen if he insisted on meeting them before she'd found the courage to tell him who they were. "We'll just take it slow with them," she said. "Everything will work out if we don't rush into things."

Ned smiled. "Just as long as we don't have to take it slow with us. I feel as if life just handed me the grand prize. I want to be with you every minute I can."

"I want that, too." Emily still couldn't believe that he was here, sitting at her round butcher-block kitchen table, sharing a breakfast of bacon and eggs. When dawn had arrived they'd been unable to say goodbye, and so the morning light found Ned borrowing her toothbrush and razor, singing in her shower and coming to the breakfast table wearing only his slacks. She rubbed her toes across his bare foot. "I wish neither of us had other obligations today."

He caressed her arm as it lay on the table. "I wish neither of us had any obligations, period. I look at you and want to give up my job, my apartment, my commitments, and run away to some South Sea island where we could lie naked on the sand."

"You're a romantic, Ned Tucker. I knew it the minute I saw that copy of Browning lying open on your coffee table."

"And you're the answer to a romantic's dreams," he said, standing and pulling her into his arms. "Warm and willing, passionate and creative." He drew the short terry robe aside to kiss her bare shoulder. "God, you smell great."

"Better than when I had smoke from the bar clinging to me, I'll bet." His lips moving over her skin aroused her once again.

"I didn't smell any cigarette smoke," he said, slipping his hand inside the robe. "Just that special scent that told me you wanted me." He stroked the curve of her breast and continued the caress down her rib cage, in the process loosening the tie belt until her robe fell open.

"You're taunting me," she said as her legs began to tremble. "You know I can't resist you."

"I'm not taunting." He nipped at the soft flesh of her breasts. "I'm celebrating."

"Ned," she pleaded, "we're in the kitchen, for heaven's sake."

"A very private kitchen," he murmured, guiding her against the edge of the heavy table. Then he unzipped his slacks.

She gazed into his eyes. "We can't," she said, even as she longed for him. "Not unless we go into the bedroom and get—"

"We can." He reached into his pocket. "You're not the only one who buys these things." In a heartbeat he was ready for her, holding her with the strong arms of an ironworker, loving her with the heart of a poet.

Her robe covered her arms and back, and as her legs brushed against the slacks he still wore, she experienced the clandestine excitement of making love partially clothed in a place meant for quite different behavior. The bud of passion quickly flowered into a release that left them gasping.

"Wow," he said moments later, resting his forehead on her shoulder.

"Did you plan that?" she asked, trying to catch her breath.

"No."

"I'll bet you didn't."

He lifted his head and gazed into her eyes. "No, honest," he said, smiling. "One thing just led to another."

"And another," she said. "That was pretty special, Ned."

"We'll have to take showers again."

"Ask me if I care."

"You won't have much time at your parents' house, and I probably won't get all the maintenance work done at my mother's house."

"I can only speak for myself, of course," she said, winding an arm around his neck and running her tongue across his lower lip, "but I think some things might be more important than visits to parents and maintenance work."

"Want to forget about everybody else today?" he asked, kneading the soft skin of her behind as he settled himself more securely against her thighs.

"That's a tempting thought, but I guess not. I think my parents and your mother would forgive us, but Monica would be crushed if I didn't make it to her place this afternoon."

"Well, damn," he said softly, gazing at her. "Then I'll have to postpone loving you again until tonight, after you leave Monica's."

"You want to see me tonight?"

"I'm surprised you have to ask. Of course I want to see you tonight. I want to take you to bed, too. Because after tonight we won't have a chance to be together until next weekend."

"I guess that's true."

"Although when I'm in this particular position—" he shifted his hips "—I feel like throwing caution to the wind and picking you up after work every night next week."

Emily shook her head. "Not when you have to get up at four in the morning. Not when you're walking around on those narrow girders all day."

"I was afraid you'd look at it that way, which means no more of this until Friday night after you get off duty. So, yes, I want to be with you after you finish with Monica and her crew. Just tell me the time and place."

"I'll drive over to your apartment," she suggested. "Then you can stay tucked in bed while I drive home."

"Or don't drive home. Why not stay until I leave for the site?"

"Because then you won't sleep."

"Sure I will."

She laughed gently. "I don't believe you. Not yet, anyway. Maybe after we've been together a few nights, the novelty will wear off and you'll sleep, but that hasn't happened yet."

"It might never happen," he said, leaning down to kiss the tip of her breast. "So I guess you're right. Ready to take a shower with me?"

"Do you think we could actually complete that assignment together?"

He grinned. "I don't know, but we could have fun trying."

BY SHOWING great self-restraint, Emily and Ned managed to leave her apartment by noon and she decided that she still had time for a brief talk with her folks. Being in a hurry might help anyway, she figured. That way they couldn't draw her into a prolonged argument.

She found them having lunch in front of their wide-screen television watching a baseball game. After her hot drive in the station wagon, Emily had trouble adjusting to the coolness of the family room with its vertical blinds drawn against the midday sun. Her mother and father were surprised to see her, touchingly pleased, and she regretted having to disturb their pleasant mood with her announcement.

After declining their offer of some lunch, she decided to work up to the subject of Ned by talking about Monica first. "I can't stay long," she said, settling into a leather armchair next to the television set.

"That's too bad," her father said absently. He'd turned down the sound a few notches in deference to her presence, but he kept part of his attention on the screen, she noticed. Perhaps that was just as well. He'd finished his lunch and was tamping tobacco into his pipe. Emily hoped that he felt as mellow as he looked.

"I'm spending the afternoon at my friend Monica's apartment, the woman who's the other waitress at Suds and Subs," she explained.

"You're socializing with her?" Emily's mother frowned. "Why would you want to do that?"

"It's a long story, Mom. She has three little boys, and her husband left. I got involved when I realized she was leaving the boys without a baby-sitter every night. I suggested she advertise for a woman to room with her and baby-sit in the evenings, and now she wants me to meet this person she's found. And her boys, of course."

Emily's mother clucked her tongue in disapproval. "They don't sound like your type of people, dear. Aren't there some women you teach with that would be better friends, considering your position? Or maybe some of your old high-school girlfriends?"

Although annoyed with her mother's snobbish attitude, Emily decided not to deal with that issue. She had more important fish to fry. Her father, it seemed, wasn't listening to much of what she'd said. Maybe her announcement about Ned would slide right by him.

"Ginny, the gal I became good friends with last semester, is out of town for the summer, Mom," she said, keeping her tone pleasant. "And my high-school friends—I don't know—they're mostly married and busy with husbands and kids. I don't have much in common with them anymore. Besides, Monica needs someone right now, and I'm handy. She's a good person who's had a bad break."

Emily's mother wiped her hands on her napkin and dabbed at her lips. "Does she know that you're a college teacher, and not just some girl off the street who needed a job at the bar?''

"She thinks I go to school, not teach it, but I may tell her the truth today. If we're going to be friends, she should know.''

"The whole thing seems so strange to me, Emily. But I guess if you're going to be friends with someone from this experiment of yours, I'd rather it be a woman than a man.''

Emily swallowed. "Uh, well, actually, I've become friends with one of the men, too.''

Her father focused on her for the first time since she'd walked into the room, as if his hearing had been selectively tuned to just such a statement and none of the others she'd been making. "What do you mean, *friends*?''

"We've had a couple of dates,'' she said, hoping frantically that she wasn't blushing.

Emily's mother cleared her throat. "You don't mean you're dating one of your father's ironworkers, do you, dear?''

"Of course that's what she means, Maria,'' her father said, clamping his back teeth on the stem of his pipe. "And I've seen it coming, ever since she thought up this damn-fool idea of studying the punks that hang out in a bar after work.''

Emily gazed at both of them, her mother looking frightened, her father furious. Emily realized that she'd entered into this discussion perhaps as frightened as her mother was now, but gradually Emily's fear was giving way to anger. She always had been more like her father. "You don't even know him,'' she said sharply, staring at her father, "and already you disapprove.''

"I don't hafta know him. All I hafta know is that he's an ironworker, and that's not good enough for my daughter. Not after all I've done to make sure you found somebody else, somebody who won't come home every night with dirt under his fingernails."

Emily gripped the arms of her chair. "How can you be so set against ironworkers? Surely you, of all people, Dad, know there are good guys climbing around on that iron—honest, hardworking, decent men."

"I didn't say there weren't!" Her father plucked his pipe from his mouth and leaned forward in his chair. "But that doesn't make them right for a girl with your kind of brains and advantages. You're too damn good for them, Emily, simple as that!" He got out of his chair and jabbed the pipe stem in her direction. "I don't wanna hear another word about this guy. I mean it."

She laughed, amazed that he'd dare to say such a thing to her. "You're forbidding me to date him?"

Her father's gaze wavered. "Yeah, yeah I am," he muttered.

"Dan," her mother said. "Maybe we should talk about this some more before we—"

"It's okay, Mom." Emily glanced briefly at her and stood up. "I'm old enough to fight my own battles." Then she faced her father. "I'm sorry if my dating an ironworker bothers you, Dad, but I plan to keep seeing Ned, whether you approve or not."

"Ned?" Her father's scowl grew blacker. "You'd better not mean Ned Tucker."

"Yes, I do," she said quietly, folding her arms.

"Son of a—" Her father gazed up at the beamed ceiling. "You would hafta pick that one, wouldn't you?"

"What *is* it with you and Danny?" Emily cried, unable to control her frustration. "Ned's a good worker, a conscientious worker, and all I hear from you two is that he's a troublemaker. I don't get it, Dad."

Her father's chin jutted as he glared at her. "That's because you don't understand this business, missy."

"Dan—" her mother interjected.

"Which is on purpose," he continued, ignoring his wife's attempts to mollify him, "because we didn't want you dirtying your pretty little hands in it. That's your brother's job, and mine, but punks like your Ned Tucker make our job damn tough." Her father's eyes narrowed. "Does Tucker know who you are?"

"No, he doesn't."

"You sure about that?"

"Yes, Dad, I'm sure." *Because if he knew, he might drop me like a hot rivet,* she thought in despair. This could be her father's ultimate weapon against the relationship. All he'd have to do would be to reveal her identity to Ned and watch the attraction disappear.

"Because the way I figure it, he might think dating you was good job insurance while he keeps hassling Danny, if he knew about who you are, I mean."

Emily's jaw clenched. "He doesn't know, and if he did, he wouldn't use that information to save his job. He's not that type of person."

"Yeah, yeah, sure. He's a prince. From what Danny's said, the guy's nothing but a pain in the butt."

Emily threw up both arms in exasperation. "Look, I came over here to tell both of you about Ned because I thought I owed you that much. You've been great parents and I don't want to sneak around behind your backs. But it seems as though you're not willing to give Ned a chance."

"Emily, dear," her mother said, casting a sideways glance of worry at her husband, "you only mentioned a couple of dates, but you're making it sound more serious than that. Goodness knows you haven't come home to tell us about every boy you've had a couple of dates with."

Disconcerted by her mother's perception, Emily grabbed for a reasonable explanation. "No, that's true, but that's because they were always people I thought you'd be pleased about. I know how you both feel about me dating an ironworker, so I wanted to be straightforward about it."

"Straightforward, you say?" Her father's gaze was piercing. "What about with him, for crying out loud? Shouldn't you tell him straight out who you are?"

Emily tried to meet the challenge of her father's stare but his accusation hit too close to home. "You're right," she said, glancing away. "I should tell him, but I'm afraid to."

"Why, dear," her mother asked. "Why would that be? You'd think he'd be pleased to learn you're Dan Johnson's daughter."

Emily glanced back at her father, studying him for a long moment. "What's the problem with this job, Dad? Why are the men so dissatisfied with what's happening?"

"I told you why. We've got a bunch of lazy punks these days who'd rather bellyache than work. Tucker's one of the worst."

"I find that hard to believe, Dad." She trembled. This was the closest she'd ever come to openly criticizing him, and she could see the hurt glowing in his blue eyes.

"Are you taking the side of this ironworker against me?"

"I don't want to take any sides. I just don't understand why the men don't seem to like you and Danny."

His gaze was belligerent. "We're the management, that's why."

"I don't remember that it was always like that, Dad."

"And what do you know about it, missy? You've been busy with school and college and all that other stuff. Now you come busting in here, wanting to know why Danny and me aren't winning popularity contests!" Despite his bravado, the hand holding his pipe wobbled.

As if sensing her husband's vulnerability, Emily's mother went to his side. "Maybe we should drop this subject for now," she coaxed, laying her hand on his arm.

"Yes, maybe we should," Emily said with a sigh. "We don't seem to be getting anywhere."

Her father didn't appear to have heard either of them. "You know I could tell that punk to stop seeing you or else take a hike."

"I know you could, Dad. I hope you don't. I'm not sure which way Ned would choose, but you and I would have some serious problems if you did that."

"I have a thought," Emily's mother said. "We're leaving next week on our cruise. Why don't we all forget about this until your father and I come back? Maybe you won't even be dating this man by then, and all the fuss will be for nothing."

"Yeah, and maybe she'll be engaged to the jerk. How would you like that, Maria?"

"Emily wouldn't do something like that in three weeks' time," her mother said, glancing toward Emily for confirmation.

"Of course not," Emily said. "I've only known him a short while." Yet she felt closer to Ned than to people she'd known for years, she thought.

Her father sighed and gazed down at his wife. "You know I don't like this one damn bit."

"I know, but Emily's twenty-five years old, Dan. She has the right to act the way she wants to."

Dan glanced back at Emily. "Okay. I won't threaten this punk. I won't even tell him you're my daughter, since I can see that you don't want that. But I'm warning you to be careful. And I still say if you had any sense you'd forget this guy. Maybe by the time we get back, like your mother says, you will have. I hope to God you have."

Emily decided that his statement was the best she could hope for at this stage. "Thanks, Dad." She went over and hugged them both. "Thanks, Mom." She stood back and smiled at them. "I hope you two have a wonderful trip."

"Yeah, well, you know how your mother likes to get out of the heat." Emily's father put his arm around his wife.

Emily took pleasure in her parents' obvious love for each other. One of the securities of her life had been the solid nature of their relationship, and she longed to exchange the same sort of devotion with a man someday. Ironically, the first man who truly seemed capable of it was someone that her loving parents were dead set against. She wondered, as she said her goodbyes and drove away, if she'd ever be able to convince them otherwise.

She had seen the look of dismay on their faces when they'd walked her to the door and glimpsed the battered station wagon for the first time. She could almost read their minds as they imagined that this was the beginning of her decline into what they now considered a substandard way of life. No matter that they had begun that way; they wanted her to be different. College was supposed to have inoculated her against material deprivation, apparently.

Funny, she thought, but in a way she felt a deprivation of experience instead. For almost as long as she could remember she'd never wanted for anything. Maybe her attraction to this study of ironworkers, and her need to help Monica, were partially rooted in a desire to understand hardship. She glanced at the seat beside her where a bag from Toys "R" Us contained three Tonka trucks. She'd bought different kinds of trucks, but tried to keep them approximately the same in size and degree of fascination. She'd resisted the urge to pick out the largest and most expensive toys and had settled for the small metal trucks, which were sturdy but fit in the palm of her hand.

Monica's apartment building was two stories, like Ned's, but there the resemblance ended. Instead of the freshly painted buff exterior of Ned's place, Monica's was a dirty gray stucco that had been patched in spots and repainted a different shade of gray. The trim and doors were a faded blue, and the doors were scuffed and scratched. Instead of a pool, the courtyard in the center of the U-shaped complex contained a rusty swing set that looked hot and uninviting.

Monica's apartment was on the ground floor, and Emily heard the blare of a television as she approached the door. When she knocked, a deep-chested barking began, followed by commands of "Shut up, Rambo." Then Emily heard scurrying sounds and the television was clicked off before Monica flung wide the door.

"You're here," she said, beaming at Emily with her not-quite-perfect smile. "Come in. The boys have been driving me crazy, asking when you'd get here."

Clutching her bag in one hand, Emily walked past Monica into a shabby but neat living room that held three very shy little boys and one enormous brown dog. The boys had draped themselves over the worn hide-a-bed and the single easy chair in a charade of nonchalance, and Emily noticed that they held on to the furniture for dear life. The dog sat alertly watching for signs as to whether she was friend or foe.

"Hello," Emily said, smiling at each one in turn, including the dog.

"That's Freddy on the arm of the couch, and Louis next to him," Monica said from behind her. "J.J.'s the one in the chair." Monica scratched behind the dog's floppy ears. "And this here's Rambo."

"I'm glad to finally meet all of you." Emily noticed Monica's glow of motherly pride as she presented to her friend what she valued most in the world. J.J. and Louis had dark hair and brown eyes, and Emily assumed Monica's husband did, too. Freddy was the only redhead in the bunch.

"You're real tall," Freddy said, staring up at Emily with wide blue eyes. His remark sent J.J. and Louis into a fit of giggles. "Pretty, too," Freddy added, which brought forth even more giggles. "What's so funny?" he asked, turning an indignant glare on his brothers.

J.J. gave him a withering look. "You're not supposed to say stuff like that, dummy."

"Why not?" Freddy jumped from the arm of the couch and stood in front of J.J., his little fists balled and ready to punch.

"Hey, boys," Monica began, "I won't have—"

"I brought you guys something," Emily said casually, glancing at the dog before sitting on the floor. She *was* tall, she thought with amusement, and sitting on the floor might be the best plan for getting to know these pint-size people. As if on cue, the dog laid down and put his large head on his paws.

Three pairs of eyes focused on her in wonder. "Presents?" the boys chorused together.

"In here." She held up the bag.

"Hey, Toys "R" Us!" J.J. said, recognizing the bag.

In a second they were clustered around her like puppies, their faces shining with expectation. Rambo thumped his tail on the floor and started to join them, but at a word from Monica he settled back on the rug.

Emily hoped that she had chosen the right toys. "I wasn't sure what you liked, so I took a wild guess," she said. "Now I want each of you to close your eyes, and hold out both hands, and when I say so, you can open your eyes, okay?"

"Okay!" they shouted together and thrust out their open hands as they squeezed their eyes closed.

Emily wished that she had a videotape of this to show her sister-in-law. Last Christmas had been a disaster, with both Jeremy and Lynette unimpressed with the toys they unwrapped and each of them eventually whining that the other one got more. Carefully Emily placed a red truck in Freddy's hands, a blue one in Louis's and a yellow one in J.J.'s. She'd checked with Monica about each boy's favorite color.

"Now you can open your eyes," she said, and watched the light snap on in each of their faces as they saw the truck nestled in their grasp. Then the room erupted into cries of delight as they all ran to show their mother the treasure they had received. This time no amount of scolding kept Rambo quiet, and he bounded around, endangering furniture with his bulk.

"What do you say?" Monica prompted amid the chaos as she shepherded the boys back to Emily. "What do you say to someone who brought you such a wonderful present?"

Her comment was followed by a chorus of "thank yous," and even a hug from Freddy. Emily hugged him back and fought an impulse to hold him a little longer than necessary. She hadn't expected to like these children so much and certainly hadn't expected to feel a twinge of envy that Carrie Simmons, and not she, was now rooming with Monica.

"Can we take the trucks outside, Mommy?" Louis asked.

"You'll get dirty, and you'll get your new trucks dirty," Monica said.

"The trucks will wash," Emily said.

Monica gazed at her boys. "So will kids, I guess. Sure, go ahead, but be careful with those trucks."

"We will," J.J. assured her, his dark gaze serious. "We're not lettin' anything happen to these trucks, boy."

"That's right," Louis added. "Right, Freddy?"

"Right." Freddy nodded his head until his short red hair quivered.

"Then go on, and take this big lug with you," Monica said, pointing to Rambo. "Emily and I will have some iced tea and visit." The boys and dog raced out the door, seemingly undaunted by the searing afternoon heat.

"Is there shade out there?" Emily asked, worried.

"They usually find some, down by the end of the building, but the heat doesn't bother them much,"

Monica replied. "They're desert rats, even Rambo." She glanced at Emily. "Thanks for the trucks, Em. As you can see, they don't get presents a lot."

"I loved giving them something. They're terrific boys, Monica. You've done a super job with them."

Her friend smiled. "I try. Ready for some iced tea? I made sun tea fresh this morning." She laughed. "In this heat it took about five minutes."

"I'll bet." Emily followed Monica into the tiny kitchen and watched her pry ice from a balky metal tray.

"It's pretty warm in here," Monica said, wiping the back of her hand against her temple. "Swamp cooling. Is that what you have?"

"No, air conditioning."

"Really? That costs a mint to run! How can you pay the electric bill?"

"Well, I—" Emily paused and decided she might as well reveal her secret before Carrie showed up. "Listen, I need to tell you about something."

"Okay." Monica handed her a plastic glass filled with iced tea. "Sugar?"

"No, thanks. What I need to tell you is—"

"Wait a minute," Monica said, taking charge as she had when Emily first began waitressing at the bar. "Before you start some big story, let's go back in the living room. The sun just beats in that kitchen window."

"Sure." Emily smiled at the assertive behavior that Monica occasionally displayed. Had she drawn different cards in life, Monica might now be head of a large corporation.

"Now," Monica said, waving Emily to the armchair while she took the couch. "Shoot."

"Well," Emily began, running her knuckles up and down the moist glass, "I'm not exactly the person you think I am."

Monica's eyes grew round. "This sounds exciting."

"Not really. The truth is, I'm an instructor in sociology at the University of Arizona, and I took this job at the bar because I'm writing a paper on the social interactions of ironworkers."

Monica sat staring at her in wonder. "You mean," she ventured at last, "that you're even smarter than I thought?"

"I doubt it. Considering some of the problems I'm making for myself, I may be a lot dumber than you thought."

"What kind of problems?"

"Well, mostly revolving around Ned."

Monica let out a breath of air. "Oh. Does he know about this?"

"Yes. I had to tell him, but that's not the real problem. The thing is . . ." Emily hesitated, reluctant to expose her parents' prejudices.

"I know what's the matter. Bookworm's pride. You're richer than him, right?"

Emily nodded.

"Yeah, Bookworm wouldn't like that." Monica thought about it for a while before she brightened. "But I have a feeling you two can work that out. He's not nearly as pigheaded as some people I could name. Like Jake."

"You still haven't told Carrie about him?"

"Nope. Today's the day."

"Then I'm glad I told you about me, first."

Monica glanced up at her in alarm. "You can't take her if Jake shows up?" She scrambled to cover her remark. "I mean, that's okay, if you can't. I understand, your being a teacher and all, so—"

"No, no," Emily protested, laughing. "My offers stands, but I thought if Jake should come back into the picture, you and Carrie should know who I really am. Otherwise there would be lots of confusion when she saw my apartment and my other car."

"Other car? What other car?"

"I, um, own a Corvette."

"Good Lord." Monica glanced at Emily and then gazed around the threadbare living room. "I'm embarrassed to have asked you here."

"No!" Emily moved to the couch and touched Monica's arm. "Don't say that. I love being here and I wanted to meet your family. Please don't hold it against me, that I happen to have more of something stupid called money."

Monica looked at her and shook her head. "Believe me, if you didn't have it, you wouldn't call money stupid."

"I guess you're right. Sorry." Emily met her gaze silently and struggled with the frustration of wanting to do something, anything, to help Monica. "The way out is through a better-paying job," she said at last.

"For me? I never graduated high school."

Emily considered that for a while. "Then that's where you start, with a GED."

"General equivalency diploma?" Monica shook her head. "That takes books, money for school. I couldn't just up and take the test."

"Monica, I'm a teacher," Emily said, becoming excited as a new idea hit her. "I've kept my old high-school textbooks for some unknown reason, maybe because I love them. I could loan you the books and tutor you on Sunday afternoons.'' She sat back with a satisfied smile.

A gleam of hope surfaced in Monica's gaze but she extinguished it. ''You should get paid for something like that. I couldn't pay you.''

Emily leaned forward again. ''Dammit, you don't have to pay me! You're worse than the ironworkers about pride, Monica. I like you—we're friends. Friends help each other. Isn't that good enough?''

Monica stared in surprise at Emily's outburst. ''Well, you don't have to get all riled about it,'' she said, grinning. ''If you want to that bad, how can I say no?''

''I guess you can't,'' Emily said, grinning back.

''But I'll find some way to pay you back. Now that you're dating Bookworm, you might want a Saturday night off sometime. I could talk Bailey into letting me handle everything once in a while.''

Emily thought about that, and the possibility of spending an uninterrupted weekend with Ned made her flush with pleasure. ''Well, maybe.''

''No maybes about it,'' Monica said. ''I've said it before and I'll say it again. You two are perfect for each other. I hope to dance at your wedding.''

''Aren't you rushing things a little?'' Emily took a long, calming drink of her iced tea.

''Oh, I wouldn't say so,'' Monica replied, smiling sagely. ''Not from the look on your face when you talk about that man.''

Emily couldn't help but contrast Monica's joyful acceptance of her new relationship with her parents' vocal disapproval. If sometime far in the future she and Ned ever had a wedding, Monica might be the only one she knew who would feel like dancing.

CHAPTER TWELVE

CARRIE SIMMONS arrived soon after Emily and Monica's discussion. She impressed Emily as a pale, timid woman who realized that she had few options in life. When Emily and Monica explained Jake's possible return and Emily's offer of a place to stay, Carrie accepted the information with the same calm resignation she displayed toward everything.

Carrie only came alive, Emily noticed, when the boys were around, and they seemed to return her affection, even after knowing her for only a short time. Watching Carrie with the boys, Emily congratulated herself on a solution that seemed to provide a better life for everyone concerned. Now both of these women had a chance, if only Jake stayed away for good.

A framed family picture resting stubbornly on top of the television set seemed to mock Emily's wish. Every time she glanced at the pugnacious expression of the man sitting next to a smiling Monica, and flanked by three grinning little boys, Emily shivered. Even in that tame, photography studio pose, Jake Spangler looked dangerous.

Supper was early and simple, wieners and beans, with applesauce and soda crackers to flesh out the meal. Emily enjoyed the company, but as the meal neared its end around six she began thinking of Ned again. In a private moment while helping Monica clear the dishes,

Emily told her about the scheduled date with him, and Monica shooed her out of the apartment within ten minutes.

A hot wind during the day had spread a layer of dust on the horizon and turned the setting sun a bright orange. It dangled like a tangerine in Emily's rearview mirror as she drove east toward Ned's apartment. A few clouds, early predictors of the monsoon rains that would splash the city in a few weeks, drifted near the sun, and the edge of heat faded as the sun slipped lower in the sky. A summer night, magic in the desert, was on its way.

Despite the problems that loomed for her and Ned, Emily couldn't remember ever being happier. Someday she'd have to tell him that she was Dan Johnson's daughter and take the consequences, but not yet. Tonight she would lie in his arms and cherish every minute of his loving.

After parking the car she hurried past the small pool and glanced up toward his door. He was waiting for her, sitting outside on a kitchen chair with his bare feet up on the railing that bordered the second-floor walkway. The sight of him sent a shock of awareness through her, as if he'd caressed her skin and left it warm and willing for more.

"Hi," she called, gazing up at him.

"Hi, yourself." He put his feet down and leaned his arms on the railing. "Want to watch the sunset with me?"

"Sure."

"I'll get another chair."

So simple, she thought as she climbed the stairs. No complicated discussions about what movie to see, where to eat dinner, how to fill the time together. The most basic pleasures come naturally—evening drives, picnics, sunsets, loving . . . and oh, the loving.

She reached his door as he came out carrying a mate to his chair. He put it down and smiled as he drew her into his arms. "I've missed you."

"I've missed you, too." She nestled against him and turned her face up to his. "Are your neighbors nosy?"

"Probably." He rubbed the small of her back and gazed into her eyes. "Do you mind?"

"Not really."

The brush of his lips on hers was light, but she felt the heat of his body pressing forward and knew that his thoughts mirrored hers.

She edged his lips with the tip of her tongue. "You're not watching the sunset," she murmured.

"Neither are you."

"I think we should," she said, nibbling at his lower lip. "We've never done that together."

He chuckled. "If that's your only reason, let's go inside. I can think of several things we've never done together, and they'd all be more fun than watching the sunset."

She gazed into the gray-green of his eyes and laughed softly. "And here I was thinking as I climbed up those stairs that you were a romantic, wanting to share the simple beauties of nature with me."

He pressed her closer. "I am, and I do."

"That's not romance," she teased as she began to ache in response to his erotic heat. "That's lust."

"Maybe it's both," he said, his gaze stirring the fires within her.

"Could be, I suppose." She knew they wouldn't watch a sunset tonight.

"I'd like to show you how romance and lust go together, if you're interested."

Her skin flushed in anticipation. "I'm interested," she murmured.

The inside of his apartment was dim and a flickering light beckoned from the bedroom. As he led her quietly through the doorway her eyes widened at the transformation he'd made since yesterday, when she'd glimpsed an ordinary bachelor's quarters with an unmade bed.

Candlelight danced over white sheets carefully folded back and the oak headboard was mounded with pillows. From the living room drifted soft music that she vaguely recognized as something classical. A delicate fragrance filled the room and she noticed that he'd moved away to light a small stick of incense.

"I'm overwhelmed," she said, looking around at the sensuous bower he'd created.

"It's what you deserve," he said softly, walking toward her. "I can understand if you think I'm driven by lust for you. That's probably what last night was about, and this morning, too." He smiled. "Especially this morning. But I wanted to show you that there's more to me, more to us, than that."

She gazed at him and felt an emotion that hadn't held her in its grip for a long time. She hesitated to acknowledge it because the last time she had her heart had been broken. He reached for the top button of her blouse and she closed her eyes, not wanting him to see the way his touch made her feel.

He undressed her slowly, almost reverently. Gone was the impatience of the night before, and when at last she stood before him without adornment, he took an unsteady breath and simply gazed at her. "I promised myself that I'd take time, this time," he said, his glance leisurely exploring every rosy inch of her. "I owe it to you and I owe it to myself." He gazed straight into her eyes, straight into her heart. "We've had sex, but I wonder if we've made love."

"I . . . I'm not sure what you mean." She began to tremble.

"After tonight, you will be." Lifting her in his arms, he carried her to the bed. The sheets were soft and cool against her heated skin, and the pillows formed a yielding cradle of comfort.

Her throat constricted as she watched him undress. Had she taken the time to appreciate him, either? His shoulder and chest muscles rippled as he pulled his T-shirt over his head and tossed it to the floor. He unfastened his shorts and flexed his arms—arms strong enough to lift her and carry her to the bed, gentle enough to wrap her in a snug cocoon of security. Then his shorts and underwear were gone, revealing the beauty of a fully aroused male, his skin bronzed by candlelight.

"We're going to take our time," he said, easing down beside her and lacing his strong workman's fingers through hers as they lay beside her on the pillow. "We're going," he said, kissing her forehead, her closed eyelids, her cheeks, "to make love." Then he touched his mouth to hers and settled into a deep kiss that fed the emotion flowering in her heart.

Silently he asked for more than passion, more than the meeting of two bodies in the night. She answered with a kiss that spoke more eloquently than words, and she knew from the soft moan deep in his throat, that he understood. Slowly he lifted his head and gazed down at her. The stakes had been raised.

Still holding her hand, he kissed her shoulder and the ridge of her collarbone. His lips cherished her, nurtured the emotion they both felt but neither could say, so new and untried were the words between them. Touching her only with his lips and tongue, he continued his journey downward. Her breasts rounded beneath his mouth and demanded to be suckled. He paid homage to them with a tenderness that brought tears to her eyes.

Candlelight picked out the sheen of his hair as he bent over her and kissed the winged outline of her ribs and the flat plane of her belly. Releasing her hand, he moved to the foot of the bed and kissed her instep, her ankle, the swell of her calf, the sensitive spot behind her knee.

She grew dizzy with anticipation as he pressed his lips against her inner thigh and moved higher. Slowly he defined all of her except the dark triangle that he saved for last. When he kissed her there, she gasped. He'd touched her that way before, but never with such slow deliberation, never with such sensuous care. *Making love,* she thought, as heat from his ministrations poured through her. *This is making love.*

His caresses gave her heightened awareness of her entire body, until the intensity of his loving blurred the clarity and she began losing consciousness of self. At that moment, as if knowing that she was slipping away from rational thought, he lifted his head and returned to her side. "Not yet," he murmured, tasting her lips once more. "Not yet."

She watched as he sheathed himself. Then he hovered over her and gently parted her thighs. His gaze never left hers as he thrust forward. "Now," he said. "Now let go. Don't close your eyes. Let me see. Show me, Emily. Show me what you feel."

His urgings were unnecessary. She was beyond concealing anything from him. Her lips parted in a whimpering cry as she arched upward and dug her fingers into the powerful muscles of his back. "I want you," she cried.

"That's not enough," he whispered, stroking back and forth, his gaze burning into hers.

"Ooh," she moaned, her head thrashing on the pillow.

"Tell me, Emily," he said, panting. "Tell me."

"I . . . Ned, oh, Ned!"

"Tell me!"

"I love you!"

"Yes!" He increased the tempo as sweat glistened on his brow. "Yes, Emily. Love. I love you. Can you feel it? Can you feel the love, every time I—oh, yes, now—Emily . . . Emily!"

They surged together one last time as a shuddering climax, more powerful than they had ever known, seized them and hurled them forward to a place where love would rule their lives, changing them forever. They held each other through the spinning ride, and at last their breathing slowed to normal. Then they gazed at each other with a sense of wonder.

"I don't take it back," Emily said softly. "I love you, Ned."

"And that's spelled l-o-v-e, and not l-u-s-t, right?" he said with a tender smile. "I love you."

Emily sighed. "And you proved your point beautifully."

"Couldn't help it. I realized after we said goodbye this morning how I felt. But my actions hadn't been those of a man in love. Instead I'd come across as some animal with a powerful sex drive. I was determined to change that tonight."

"I'd say that you did."

He combed his fingers through her hair. "I do love you, Emily, and it's important to me that you know, but beyond that..." He gazed at the candle burning down to a stub on the beside table. "I just can't make any promises," he finished, glancing back at her. "I wish—"

"Hush. I know." She caressed his cheek. "It's too early for promises. For both of us."

He frowned, his expression troubled. "The hell of it is, I want to promise you the world. And I can't. I love you and I'm in no position to be loving a woman."

She smiled at his choice of words. "I think you're in a wonderful position."

In spite of his concern, he grinned. "Okay, smarty. And speaking of my position, I'd better change it and blow out these candles before we start a fire."

"I loved the atmosphere. Not that I would have minded, but I expected an unmade bed and untidy closets."

Ned laughed as he eased away from her and headed for the bathroom. "The closets are still untidy. I just closed the doors."

"Do you always sleep with this many pillows?" She snuggled into the fluffy depths and pulled the sheet over her.

"No," he said from the bathroom. "K-Mart had a sale and I thought it would be kind of nifty, having all those pillows."

"It was."

"And will be," he said, emerging from the bathroom and climbing back into bed with her. "You can do all sorts of interesting things with extra pillows."

"Oh, yeah?"

"Mmm." He cupped her breast and leaned down to flick his tongue against her nipple.

"Where did you learn that you can do interesting things with pillows?"

"Books," he said, laughing.

"Sure you did, Ned Tucker."

"Why do you doubt me? You know I'm a scholar," he said, nuzzling her neck as he kneaded the soft flesh of her breast.

"Then I guess you could show me the book where you learned this."

"Well..."

"Just as I thought." She caught his face in both hands and made him look at her. "You learned it from a woman, didn't you?"

"Is this true confession time?" His hazel eyes were bright with humor. "When we reveal our pasts, yours and mine? Because for everything you wring out of me, I get a similar bit of juicy information from you."

"Oh, well, uh..." Revelations about her love life didn't worry her, but she had other secrets that did.

His expression grew serious. "Let's save that one, okay? There's only one person in my past that you should know about, and I'll tell you about her pretty soon, but not now. And then you can tell me all about your one, or two, or half a dozen, or—"

"Hey!" She grabbed a pillow. "Half a dozen?"

He shrugged and smiled and she hit him with the pillow.

"That isn't one of the ways," he said, laughing as he grabbed an edge of the pillow. "If you'll be a little patient, I'll show you, but you don't have to get violent."

"Give me that," she said, wrestling with him over the pillow. "Half a dozen. Honestly. If you think that I've been to bed with—"

"No, I don't," he said, rolling her over and pinning her arms to the mattress. He gazed gently into her face. "No, I don't," he whispered, kissing her pouting lips until the pout disappeared. "And now let's find a better use for that pillow," he said with a wickedly sensuous smile.

MUCH LATER, as Emily was dressing to leave, Ned pulled on his underwear and shorts and went out to retrieve the kitchen chairs from the front walkway.

"I guessed we missed the sunset," Emily commented, buckling the belt of her slacks as she wandered into the small kitchen where he was returning the chairs.

He smiled at her. "Think there'll be another one next weekend?"

"Could be."

"Then we could try catching it, if we don't have anything more important to do." He shoved the second chair up to the table and walked toward her. "If we made love all afternoon next Sunday, we might feel like watching the sunset, for a change of pace."

"Oh, Ned, I can't," Emily said, remembering with a pang of regret that she'd promised Monica her Sunday afternoons for the next few weeks.

His expression changed from open to wary. "Sorry. I shouldn't be making those kind of assumptions. I just—"

"Ned, I wish I could spend every minute with you." She slid both her arms around his bare torso and gazed up at him. "And I'd be free on Sunday, except that this afternoon I promised Monica I'd tutor her once a week. She's going for her GED."

"Hey, that's great. Really." He gathered her close. "I'm just a selfish punk who'd like more time with you."

"I want time with you, too, and I offered my Sunday afternoon to Monica without thinking. As much as I want to help her, now I regret offering, to tell the truth."

"No, you did the right thing. Maybe it's just as well." His smile was bittersweet. "The more I'm with you, the more frustrated I'll probably get over all the restrictions on me right now. For both our sakes, we need to take this slow."

Emily thought of the giant task of overcoming her father's antagonism and the even more threatening prospect of revealing her identity to Ned. "I suppose so," she agreed, wanting to tell him everything and end the agony of deception, yet knowing she would be unwise to do that.

He hesitated. "Did you say anything to your parents today?"

"Yes, I did." She glanced away from him.

"They're not pleased."

"No."

Ned sighed. "Is that going to be a problem for you?"

"I won't let it be a problem," she said, meeting his gaze. "I love you. They'll have to learn to deal with that."

His eyebrows rose. "You told them that you love me?"

She smiled and shook her head. "No. I wasn't admitting to myself, even, that love was what I felt about you until tonight. You were the first to hear."

"Thank goodness for that," he said, chuckling. "Not that I wouldn't like you to shout it from the rooftops, but with parents I think you're better off letting out the information gradually. Especially in this case, when they already dislike me before we've even met."

"Ned, I apologize for their prejudices. I can't imagine how they—"

"Hold it. How they react isn't under your control, so you have no reason to apologize."

"But I feel terrible, as if it's a slap in the face to you."

"Would it help if they met me?" He traced the line of her jaw with his finger. "I'd promise to dress like a human being and watch all my verb tenses."

Emily panicked. "Um, let's wait on that for a while," she said, looking away from him. "They're leaving in a couple of days for a cruise, anyway, and won't be back for three weeks."

"A cruise, huh?" He nestled her head against his shoulder and kissed her hair. "Oh, Emily, I don't know if I'll ever be able to give you advantages like that. Your parents may have a point, objecting to a guy like me."

She lifted her head and glared at him. "That's nonsense, and you know it, Ned Tucker. If you keep talking that way, I'll just have to...to..."

"To what?" he asked, gazing at her with amusement.

"To kiss some sense into you," she said, grasping his head in both hands and pressing her lips hard against his.

"Mmm." He cooperated immediately, softening the firm line of his mouth to meld with hers and create a moist channel for the sensuous movement of tongues, the gentle mingling of breath. Soon the gentleness faded as their bodies warmed in response to the suggestive exploration of eager hands.

When Ned's fingers started on the buttons she'd recently fastened down the front of her blouse, Emily gripped his hand and stopped his motion. "This is crazy," she said, taking her mouth from his. "I have to leave so that you can sleep."

"Says who?" He reached for the buttons again.

"Says me." She pushed his hand away and wiggled out of his arms. "The point I was trying to make was that money doesn't matter," she said, breathing hard as she rebuttoned her blouse. "Do you agree with me?"

"I don't know." He smiled and stepped closer. "I always think more clearly when I'm undressing you," he said, reaching for her again.

"The heck you do." She backed away from him.

"Spoilsport."

"Ned, be sensible. I won't have you wandering around on those beams on no sleep."

"But I won't be able to hold you like this until Friday night. That's a lifetime away."

"I know." She gazed at him. "I'll be just as lonely as you are. Should I reconsider this deal with Monica, so that we'll have more time?"

"Absolutely not." He put both hands into his shorts pockets, as if to tame them into submission. "Will you be staying for supper each time you tutor her?"

"No. That wasn't mentioned, and I won't agree to that."

He regarded her silently for a moment. "Then how about having supper at my mom's next Sunday?"

"Your mother's house?" Emily paused, thrown a little off guard by his suggestion.

"Sure." His tone was casual, but his gaze was anything but. "You weren't the only one who spilled the beans about us today, although my mom's reaction was a little different from your parents'. She's delighted that I'm interested in someone and she's dying to meet you."

"Well, I . . . I guess that would be fine." Gradually Emily became used to the idea. "Yes," she said, smiling at him, "I'd like that."

"Curt will be there, too, I expect, once he finds out you're coming. It's a good thing he's my brother and I can trust him, because he has a massive crush on you."

"That's flattering."

"Yeah, well don't be too flattered or I'll have to reconsider this invitation."

"You're not really worried about your brother, are you?"

"No." He smiled. "I'm glad that you already like each other."

Emily studied him while she thought about his invitation. "You're taking me home to meet your family, aren't you?" she asked finally.

"Yes," he said, his expression serious. "And if you think that's significant, you're absolutely right."

CHAPTER THIRTEEN

ON MONDAY Emily brought her high-school textbooks to the bar and gave them to Monica.

"God, they're in beautiful shape," Monica exclaimed, leafing through an algebra book as the two of them sat in the storeroom during a break. "Why didn't you sell them back?"

"I didn't want to."

"Most of the kids I knew had to sell them. They needed the money."

"I was lucky," Emily said, realizing more and more how true that was. "My parents knew that I loved school and the books were special to me, so they let me keep them."

"I can see they were special," Monica said. "You didn't write in them or nothing." She glanced up from the book. "I won't mess them up, either," she promised. "I won't smoke while I'm reading them, and I won't let the boys get anywhere near them."

"I'm not worried about that, Monica. I trust you with the books, and besides, they should be put to use. They've just been sitting on my bookshelf gathering dust."

"Well, I'll take very good care of them, all the same." Monica picked up the textbooks as if handling gold bullion. "If you'll cover for me, I'll lock them in my car right now, so nothing can happen, like food getting on them or anything."

"Sure, I'll cover." Emily smiled and headed back through the kitchen. She needed to gather more information for her study, anyway, although her enthusiasm for it had evaporated somewhat. Nothing in her life these days seemed as important as being with Ned. Other than the few moments she could steal to talk with him each night at Suds and Subs, she had to wait until Friday after work to satisfy the longing to nestle in his arms.

He'd left the bar a half hour before. His presence had suffused the smoky room with excitement for Emily, but it was a frustrating sort of excitement. She wondered if life would be easier if they couldn't see each other at all until Friday. They were like spies, snatching a few moments to talk, to communicate their love with a glance or the merest feather touch that had to look like an accident.

But of course she didn't have the choice of seeing him or not. He was part of a work gang and the social interaction at Suds and Subs meant something to him and to the other men. Besides, she really wanted to see him each night, even for such brief contact. She had no doubts now—she was head over heels, wildly, passionately in love with Ned Tucker.

Yet she couldn't simply drop the other elements in her life. The ironworker study had been a good idea, was still a good idea. Publication of her findings would help as she moved toward a tenured position at the university, and she wanted that security even more now so that she'd never become an additional financial burden to Ned.

Taking notes was much easier because Monica knew about the research, and Emily could scribble her observations when Monica was around. Monica was curious, and often peered over Emily's shoulder as she wrote. Emily didn't care; she welcomed Monica's input concerning the social structure at the bar.

Later that evening she and Monica met by chance, as they often did, when both had orders to fill at the same time.

"I still can't get over you loaning me those books," Monica said for perhaps the fourth time that night.

"You're making too much of it," Emily said with a smile. "It's no big deal, really."

"Yes, it is, and I meant what I said about convincing Bailey to give you a Saturday off now and then. How about this weekend?"

Emily laughed and shook her head. "Thanks, but I think we should start you on a plan of study, and Sunday afternoon is the time to begin. Besides, Ned has invited me to have dinner at his mother's house Sunday night, so he and I couldn't go off somewhere together, anyway."

"His mom's house, huh?" Monica grinned. "Good for you. When are you taking him to meet your folks?"

Emily's smile vanished, along with her cheerful mood. "I don't know."

Monica frowned. "Wow, what did I say that turned off the sunshine."

"Nothing." Emily picked up her tray of drinks. "Thanks, Henry," she said, and glanced at Monica. "There are a few problems with my parents, that's all."

"Oh." Monica gazed at her. "Sorry to hear that, Emily. That could be a real bummer."

"You're telling me."

"Well, what about the weekend after next, for Saturday night, then?" Monica asked brightly in an obvious attempt to change the subject.

Emily smiled at her friend. "Maybe," she said. "Let me think about it."

"You do that."

As the evening wound to a close, Emily did think about Monica's offer. A weekend with Ned sounded like a fantasy come true. What she'd really like was to take him to the family cabin on Mount Lemmon. She already knew how he loved the mountains, and both of them could escape the heat that bore down on Tucson day after sweltering day.

She wouldn't have to tell him who owned the cabin, just that she'd been allowed to use it for the weekend. With her parents out of town for three weeks, the only person who might have plans to go up would be her brother.

The next day Emily thought about her idea, and the more she thought the more she liked it. She dreamed of time alone with Ned, making love beneath the beamed ceilings on the king-size bed in the loft, walking hand in hand through pine forests, sharing the privacy of an entire house without worry about neighbors on the other side of the wall. That evening she called Danny from work and let him know that she'd need the cabin weekend after next. Fortunately Danny didn't ask her why.

SHE KEPT HER PLAN a secret as a surprise for Ned. She decided not to tell him until Sunday night, just before she left his apartment. All weekend the prospect of a mini vacation together elevated her mood. On Saturday they swam in the large pool owned by her complex and made love until she had to leave for work. Sunday morning they ate Dunkin' Donuts and read the Sunday paper before making love again amid a crinkle of newspapers. Then Emily left for Monica's and drove from there to Ned's apartment, where they took his old Pontiac over to his mother's house.

"Something's going on," Ned finally said as they drove through shimmering desert heat that refused to abate, even at five-thirty in the evening. "You've got something up your sleeve, Emily. I can sense it."

She didn't answer and merely gave him a smiling glance.

"When are you going to tell me?"

"Later."

"Come on, Emily. I hate surprises."

"You do?" She looked at him, considering this. "I thought everyone loved surprises."

"Not me. Good things, bad things, it doesn't matter. I like everything out on the table, where I can see it."

"My goodness," she exclaimed, trying to banish her uneasiness. "You mean, even for your birthday, even for Christmas?"

Ned laughed. "Yep. It got to be a joke around my house when I was a kid. I'd make a list of what I wanted, and my folks would tell me what out of the list they could afford, and that's what I got, no deviations."

"Seems pretty stark to me," Emily said. The word *inflexible* also occurred to her, but she didn't say it aloud. "What about Santa Claus?"

"That might have been the beginning. I was furious when I found out that my mother bought the presents that I'd imagined were made by little elves at the North Pole."

"But what about the beauty of fantasy?"

He squeezed her hand. "I have that," he said softly. "When we make love, we create a fantasy that's far sweeter and gentler than the rest of life. That's all the escape from reality I need."

"You read books," she continued, determined to poke a few holes in his logic, more for her sake than his. "Novels, for example. They're not true."

"The good ones are. I don't mean the characters are real, but the emotions and the human situations are. That's another reason I like Browning. He was dedicated to the truth."

Oh, God, Emily thought. Hot wind blew in through the open windows of the car, matching the dry desolation she felt as she imagined what would happen when Ned learned the truth about her. Her only hope was to build their love solid and strong now, so that it could withstand the storm later. "So, to make a long story short, you want to hear about my surprise," she said.

"Please."

"Okay. First of all, Monica feels terribly obligated to me because of the books and the tutoring. She's offered to cover for me next Saturday night so that we can have the weekend together."

Ned grinned. "I like this already."

"There's more. Some...friends of mine have a cabin on Mount Lemmon, and I've been able to get the key. The place is very quiet and very cool."

Ned gave her a loving glance. "Sounds pretty terrific. You can let your hair down, literally and figuratively."

"Yep." Emily reached for the single braid that hung down her back. "I know how much you like my hair loose, but today was just too hot."

"I understand, and please don't think you have to make yourself miserable to suit my preference. I have an obsession about your hair, but not an incurable one."

"Oh? Then you won't mind if I have it cut next week?"

"You're testing me, but no, I'll love you every bit as much, hair or no hair."

Emily chuckled. "Luckily for you that won't be an issue, at least not soon. I like my hair the way it is, except on days like today."

"Yeah. Next weekend in the mountains will be a treat, all right. Much as I hate to admit it, dating a rich girl has its advantages."

"Oh, Ned, lots of people have cabins in the mountains," she protested, uncomfortable as always with his rich versus poor statements.

"Nobody that I know."

"Well, it's no big thing, but I thought you'd—we'd—enjoy it."

"I'm sure we will," he said quietly. "Thanks, Emily."

She swallowed the dryness in her throat. The eager anticipation for next weekend had been dimmed a little, or perhaps it had been dimmed a lot, she thought. The more she learned about Ned, the more she dreaded their inevitable confrontation at the end of the summer when she told him who she was. Despite the joy of being with him now, she was unable to forget the problems looming in the future.

"You're quiet all of a sudden." He brushed her cheek with the back of his hand. "I guess I spoiled your surprise."

"No, not really," she said, adding yet another untruth to the growing pile. "I was going to tell you tonight, so a few hours doesn't make any difference."

"I'm touched that you planned all this for us. Just think, we'll be able to spend two whole days together with nothing to do but eat, sleep and make love." He laced his fingers through hers. "Especially make love." He sighed. "Even that time won't be long enough for me to show you how I feel about you."

His words fanned a glow of sensual excitement between them, and the chill of Emily's misgivings began to disappear. "I know it won't be long enough," she said, squeezing his hand, "but it will be more than we've had."

"Someday," Ned vowed, rubbing his thumb across the back of her hand, "someday we'll have all the time in the world. It's got to happen for us, Emily. We're so good together."

"Yes," she said, storing away every word he uttered. "Yes, we are."

They rode in silence the short distance left to his mother's house. As they pulled into the driveway Emily concluded that the small ranch-style house with the single carport was about the way she'd pictured it. Made of concrete block textured to look like adobe, the house had a straightforward rectangular design—living room and kitchen on one end, front door in the middle, bedrooms on the other end.

The front yard was gravel and cactus, as were most of the yards in the subdivision, and Curt, shirtless, was pulling a few stray weeds. He waved as they drove up.

"I'm warning you that the house is like a furnace," Curt said, smiling in welcome. "Mom thinks the only meal to cook for company is pot roast, so the oven's been blasting all day. I tried to convince her that we could simmer the darn thing on the roof instead. I voted for cold cuts and salad. She wouldn't listen to a word I said."

"That's okay," Ned replied. "We're tough. Don't forget that the Pontiac doesn't have air conditioning."

"I wasn't worried about a he-man like you, but I thought maybe Miss Johnson might object." Curt glanced shyly at her.

"You're going to have to call me Emily," she said, "and I'm used to the heat, too. I've lived in Tucson all my life, just like both of you."

"Emily, huh?" Curt looked doubtful. "That doesn't sound right."

"That's because you're not used to it," she said. "Practice saying my first name enough times, and the foreign sound will wear right off."

"If you say so, Miss Johnson."

She glanced at Ned, who was watching them with amusement in his hazel eyes. "If you say so, *Emily*," she prompted.

Curt grinned. "If you say so, *Emily*. And I think all of us could enjoy this discussion lots better on the back porch with a cold drink in our hands. What do you say?"

"Sounds good," Ned replied. "Let me take Emily in to meet Mom and we'll try to drag her outside, too. I didn't intend for her to get heat prostration when I invited Emily over for a meal."

"Well, you know Mom," Curt said, leading them through the carport to the side door.

Emily wondered if Curt and Ned's mother preferred that they bring guests through the front door instead. Apparently she did, judging from the shocked look on the face of the woman glancing through the kitchen window as they passed. At the door the men weren't quite sure how to proceed, knowing that Emily as the woman should go first, but that they shouldn't shove her into the room ahead of her introduction.

Finally they managed to pile in almost all at once, something like a gang of little kids, Emily thought with a chuckle. Ned's mother faced them with a determined smile as she dried her hands on a dish towel. Sweat dampened her hairline and Emily estimated the temperature in the kitchen at well over a hundred and ten degrees.

"I'm glad to meet you, Mrs. Tucker," Emily said, stepping forward to shake hands after Ned and Curt's chorus introduction.

"Oh, just call me Lee. Everyone does, except the boys, of course," Ned's mother said. Her handshake was firm and capable, although Emily noticed a wincing crinkle around her eyes when she moved. Ned's mother had some sort of chronic pain, Emily guessed.

"Lee?" Emily said, smiling. "That's pretty."

"Short for Rosalee," she explained. "Eddie—that's my late husband—he liked nicknames, so I was Lee from the minute he met me. It stuck."

"Well, I like it," Emily said, noticing that Ned had inherited his mother's eyes. Emily had no trouble seeing beyond the few extra pounds and the lines and worry to a time when Rosalee Tucker had been a lovely woman. But unlike Emily's mother, whose problems had lessened over the years, this woman's had multiplied, beginning with the death of her husband. "Something sure smells delicious," Emily commented. One thing both mothers had in common was their love of cooking.

"Yeah," Curt added, "and this place is sweltering, Mom. I was cooler out weeding the front yard."

"The living room's better," his mother said, her tone slightly scolding. "I would have thought you'd bring Ned and Emily in through the front door, Curt."

"No reason," Curt said. "We're on our way out to the backyard, and this is the closest way."

"And we want you to come with us," Ned added. "Can you leave dinner for a while? Curt's right, this kitchen is blazing, and you've probably been on your feet too long already."

"I feel responsible," Emily said, "having you go to all of this trouble for me."

"Heavens, it's not trouble," Ned's mother said, waving the dish towel. "I asked Ned to invite you." She smiled sheepishly. "But it is pretty hot in the house, isn't it? Maybe we should eat outside, if the flies aren't too bad."

"I'll take the flies. Come on, Mom," Curt said, guiding her by the elbow. "I have a lounge chair out here with your name on it, and Ned's going to fix us all something cold to drink."

"Well..." The older woman glanced around the kitchen. "I guess everything's in pretty good shape. The salad's unmolded, and the coleslaw is made, and the roast will keep for a while."

"Then go and relax, all three of you." Ned ushered them out the back sliding door to the covered porch. "I'll play waiter."

"I'll help you," Emily volunteered.

"No, you won't." He smiled at her and gave her a little push out the door. "Six nights a week is enough. Tonight I'll wait on you, for a change. What's everybody want?"

"Iced tea, please, Ned," his mother said.

"Lemonade," Curt called through the door.

"I'll have lemonade, too," Emily said.

"Coming up," Ned replied and closed the sliding door.

Emily sat on a webbed lawn chair next to the lounge where Curt was settling his mother with a pillow for the small of her back.

"Oof," she exclaimed softly as she eased onto the lounge. "This back of mine is such a nuisance. Getting old is a nuisance, Emily."

Emily wasn't sure how to respond. Her parents, who were probably about the same age as Lee Tucker, didn't find age a nuisance, at least not so obviously. What a difference circumstances made, Emily thought. "Your house is very nice," she said, grabbing for a different topic of conversation.

"Why, thank you." Ned's mother looked pleased. "You didn't get to see much of it, with Curt bringing you in the back way, but I'm happy with it. Eddie and I bought this place before Ned started high school, so he'd go to the same place all four years. The boys used to beg us to put in a pool in the back, here, but I'm glad we didn't, now that Eddie's not around to take care of it."

"I suppose pools are a lot of trouble," Emily ventured, not knowing in the least what she was talking about. Her parents had a pool service and her apartment pool wasn't her concern, either.

"They sure are," Ned's mother said. "We have enough trouble keeping the little bit of grass trimmed and the bushes and trees watered. And the mulberry there, that Eddie and I planted, cools the yard considerably. A pool in the middle would mean no tree."

"It's a nice tree," Emily said, again hearing herself sounding like a conversational robot.

"How do you like your job at Suds and Subs?" Ned's mother asked. "I used to have a job something like that, at a cafeteria, until my back gave out for good."

"Waiting tables is hard work," Emily said, speaking for the first time with real feeling. "I don't understand how women keep it up, year after year."

"Sometimes they have no choice," the older woman commented.

"I guess not, but I'm sure glad I won't have to do it for the rest of my life."

"I hope you'll teach the rest of your life," Curt said with a trace of worship in his tone. "You're great at it."

"Thanks, Curt," she said. "But I'll tell both of you something. If I was a good teacher before, I'll be a much better one next semester, after this experience. Before I only talked about different social stratas, and how environment shaped people. I didn't understand it firsthand, but I'm beginning to now, after working in the bar."

"That's good." Ned's mother nodded. "I always thought that people from one way of life should go through a program to see what it's like for people in another." She laughed. "Of course I'd be first in line to try out the country-club life."

Emily squirmed, searching for a comment that wouldn't seem patronizing. After all, she represented the country-club life that Lee envied. Fortunately Ned opened the sliding door at that moment and produced a tray of iced drinks, saving Emily from having to say anything.

"Your drink, ma'am," he said, handing her a lemonade with a flourish.

"I suppose you'll expect a tip," she said, chuckling.

"Sure will," he replied, and winked.

Emily blushed and wondered if either Curt or his mother would read anything suggestive into Ned's response. Emily found that she read something suggestive into almost anything concerning Ned.

"Well, you're lucky," Ned's mother said when each person had a drink and Ned had pulled up a lawn chair next to Emily's. "You've been able to go to college and get the kind of training that will keep you from having to wait on tables or stand in an assembly line."

"Yes, I have been lucky," Emily said for the second time that day.

"I believe in college," Lee went on. "I wanted Ned to go, even after his father died and we were so strapped. I told him we'd find a way. My back wasn't so bad then, and I was ready to take on a second job, but he wouldn't let me."

"Mom, you know I didn't want more school," Ned said. "Curt and I are two different animals."

"Yes, but what about your future, Ned?" his mother asked. "It's tied to the construction business, which goes up and down like crazy. And then, when you're older, you won't want to keep climbing around up there...." She paused and cleared her throat before launching into a litany of the dangers inherent in Ned's job.

Although Ned tried to change the subject and then discount the risks of ironworking, his mother continued expressing her concern. Emily listened, refusing to acknowledge Ned's glances and resigned shaking of his head. Emily was on his mother's side in this discussion, although as a newcomer to the family group she was reluctant to voice an opinion.

Ned's mother was saying the same thing her parents would have said, Emily realized. In his present situation, Ned didn't have a particularly promising future. He'd been too busy helping his family to set any goals for himself, a sad omission for a man with his intelligence and ability.

In their only conversation on the subject, Emily remembered that Ned had rejected the prospect of advancing into management and eventual ownership of a construction company, the path that Emily's father had followed. Instead Ned had confessed almost shyly his desire to write something about his experiences as an ironworker.

Emily would imagine how her parents, and probably even Ned's mother, would look at that ambition. They'd consider it a foolish long shot, and perhaps it was. But Emily recognized a yearning in Ned that made her believe he might be successful.

She'd known of a few people in similar circumstances—a longshoreman and a fire fighter came to mind—who had combined a physically demanding job with the ability to write about it and become successful authors. Perhaps she ought to ask Ned if she could look at his notes when they spent the weekend at the cabin. That would tell her something about his chances.

"Mom, I think I smell the roast burning," Ned commented, finally as a last-ditch effort to interrupt the tirade about ironwork.

"I don't," his mother said, although she sat up in the lounge chair and sniffed apprehensively. "But I guess I should check on it."

Ned got out of his chair and helped her up. "Tell us what to do and we'll all pitch in."

"Yes, definitely," Emily said, also leaving her chair.

"Oh, you all just sit out here and enjoy yourselves. There's not that much to do," Ned's mother protested.

"Come on, Mom," Curt said, shepherding them all into the kitchen. "You didn't raise us to be waited on."

They carried the dinner out to the patio and laughingly fought off flies during the meal. Curt kept them entertained with stories about his fast-food restaurant job and the topic of Ned's future didn't come up again.

Emily enjoyed herself, yet she couldn't help thinking how these two people that Ned loved had circumscribed his potential. Ned had, of course, participated fully in the limiting of his horizons for the sake of his mother and brother, but Emily wondered if, now that the obligation was nearing an end, he'd forgotten how to dream. She vowed to begin teaching him tonight.

Later at his apartment, as they lay together surrounded by pillows and sated with lovemaking, she decided to broach the subject. "Remember the day of our picnic, when you mentioned something about writing a book?" she asked, turning on her side to face him.

"Yeah." He gazed at the ceiling and chuckled.

"Why are you laughing?"

"Because the idea's ridiculous."

"Is it?"

He turned toward her. "You should realize that it is. I don't know why I even mentioned it that day. Maybe I was trying to impress you."

Emily took a deep breath. This wasn't going to be easy. "I don't believe that's why you told me. I think you'd really like to write a book."

"So what if I would? That doesn't mean I could, or that anyone would want to publish it."

"That's not a very positive attitude," she said.

"It's a realistic attitude."

"Maybe, Ned, but the excitement in life comes from being a little unrealistic. I know you can't afford to be unrealistic right now, but in a matter of months Curt will graduate, and you'll be able to take a chance."

His gaze softened. "I was hoping that in a matter of months you'd agree to be my wife."

Excitement awoke within her at his statement. Even though she'd imagined him saying it many times, the words, spoken aloud, were like a jolt of electricity. "I was hoping you'd ask," she murmured.

He smiled. "Don't worry, I will. But that hardly seems the time to be taking off on some tangent like writing a book."

"Now, wait a minute." Emily cupped his face in both hands. "I won't have you trading one obligation for another, and leaving yourself out again."

He turned his head to kiss her palm. "I wouldn't call marrying you an obligation," he said, rubbing her hand along his cheek. "I want you with me for very selfish reasons."

"But Ned," she persisted, "you're not giving yourself a chance to find out what you might really want from your life."

"I want you."

"That's not enough."

He kissed the pads of each finger. "I don't think you're the one to judge. If I have to choose between writing this crazy book or marrying you, there's no choice."

She pulled her hand away and gripped his shoulder. "You don't have to choose," she said, wanting to shake him. "You can do both."

He lifted both eyebrows derisively. "How? By living on your salary?"

"What's wrong with that?"

"A hell of a lot."

Emily sat up and stared at him. "Would you care if I quit my job and lived off your salary?"

"That's different."

"No, it's not!" She knew they were fast approaching a fight, and she didn't want that. "Okay," she said, gazing down at his frowning expression. "I've gotten ahead of myself. I meant to ask you something before we ever got into this business about who pays the bills."

"What's that?"

"You said you have lots of notes from your years on the job. Would you consider bringing them next weekend and letting me look them over? Then we'd have a better basis for discussion. If I think the material isn't worthy of a book, I'll say so. But if I like what I read..."

Ned sighed. "I shouldn't have mentioned any of this."

"But you did, and I can't forget it. Ned, I agree with your mother. You should have something more in mind than being an ironworker for the rest of your life."

Ned laughed. "I don't think Mom would be excited about this plan, either. Her son the free-lance writer. Talk about an unsteady future, that's worse than ironwork."

"Maybe she wouldn't approve, but I do," Emily said, determined not to let him wiggle away from the idea. "Let me look at your notes next weekend. Please."

"And if they're lousy, do you promise to drop the subject forever?"

"I promise."

"I have a fair pile of them. I wouldn't want your reading to interfere with—" he reached up and pulled her down beside him "—other things."

"I'm a fast reader. Besides, we can't make love every minute."

He grinned. "Want to make a bet?"

CHAPTER FOURTEEN

THEY TRAVELED up the Mount Lemmon Highway early the following Saturday morning in Emily's Corvette. Ned drove so that Emily could get a head start on the stuffed folder of notes that he reluctantly brought along. Once again he made Emily promise that she'd be brutally honest in her evaluation.

As they drove, he kept glancing anxiously at her. "You may have trouble reading that chicken scratch," he said. "Mrs. Pembroke used to complain about my handwriting."

She looked up with a smile. "I'm not having trouble."

"I doubt if the pages are in order," he said, later, interrupting her again.

"Ned, the pages are in meticulous order. Don't be so nervous. I'm enjoying this. It's as if I had a chance to read your diary, and I'm really getting to know you."

"Great. A diary, like a teenage girl would keep, right?"

"No, that's not right. You know better than that, with all the reading you've done. Without Samuel Pepys's diary, we wouldn't know as much about London during his day. So be quiet and let me read."

Ned let out a noisy sigh. "I didn't know this would be so tough, letting someone else read what I've written."

Emily picked up the next page of his notes. "I think you'd better get used to it," she said and continued reading. His firsthand account of life as an ironworker was incredible, she thought, but she wasn't going to make a final statement until she'd finished. The notes were almost good enough to publish as is, but they needed some polishing. She would have to caution him, however, to retain the vitality as he wove a tighter narrative.

Already she was thinking in terms of working together on the manuscript—he as author and she as preliminary editor. She would want to suggest it, even if she and Ned had been only friends. The fact that they were more than friends made the prospect even more exciting.

Vaguely she realized that the Corvette had left the desert and they were gradually climbing through the vegetation zones along the highway that led to the mountain's nine-thousand-foot summit. The trip wasn't new to her; she'd made it many times with her family, so she remained absorbed in her reading.

Parts of the narrative caused her stomach to clutch with fear as Ned described close calls that he or his friends had experienced. His description of how Mando saved his life claimed her complete attention.

As the Corvette neared the small mountain community of Summerhaven, Ned interrupted Emily's reading to ask for directions. She provided them quickly and immediately returned to his diary. The story had taken a different turn, one that made her mouth dry with apprehension. Ned was describing his current job working for Johnson Construction.

"Is this the place?" Ned asked, slowing the car beside a winding driveway.

Emily glanced up briefly at the two-story chalet partially hidden by large ponderosa pines. "Yes," she said, and kept on reading. "Just go up the driveway and park in front."

"Some cabin," Ned muttered as he steered the car up the narrow dirt road. He parked where Emily had instructed and turned to her. "We're here," he said unnecessarily.

She dragged her gaze from the papers on her lap. "Is this true?" she said in a voice that grated in her ears like the rasp of a nail file.

His expression was questioning. "Yeah."

"It sounds like—" She paused to clear her throat. "It sounds like this company isn't particularly worried about the safety of the workers," she managed to say.

Ned shrugged. "They're not. It's a nonunion job, so they can take advantage of us more easily."

"Have you . . . ever worked for this company before? Your notes begin about two years ago, but you've been an ironworker for nine, right?"

"That's right, and yeah, I worked for Johnson a little over two years ago, now that you mention it."

"Were conditions the same then?"

"Not really. At least I didn't notice that they were. Things have changed, though, and I figure the son has some responsibility for it."

"Ned, something should be done about this," Emily blurted out, unable to contain her indignation.

He smiled. "First you want me to write a book that probably won't sell, and now you want me to blow the whistle on Johnson, which will mean the end of my job."

"They couldn't fire you, not if the charges were true."

Ned's gaze was tolerant. "And what kind of a situation would I have, working for someone I'd turned in to OSHA?"

Emily stared at him for a long time as she sorted out her thoughts. Gradually her course became clear. The person who should intervene was her. She wished that her father was in town, but because he wasn't, she'd have to go straight to Danny herself. She'd make some excuse to leave Ned's apartment early Sunday night and stop at Danny's house on the way home.

Either Danny would agree to improve working conditions immediately, or Emily was prepared to call her father on the ship-to-shore telephone. Her call would ruin her parents' cruise, but that hardly seemed significant compared to the safety of the men working for Johnson Construction—in particular the safety of the man who sat beside her in the Corvette.

She realized that most of the safety violations were minor, and perhaps the job could be finished without anyone being crippled or killed. So far the men, including Ned, were willing to take that calculated risk. But Emily, daughter of the man responsible for those risks, was not.

Slowly she closed the folder containing Ned's papers. "I guess you're right," she said. "I can't expect you to jump in there right now."

"If and when I'm convinced it's necessary, I will. So far the danger has been borderline."

Emily clenched her jaw against saying that even borderline danger was a humiliation, an indictment of those she loved. "I'm glad you're careful," she said.

"I am." He paused. "You . . . haven't said anything about the notes. I guess they're pretty lousy, right?"

"Oh, Ned, they're not lousy at all," she said, chagrined that she'd allowed herself to forget that he was waiting for her evaluation. "This material is wonderful, almost as is, but with some editing and polishing, some narrative direction, I think you've got something really worthwhile here."

"You do?"

"Yes, I do." She watched the glimmer of hope and pride gain force in his expression. "Despite the handwriting, Mrs. Pembroke would be proud of you."

At last his smile broke through and he reached across the console and pulled her into his arms as best he could under the circumstances. "Thanks for saying that. It means a lot."

"I'm not just saying it, Ned. You have a facility with the language. I guess you picked it up with all of your reading. This would make a great book, or maybe more than one. You could go the fiction or nonfiction route, whichever draws you the most."

"It sounds crazy to talk like this, as if I might really do it."

"Of course you're going to do it," she said with deliberate assurance. Maybe by sheer force of will she could convince him. "Too much is at stake not to."

He frowned. "What do you mean?"

"Ned, this is what you were meant to do. Through your writing people who have never walked twenty stories above the ground on narrow beams will understand something of what that's like. They'll gain appreciation for the work you and others like you accomplish."

"You make it sound so noble, but I just wrote that stuff for fun."

"Don't you see? That's all to the good! What more could you want than to have fun doing something, make money at it and contribute to society, all at the same time?"

Ned laughed, but there was a brightness, an excited quality to his laughter that told her he might consider the idea. "I'll tell you what more I could want," he said, smiling down at her in his arms. "I'd like to leave this cramped car and get on with the weekend we planned."

"This isn't the most comfortable place we've ever been, is it? Let's go in," she agreed, untangling herself. "I'll unlock the door if you'll bring the groceries."

"I'll be right behind you."

Moments later they'd unloaded the car of two small suitcases and the groceries they'd bought together before they'd left town. Ned agreed to leave the kitchen organization to Emily for the time being, and he explored the lower level of the house while she put the perishable food in the refrigerator.

"Some little mountain cabin your friends have," Ned commented, surveying the television, VCR and sound system set into the wall beside a huge stone fireplace. "Is this what they call roughing it?"

"It is nice," Emily agreed, although she was so used to the place that she didn't look at it the way Ned did, obviously. She took for granted the elegant living room with its butterscotch leather sofas, the two back bedrooms, each with its own private bath, and the master bedroom in the loft that looked down over the living room. Folding doors closed off the loft for privacy, but with only two of them staying here, the doors wouldn't be needed and they could enjoy the open design of the house.

The place was familiar to Emily—almost too familiar, she'd realized after asking Ned up here. During the week, she'd taken a quick trip up the mountain to remove family pictures, magazines with her parents' name on the subscription label—anything that might reveal the owners of the cabin to Ned.

Soon she would have to tell him the truth, she knew, but she would put that day off as long as possible. Now that she faced the showdown with Danny, she needed more than ever to conceal her identity from Ned, at least until conditions at the work site had been improved. If her behind-the-scenes efforts paid off, there might be a chance that Ned and her family eventually would get along, especially if it seemed to Ned that Danny voluntarily had cleaned up his act.

"I guess somebody around here smokes a pipe," Ned remarked, glancing at a shelf with a collection of Meerschaums and a can of Borkum Riff tobacco.

"Yes, I guess so," Emily replied casually, although she experienced a moment of panic. The pipes and tobacco belonged to her father, but she hadn't thought to put them away. Would Ned remember that the owner of Johnson Construction smoked a pipe?

Then she sighed and rebuked herself for unnecessary paranoia. Lots of men smoked pipes and used that brand of tobacco. "Are you hungry?" she called to Ned as she put away the last of the food.

"No." He leaned in the kitchen doorway with his arms crossed, and his gaze flicked over her.

Every once in a while when she glanced at him, she caught her breath at how magnificent he was. This was one of those times. His short-sleeved cotton shirt, a Hawaiian print, exposed biceps that strained the hem of each sleeve. Below the ragged edge of his cutoffs his thighs were equally impressive. His shirt hung loose over his shorts, not quite covering the inviting bulge of his crotch. At times like this his appeal had far less to do with his mind than she'd like to admit.

"You're sure you don't want lunch?" she said. Her heartbeat told her that she would soon be making love to Ned Tucker.

He shook his head before glancing up toward the loft above the living room. "Ever slept up there?"

"Yes."

"Ever made love up there?"

"No."

"I'd like to change that." He unfolded his arms as he walked toward her. "Right now." Without warning he scooped her up and headed for the narrow wooden staircase.

"Hey," she said, laughing, "what do you think you're doing, carting me off like a sack of potatoes?"

He adjusted her weight as he began the climb. "Some sack of potatoes," he murmured, his gaze traveling lovingly over her. "Your lumps are all in the right place."

"How poetic." The strength of his arms supporting her so easily created a languid heat that made her limp with desire.

"Browning would be jealous," he said, reaching the loft and crossing to a king-size bed covered with a furry zebra-striped throw.

"Of your language?"

"No." He nestled her against the imitation pelt and began stripping off his clothes. "Of the chance to make love to you."

He was fully aroused and Emily feasted on the visual banquet he provided with the supple power of his body as he approached the bed. "I love you," she murmured.

"And I love you." He slipped her shoes from her feet and rested his hip on the bed while he unbuttoned her sleeveless blouse. "You have no idea how much I—" He paused and glanced at her in pleased surprise as the blouse parted to reveal her naked breasts.

"I left the bras at home," she said softly.

"Mmm, what an idea," he said, leaning over to nuzzle her rosy nipples. "You could have left all your clothes at home, come to think of it."

"I thought—" She stopped to catch her breath as he cupped her breasts in both hands. Gently his strong fingers kneaded her flesh while he suckled the darkened tips that seemed to reach upward for his mouth's caress. "I thought we were planning...to take walks in the woods," she said faintly.

"Might not have time." He continued nibbling at her breasts while his hands became busy elsewhere removing the rest of her clothes. When he was finished he stopped kissing her and sat back. His powerful chest rose and fell with the rapid breathing of passion, but he seemed determined to rein it in. "Just give me a minute to appreciate this," he said.

She gazed up at him, not understanding.

"You can't imagine the beauty," he continued, "of you lying on this black-and-white fur, with your ebony hair spread out. And to look in those blue eyes...there's something untamed, something—" He shook his head. "Beyond words," he finished, his tone husky.

"I feel untamed," she admitted, moving her hand along his thigh. "For the first time we're truly alone. We can do anything we want." She tantalized him with a feather touch on the baby-soft skin stretched tight by his need.

He closed his eyes. "Again," he whispered.

Instead she changed her position and kissed him there, with her hair tumbling over his thighs.

"Emily..." He buried his fingers in her hair and moaned when she took possession of him.

Their seclusion loosened her inhibitions and she resisted when he tried to pull her away. Quickly, from his gasps and his trembling thighs she knew that the moment of resolution had passed and he had given himself up to the seduction of her lips and tongue. She gloried in his cry of release and the sea-water taste of him.

At last he lifted her up to meet his kiss. "Oh, my love." He sighed, drawing back to gaze into her eyes. "My sweet love."

She smiled, basking in his tenderness.

"There's only one thing wrong with that fantastic experience." He eased her back against the fur throw. "You were left out."

She caressed his cheek. "I can wait," she said softly, although the sensuous friction of the fur against her skin made her wonder how long.

"Maybe you can," he murmured, his kiss suggestive, his hand slipping between her thighs. "But you're not going to."

THEY SPENT MOST of the afternoon abandoning themselves to the erotic atmosphere of the loft bed. Finally they talked themselves into a walk before dinner, but early evening found them back in each other's arms making love on the butterscotch couch. Much later they returned to the loft bed, this time to sleep curled together like the ancient Oriental symbol of yin and yang, female and male.

Ned awoke just before dawn, a habit he might never break, he thought, staring up at the beamed ceiling and gradually remembering where he was. They'd left a window open, and the pine-scented air beckoned to him. One benefit of his job was the joy of experiencing early morning.

He turned his head to gaze at Emily, her magical blue eyes closed in sleep. She didn't wake up as early as he; he'd already learned that about her. It didn't matter. Nothing mattered but the wonder of finding this warm and intelligent woman, whose physical beauty was matched by her loving nature.

Because of Emily, his world resembled a pop-up picture book with full-color surprises on each page. He'd even begun to seriously consider a writing career, although he wasn't ready to let Emily support him. He'd give up some reading time in the evenings and start the book now. Perhaps by Christmas he'd have something worth submitting, and by Curt's graduation in June he'd have some idea of his publishing chances.

Too restless to sleep and unwilling to disturb Emily, Ned eased out of bed and pulled on his clothes. Downstairs he left her a note explaining that he was out for a walk and would be back soon. Then he opened the front door and then quietly closed it behind him.

The dew-damp pines smelled like Christmas. Ned supposed that if you lived in the mountains for any length of time you got over that association, but in the desert a fragrance this strong happened only once a year on Christmas-tree lots strung with colored lights.

He decided the wave of holiday cheer that washed over him was appropriate, anyway. Emily's love was the best gift he'd ever received. As he descended the steps from the wooden deck and followed a footpath up a slope behind the house, Ned pictured a Christmas morning in the future, with a toy train racing around the tree and a couple of kids working the controls while he and Emily cuddled by the fire and watched them play.

Ned paused in his trek as a squirrel darted across the path in front of him and scooted up the trunk of a giant ponderosa. "Nice morning," Ned addressed the squirrel, and it clung to the side of the tree and glanced over its shoulder with such human surprise that Ned laughed. Startled, the squirrel raced barber-pole style up the trunk and out on a branch where it chattered with indignation.

From behind him a dog yipped, and Ned turned to face a wiry, white-haired man holding a taut leash with a wiggling beagle at the end of it.

"Snoopy loves to chase squirrels," the man called in explanation. "That's why I have to walk him on a leash, or he'd be all over the mountainside and get himself lost." The man reeled the dog in and ordered him to sit, which the beagle didn't do. "Beautiful morning," the man said as the dog pranced at his feet.

"Yes, beautiful," Ned agreed, a little sorry to have his idyllic reverie interrupted.

"You staying at the Johnson place?"

"I don't know," Ned replied and then decided that sounded foolish. "I mean, the cabin belongs to friends of my—" he hesitated and plunged boldly on "—of my girlfriend. I didn't ever find out the owner's name."

"Well, that there," the man said, jerking a thumb in the direction of the house on the hill beneath them, "is the Johnson place. I've met them a few times. Nice people."

"I guess so. They were generous enough to loan the cabin to us for the weekend." Ned wondered at the coincidence that Emily's friends had the same last name that she did. "By the way, how old a couple are the Johnsons, would you say?" he asked as a suspicion entered his mind.

"Oh, late fifties, maybe, early sixties. They have a couple of grown kids, I think, although I never did find out too much about them. A lot of people come up here for privacy so we let each other alone unless there's a problem."

"Sure, I can understand that." Ned's suspicion grew. He wished, if Emily's parents owned the cabin, that she'd told him, instead of implying that it belonged to friends. But the more he thought of her familiarity with the place, the more he became convinced that it belonged to her mother and father, who didn't approve of him.

The beagle lunged at the end of his shortened leash, throwing the man off balance. "Guess I'd better head on up the trail, if you don't mind," he said, regaining his footing.

"Sure thing." Ned stepped aside to let the man and dog pass.

"Enjoy your stay," the man said, looking back once more before the dog tugged him forward.

"I will." Ned gazed after the man and dog and wished he'd never met them. It seemed that once again Emily had disguised the truth, probably from her parents, as well. He doubted that they knew the identity of Emily's houseguest this weekend. Minutes ago Ned had felt a part of the refreshing mountain scenery around him; now he felt like a trespasser.

With a sigh he retraced his steps down the path to the house where Emily slept. They'd shared such joy in the past twenty-four hours that the pain was twice as sharp when he realized that none of it would have happened without Emily's deception. Had she told him the truth about the cabin, he wouldn't have been able to stay in it without first meeting her parents and clearing the air about his relationship with their daughter. He opened the front door and wearily climbed the stairs to the loft.

In the tousled bed, Emily stirred under the zebra-striped throw and opened her eyes. She smiled, but her smile disappeared as she saw the look on his face. "What's the matter?"

"Your parents own this place, don't they?" he asked, knowing the answer immediately from the flicker of fear in her blue eyes. "Why didn't you say so?"

She didn't answer, but her throat moved in a convulsive swallow.

"Did you have to make up some sort of story about who you were bringing here? Obviously you didn't tell them the truth, after their original reaction to me."

"I—I didn't tell them anything." She looked away for a moment. "They're on a cruise."

"That's right. I forgot that. So they never have to know that their daughter brought that damned iron-worker to the family cabin." Ned felt sick to his stomach.

She pushed up on one elbow and the throw fell away, exposing one alabaster breast. "Ned, please."

He closed his eyes. Even though she'd done something underhanded, he still loved her, still wanted her. "I just wish that you'd been straight with me," he said, gazing down at her. He tried to read the expression on her face and failed.

"You wouldn't have spent the weekend here if you'd known," she said.

"Probably not."

She reached out and caught his hand. "I knew that, and I also knew we could have a wonderful time."

"I feel like some sort of thief, stealing up here while your unsuspecting parents are out of the country." Ned tried to maintain his anger, but the plea for understanding in her blue eyes, the warmth of her touch, the temptation of her body waiting for him beneath the zebra throw, conspired against his righteousness. "Dammit, Emily, sneaking around is not my style."

"I know." She met his gaze in a mute appeal. "Please forgive me."

"When your parents come home, I want to meet them. I don't care how rich they are, or how well educated, or how much they hate construction workers. I won't have this hiding business anymore."

Fear leaped once more into her eyes, but to her credit, she didn't waffle. "All right," she said, although her tone was tremulous. "All right, you will meet them."

"Good."

She gazed at him steadily, her hand still holding his. "Would you feel better now if we went home?"

He stood before her, torn between the desire welling up as he imagined her stretched out beneath him once more, and the principle of rejecting something, namely this cabin, that wasn't his to enjoy. Slowly she drew back the covers. Without speaking, he released her hand and began unbuttoning his shirt.

CHAPTER FIFTEEN

AS THEY RODE down the winding Mount Lemmon Road in the late afternoon, Emily's thoughts whirled and tangled together like clothes in a dryer. When Ned had confronted her that morning she'd been certain that he knew everything. In fact he'd only guessed the most obvious, that the mountain cabin belonged to her family. He still hadn't considered that she might be the daughter of his boss.

She owed that to his love for her, she knew. The facts would have to be spread out in plain view before he'd suspect her of a subterfuge that enormous. But her time for hiding that final secret was running out, no doubt about that. She intended to keep her promise to introduce him to her parents when they returned from their cruise. Sometime before that she'd tell him the truth about her father.

In the meantime, she'd talk with Danny about conditions on the job, and perhaps the entire matter could be taken care of before she hit the turbulence of bringing Ned and her parents together. She prayed that Ned loved her as much as he seemed to, and that his love would hold together during the difficult days ahead of them.

She was encouraged that he planned to start on his book right away. During lunch he'd discussed his idea of writing each evening, and she'd given him enthusiastic support and offers of editing help. She'd reiterated her belief in his ability and watched with joy as his self-confidence increased with her praise. Everything had to work out for the two of them, Emily thought as Ned guided the Corvette down the mountain. As he'd said, they were so good for each other.

They picked up a bucket of fried chicken on the way to Ned's apartment and ate it while they finally watched a sunset together. Then Emily left. She'd explained earlier that she needed to stop at her brother's house. Ned had remarked that here was another relative he should meet, and she'd told him that he would, after the two of them braved her parents.

By eight-thirty Emily was ringing her brother and sister-in-law's melodious doorbell that was equipped with Westminster chimes. Danny and Gwen's house was easily as elegant as Emily's parents', and it looked more spectacular because it was two stories instead of one. In the rolling foothills area where they lived, multistoried homes were the exception rather than the rule, but Emily hadn't been surprised by Gwen and Danny's choice of elevations. Both of them seemed anxious to impress the world.

Jeremy answered the bell after peering through the child-height peephole in the lower half of the heavy door. "It's Aunt Emily," he called over his shoulder.

"Hello, Jeremy," she said, although he hadn't exactly greeted her. "How are you?"

"Okay," he said.

From upstairs Emily heard Gwen yell, "Let Aunt Emily in, for God's sake, Jeremy!"

The small boy opened the door and stepped back.

"I thought you might be in bed by now," Emily said to Jeremy as she stepped into the dimly lit front hall.

From the floor above came the sound of fretful crying, which she supposed was Lynette.

"Nope," Jeremy replied. "Me and Lynette were playing, but she started smashing something and cut her finger."

"Oh. Not bad, I hope?" Emily couldn't help thinking that Lynette had probably been smashing one of the many toys Emily had given her. Nothing seemed to stay in one piece around these two kids.

"Naw, just a little scratch," Jeremy said. "She's a big baby."

Emily glanced toward the living room. "I came to see your daddy," she said, turning toward Jeremy, but he was already gone, racing up the stairs toward the hubbub created by his sister. Emily shrugged and decided to find Danny for herself. She headed for the living room and called his name.

As usual, unless the maid had recently cleaned, the room looked as if it had been vandalized. Pieces of toys and sections of the Sunday paper were strewn around the room, along with a couple of wet bathing suits dampening the plush gray rug and wet towels piled on the gray-and-magenta sectional. Emily knew from previous visits that the couch had at least three permanent stains on it and a rip in one cushion.

Hearing no answer to her call, Emily walked through the kitchen, which was in similar disarray, and glanced out the sliding glass doors to the patio. The growing darkness had activated the landscaping and pool lights. The turquoise glow of the pool illuminated a bathing-suit-clad Danny on his knees by the skimmer trying to pull out some object that had become wedged inside. Emily walked out on the patio and he glanced up at her approach.

"Problems?" she asked.

"Jeremy stuffed Lynette's swim ring in here," Danny said, returning to his task. "It's her favorite one, so I'm trying to work it out without putting a million holes in the damn thing."

"Good luck."

"Yeah. So how was your weekend in the mountains?" he asked without looking up.

From his tone she knew that he'd guessed who she'd taken there. "Danny, I've got to talk to you. It's important."

"Look, if it's about you and Tucker, I don't wanna play, okay? You know Mom and Dad will be steaming, and I don't want them to be mad at me, too. I'm already taking that chance with what you've already told me."

"It's not that. This is more important, Danny. Can you stop that for a minute?"

"I've almost got—hell! I'll never be able to patch that rip." Danny held up a deflated tube with blue and gold unicorns printed on it and a jagged tear in one side.

"Danny, for God's sake, listen to me!"

"What?" He glanced up, and the quivering water in the pool made rippling patterns of blue light on his face. "What are you raving about, sis?"

"Put that thing down and come over here," she said, surprised at how easily the order came out of her mouth. She walked over to an arrangement of patio chairs and moved another damp towel so that she could sit down.

Danny, looking surprised himself, followed her example and sat in a chair next to hers. "Okay, what gives?"

She looked him straight in the eye. "Something has to be done about the safety standards at the construction site."

He drew back as if slapped, and then he leaned toward her, his chin jutting in the same way her father's had the last time she'd seen him. "And what do you know about stuff like that, college teacher?"

"I know enough. I know the danger when chokers are so frail that they might break any minute and somebody gets crushed under a load of iron. I know that safety goggles should be provided at all times, and flooring put down every three stories, and guardrails, none of which you've been too concerned with."

"It's Tucker, isn't it?" Danny growled. "He's filled your head full of chicken-livered lies."

"I don't believe they're lies, Danny."

"Oh, you don't, huh? Then would you like to risk your little fanny and climb up there to prove it?"

"I don't have to. Ned's been keeping notes for two years on every job he works. I read those notes yesterday, and when I came to the part about this job, I wanted to throw up."

"Yeah, and I bet Tucker begged you to read that sewage," Danny sneered, "especially after he stayed awake nights making it up. He knows who you are. I'd lay bets on it."

"No, he doesn't, and his notes are real," Emily said, her anger growing in proportion to Danny's denial of the facts. "And I asked to read them, not the other way around. I had no idea what I'd find."

"You have no idea what you're talkin' about, period."

"Yes, I do." Emily kept her voice even, but each word was laced with fury. "And I want the things I've mentioned changed."

"Oh, you do, do you? And what if I don't feel like following the orders of some prissy college teacher? What then? You gonna sick your boyfriend on me?"

"No." Emily's grip tightened on the arms of the chair. "I'll call Dad."

"You seem to forget he's out of the country."

"Cruise ships have telephones, Danny. I'll call him, and don't think I won't."

"He'd stick by me," Danny asserted belligerently. "He knows those guys are all a bunch of wimps who can't—"

"Danny, that's enough! Either those violations are cleared up by the end of the week, or I'm calling Dad and telling him to come home and take care of it himself."

Danny gazed at her for a full minute. His face was in shadow, and she couldn't read his expression very well. Finally he shifted in his chair and looked away. "Talking about blackmail, what if I decide to tell your boyfriend who you are?"

Emily cringed. She'd thought of this, of course. Playing tough with Danny meant he had every right to do the same with her. She swallowed. "That's a chance I have to take. But I won't put the safety of those men ahead of my own interests." She looked at her brother and wondered who he'd become in the past few years. "Danny, for God's sake, how can you take chances like this with people's lives?"

His gaze swiveled to meet hers. "You don't know anything about what it takes to run a company like this, in these times," he said bitterly. "You've had everything handed to you on a silver platter, and now you sit in your cushy college job and think you know about ironwork. The whole damned job is a risk!''

''I know, but you're responsible for minimizing that risk!'' She got to her feet. ''Danny, I want your word that the violations will be corrected by the end of the week. Do whatever you want about telling Ned, but promise me that the rest will be taken care of.''

He glanced away again and didn't answer.

''I mean it, Danny. If everything's not done by Friday, I'm calling Dad.''

''Okay, okay.''

''You'll do it?''

''Yeah.''

From inside the house came another yowl, and this one sounded like Jeremy, followed by Gwen's angry voice. Emily glanced at the torn swim ring lying beside the pool and thought of the unkempt, expensive house and the destructive children and materialistic wife. Danny wasn't happy with his life, Emily realized, and felt a moment of pity.

She walked over and touched her brother's bare arm. ''If there's ever anything...''

He looked up at her and the pain of smashed dreams was in his gaze. For a moment he seemed about to say something, then he glanced away again. ''You just climb back to your ivory tower,'' he said. ''People like me will take care of making everything nice for you, so you don't have to worry about anything.''

She recoiled from his hostility. She'd been aware of his jealousy, but never of its depth. She stood in the semidarkness of the lamp-lit patio and wondered if they could ever be friends, if there was anything she could say that wouldn't sound ridiculous in the face of the widening gulf between them.

Gwen shouted from an upstairs window. "Danny, I need you up here!"

Danny glanced up at the window and didn't move. With a sigh, Emily turned and walked toward the patio gate that led to the front of the house.

On the drive home Emily debated whether to call Ned and tell him everything. The prospect of having him find out through Danny worried her tremendously, but she couldn't be certain that Danny would take that vindictive step. Despite his faults, Danny had never deliberately tried to hurt her and she didn't really believe he'd do it now.

She had trouble dealing with his disregard for the safety of his workers, although she had to admit he was putting himself in jeopardy at the same time. The only explanation was greed. She could blame Danny's behavior on Gwen's influence, of course, but that wasn't entirely fair, either. Danny was an adult. He didn't have to cater to Gwen's demands for more and better of everything. Because he had, Emily concluded that possessions filled some deep need in Danny, too. A need to compete with his brainy sister, perhaps? Emily shuddered.

Still deep in thought, she arrived at her apartment complex and turned into her regular parking space. As she got out and locked the Corvette, someone called her name. She glanced up and saw Monica climbing out of her battered car parked on the other side of Emily's station wagon. Carrie emerged from the passenger side.

Startled but glad to see them, Emily walked quickly forward. She'd meant to invite them all to her place soon, but her involvement with Ned had taken precedence. She wondered if the boys were still in the back seat where they'd been told to sit quietly. Emily was surprised that Monica had them out so late. And how had she known when Emily would come home?

"What a surprise," she said, smiling as she approached the two women. "Are the boys in the car?"

"The boys are at home," Monica said, not returning Emily's smile. "With Jake."

THE NEXT AFTERNOON as Suds and Subs began to fill with ironworkers, Emily reviewed the drink orders she knew by heart and brought them to the men as soon as they arrived. Tonight she'd work harder than ever before in her life. At Jake's insistence, Monica had quit.

Emily prayed that Jake wouldn't be among her customers in the bar, because she didn't trust herself to be around him. She knew he'd been rehired; apparently he'd called Danny at home and asked to be taken back. Emily raged inwardly at the injustice of his easy return to work and his family. After weeks of deserting his responsibilities, he was accepted again without a ripple of protest it seemed.

Anger gave Emily extra energy, and her skill as a waitress had improved sufficiently so that she handled the orders better than she'd expected. By the time Ned came in she was caught up.

She met his glance boldly, determined not to show any fear of what he might find in her expression. His smile was as welcoming as ever, and she relaxed. At least for today, Danny hadn't revealed her secret. She brought Ned's and Mando's drink order to the pool table area.

"I guess you have a roommate," Ned said in a low voice after she handed him his beer.

"Yes." Emily allowed herself the luxury of pausing a moment to talk with Ned. "Nobody's asked where Monica is, so I suppose they all know he made her quit."

"They know." Ned's mouth compressed into a hard line.

"Will he come in here for a drink? I really don't want to have to serve him. I might throw his beer in his face."

"He won't be in. Danny-boy may have hired him back, but most of the guys wish he hadn't and wouldn't be too likely to drink with him. They much prefer having Monica around than Jake."

Emily frowned. "That's another thing. She shouldn't have quit this job. No telling when Jake might take off again."

"I'm sure Jake gave her no choice."

"No choice?" Emily bristled. "What do you mean, 'no choice'?"

Ned shrugged. "A lot of the guys are like that. They don't want their wives to work, especially not waitressing in a bar."

"But that's hypocritical!" Emily burst out, then lowered her voice when the pool players looked up from the table. "When he left her, she had to work or she and the kids would have starved," Emily said, tense with anger. "If he leaves again, she'll have to scrounge for another job."

"I guess he thinks he's not going to leave again."

"Surely you're not defending him?"

"No." Ned sipped his beer and gazed at her over the rim of his glass. "Jake's the worst example of the macho attitude you find around here, but I have lots of friends in the trade who think like Jake. They don't happen to leave their wives in the lurch the way he does, but they maintain control in the household."

Emily studied his expression. "I couldn't live like that."

"I know."

She hesitated. "Could you?"

"Not now. Not after knowing you."

Emily let out the breath she'd been holding. "I'd better get back to work. I really miss Monica, in more ways than one."

"Yeah." He angled his head for her to step closer. "I guess it's my place this weekend," he said softly.

She gazed into his eyes. "I guess so. Unless you want to work around Carrie's schedule."

Ned shook his head.

"Sorry about this inconvenience," Emily apologized.

Ned grinned. "That's okay. You don't have enough pillows, anyway."

Warmth rushed over her. "Careful, someone might hear you."

"I want to shout it from the rooftops," he said, keeping his voice just above a whisper.

Emily smiled uncertainly. "Soon," she said, and wondered if he'd still feel that way when her parents returned and he found out who she was.

THAT NIGHT and the next at the bar were exhausting for Emily, and she wondered how she'd continue taking notes for her study while serving drinks to the whole bar full of people instead of half of it. In addition Emily worried about conditions on the job site, and whether Danny was taking the steps she'd laid out for him on Sunday.

She also wondered if in the process he'd lose his temper and tell Ned everything. On Tuesday and Wednesday nights Ned seemed unchanged in his attitude toward her and even mentioned that he was working on the book. Emily began to hope that her brother wouldn't betray her, after all.

At about ten on Wednesday night, long after Ned had left to go home and write, Emily retreated to the storeroom for a quick break. She came to an abrupt half in the doorway when she discovered Monica, disheveled and red eyed, sitting at the card table with a shopping bag in front of her.

"My God, what's wrong?" she cried, hurrying over to her friend.

"Everything," Monica said, her lower lip trembling as she took the cigarette from her mouth. Then she sniffed and clenched her jaw. "That bastard. I'm sorry, Emily. He ruined some of your books. I brought them all back, but some are ripped. I'll pay for them, but maybe you can't buy—" Her eyes filled with tears and she turned away to take another angry puff of her cigarette. "Damn bastard."

Emily lowered herself to the folding chair nearest Monica. "The books don't matter," she said, putting her hand on Monica's arm. "I'm more worried about you than any stupid books. What happened?"

Monica's face contained a fierceness that Emily had never seen before. "He said he didn't want me studying anymore, and I told him to get lost." Monica's empty hand closed into a fist. "Then he started tearing up your books. I only had three out—the others were put away. I tried to get them away from him, but he tore the English reading book, and the grammar one, and—"

"I don't care," Emily said urgently. "We'll replace them. Are you all right?"

"Yeah." Monica's eyes were bright with cold fury. "I'm no match for him, so I stayed out of his way until he calmed down and had a few more beers. When he went to sleep in his chair, I took all the books, even the pieces, and came here." She grimaced. "I felt like bashing his head in while he was sleeping."

Emily shuddered. "I'm glad you didn't."

"I had to think of the boys." Monica's tone had become dispassionate, now that her recounting of the damage to the books was over. "I'm divorcing him."

"Oh, Monica." Emily went cold as she realized her own part in this dangerous decision. "Monica, he might hurt you."

Monica's smile was thin. "No, he won't. I'm not stupid. I'll wait until he's at work tomorrow and change the locks on the apartment. If he's any trouble, I'll call the police."

"I can't believe you're saying this. You always—"

Monica looked at her as if Emily had some brain defect. "He ripped up your books," she explained patiently. "When he did that, something snapped in me. I finally got it through my thick head that he doesn't love me, never did."

"Monica, you're far from thickheaded."

Monica stubbed out her cigarette and stared thoughtfully at Emily. "You're right," she said at last. "I'm not, and I'm tired of that jerk telling me I am."

"I'm still afraid for you, though."

"I can handle it." Monica glanced in the direction of the bar. "Don't forget that I've made a lot of friends out there, guys who talk Jake's language real good. Once he knows the score, he'll stay in line."

Emily thought about the burly ironworkers, about men like Mando and Smiley, Al and Rooster. Even Ned might get a little rough with someone who threatened Monica, Emily acknowledged. "Maybe you're right."

"I'm going into the bathroom and comb my hair, make myself a little more presentable," Monica announced, getting up. "Then I'm gonna ask Bailey for my job back, that is, if you don't mind giving up a few tips."

"Are you kidding?" Emily stood up and hugged her. "I've been going crazy around here without you. But are you sure this is the job you want?"

"For now," Monica answered, picking up her purse. She glanced longingly at the sack of books on the table.

"You can have them back, you know."

"But I told you that I'd take care of them, that nothing would happen, and something did."

"That's not your fault. Listen, I want to keep on with the tutoring, if you do."

Monica gazed at her eagerly. "God, I sure do. I want that GED more than ever. I loved studying. That's why I got so mad when Jake told me to stop."

"That's *why* he told you to stop. He didn't want you to improve yourself. He knew what would happen."

"Yeah, I see that now. And he wasn't much of a father, either, you know? He never once brought the boys trucks or something like you did."

"Speaking of the boys, what if Bailey gives you the job back? Would it be safe for them, and I guess Carrie, at night?"

The twinkle returned briefly to Monica's eyes. "Rambo doesn't take kindly to Jake. Only reason Jake got away with ripping up the books is because he tied that big old dog outside."

"You mean Rambo would bite Jake?" Emily remembered the lumbering dog as an affectionate teddy bear, but she wouldn't want Rambo mad at her, she decided.

"If I give the signal, or Carrie either, Rambo would tear Jake limb from limb," Monica said. "Jake knows it, too. He wanted to get rid of Rambo the minute he came home, but the boys cried somethin' pitiful, and even Jake, mean as he is, couldn't do it in front of them. He said Rambo would be an outside dog, though, and I think he was figuring on letting Rambo loose one of these days and hoping he'd wander off."

"Where's Rambo now?"

Monica grinned her endearing, imperfect grin. "In my car. He's gonna be an inside dog, now."

"Well." Emily smiled, too. "What about tonight?" she asked. "Are you going back there?"

"Sure. Once Jake goes to sleep in his chair he's a pussycat for the rest of the night. And he's not usually much for conversation in the morning. He'll just stumble off to work. Once he's gone I'll call the lock shop."

"You seem to have it all planned," Emily said, still amazed by Monica's cool assessment.

"I do."

"If you're the least worried, you can stay with me tonight."

"Thanks, but I'll be okay. I know the jerk pretty well by now, unfortunately. He has a pattern."

"Promise to call me in the morning to let me know you're okay, though." Emily hoped that Monica knew what she was talking about.

"I'll call. And tell Carrie to pack her things if she wants to move back. 'Course, she'll probably hate to leave the Ritz."

Emily shook her head. "Nope, she'll be delighted. We haven't talked much, but when we have she always tells me how much she misses those boys."

"And that's another thing," Monica said, pausing on her way to the bathroom. "The boys didn't seem happy to have their dad around instead of Carrie. I didn't want to think about it, I guess, but they don't like him much."

"Obviously he hasn't given them reason to."

"Well." Monica sighed and straightened her shoulders. "He's had his chance."

"Right. Be tough."

"I have to." Monica left the storeroom and Emily glanced quickly at her watch before hurrying back to her job. If she didn't watch out, Bailey would hire Monica back and fire her for taking too long a break.

CHAPTER SIXTEEN

BAILEY TOOK MONICA on again, as Emily had been sure that he would. Emily knew that she'd performed adequately alone, but she couldn't handle the entire bar nearly as well as Monica and perhaps never would be able to. Emily gratefully welcomed Monica back on Thursday afternoon. Maybe her study of the ironworkers could be accomplished now that life had settled down a little.

Carrie had managed to get the day off and the three women had moved her belongings back into Monica's apartment with its shiny new locks. Monica had packed all of Jake's clothes into a battered suitcase, along with a note of explanation, and on the way to work that day she'd put the suitcase in his old truck, which he never worried about locking up.

"He could come in here looking for you with fire in his eyes," Emily warned when she heard how Monica had disposed of Jake's clothing.

"I hope he does," Monica said. "I plan to tell Smiley and Al to be on the lookout for him. But I doubt if he'll show, 'cause he knows he's not popular around here. If I know Jake, he'll head for some other bar and get drunk."

"And then head for your apartment?" Emily asked, picking up her order pad.

"Maybe."

"Look, I know Rambo's a good guard dog, and the locks are sturdy, but I'd feel better if Ned stopped by after he leaves here and stays for a couple of hours."

Monica chuckled and shook her head. "Carrie wouldn't know what to do having someone like Ned around. She'd think she had to entertain him or something."

"All the same, I'd—"

"It'll be fine. You should see Rambo when he's fired up. Even Jake's scared of him." Monica stuffed her order pad into her pocket and put a pencil behind her ear. "Time to get out there and work, gal. Y'know, it's funny, but with all the complaining I used to do about this job, I missed it." She pushed through the swinging doors into the bar.

Emily thought about what Monica had said as they both entered the friendly noise and confusion of Suds and Subs. Would she miss the rowdy, good-natured atmosphere when her study was completed and she returned to the sedate halls of the university? Emily had a feeling that she would.

With her mind somewhat relieved about Monica, Emily could think about other things. Tomorrow was the deadline she'd given Danny for improving safety conditions. Emily decided to casually ask Ned if he'd noticed any changes this week. She prayed that he would have good news.

Before she had a chance to talk with him she noticed him deep in conversation with Monica. From Monica's gestures Emily guessed that the red headed waitress was filling Ned in on the events of the night before. Good, Emily thought. Maybe he'll convince her that someone should stay with Carrie tonight, at least during the time when Jake might show up at the apartment.

Later, when orders slowed down, Emily found a moment to wander over by the pool tables.

Ned immediately handed his cue stick to Mando and walked toward her. "I talked to Monica."

"I saw that. I hope she's not being foolhardy. I'm a little afraid for her and Carrie."

"Yeah, well, I thought I'd go over there in a little while," Ned said, leaning against the wall.

"And risk flustering Carrie?"

Ned smiled. "No, I wouldn't want that."

"So what are you planning to do?"

"Spend the night in my car, in the parking lot. I'll be able to hear if there's a ruckus."

"Oh, Ned. You won't get enough rest, and I—"

"Hush, Emily," he said gently. "It's the best way. A few of the other single guys have agreed to take turns for a few days, doing the same thing, until we figure Jake's cooled down. We're just a backup for Monica and Carrie, and the dog, of course. They probably can take care of it alone, but one of us might come in handy."

"I agree, but sleeping in your car?"

"With the new upholstery, the back seat's as comfortable as a bed." He winked. "In fact, I was thinking it might be fun sometime if we—"

"Never mind." Emily glanced away from his teasing expression before he managed to embarrass both of them. With difficulty she focused on the other items she had to discuss. "How's the job going?" she asked, in as offhand a manner as she could.

"The job? Okay."

"Has, um, Danny-boy improved any on the safety measures?" she asked, forcing herself to use the nickname that Ned had adopted for her brother.

Ned's chuckle lacked humor. "I'm afraid not. This job is liable to make an interesting chapter in my book. I just hope not too interesting."

Emily couldn't speak as the reality of his statement pricked her like hot needles. Danny had ignored her demands, apparently believing that she wouldn't check on his progress. She'd given him a deadline, and he was calling her bluff.

"Hey, I didn't mean to upset you." Ned touched her arm briefly. "This is nothing new. So far the guys are surviving all right, and if it gets bad enough, I'll go to OSHA, I promise."

"And risk your job," she said bitterly, furious with Danny for putting Ned in a no-win situation.

"Yeah, well, we don't know that. Anyway, let's forget about the job and talk about this weekend. Now that your roommate's gone, would you rather stay at your place?"

She gazed at him and knew that this probably would be their last weekend together before Ned learned the whole truth. Tomorrow she'd call her parents and ask her father to come home and deal with Danny. Once that happened, she'd be wise to tell Ned who her father was, before Danny, seeking revenge, did so. The picnic was over, but she and Ned could enjoy one last weekend, at least.

"My place would be fine," she said, thinking of the romantic touches she'd add to her apartment before she and Ned arrived on Friday night. She'd make this a weekend to remember, and she hoped that he would remember it when the going got rough.

"Great." Ned glanced at the Coors beer clock over the bar. "I'd better take off, so I can pick up a hamburger on my way over to Monica's."

"Be careful, Ned. I've only seen Jake's picture, but he looked as if he could be a handful. Get Carrie to call the police right away if he shows up, okay?"

Ned only grinned at her.

"Ned Tucker, I mean it. None of this macho stuff."

"Who, me? The guy who reads poetry? I wouldn't hurt a fly."

"You're almost hoping he'll come around, aren't you?" Emily grew worried about the wisdom of this plan. "Ned, take one of the other guys, so there will be two of you if something starts."

"Nope." Ned pushed away from the wall. "See you tomorrow night, love," he said softly, and walked out of the bar.

Frustrated, Emily hurried over to Mando. "Shouldn't someone go with him over to Monica's?" she asked. "Shouldn't you?"

A smile twitched under Mando's bandit mustache. "What did I hear you say? You think that guy Jake is a handful?"

"Yes, and Ned—"

Mando pointed his cue stick toward the door closing behind Ned. "He's a bigger handful, *señorita*."

THE MOON was a brief comma in the night sky, for which Ned was grateful. Too much light would make his car easier to spot, and he wanted to stay in the shadows and surprise Jake if he came around. He'd parked at the end of the building, only two doors down from Monica's apartment where he could hear anything unusual going on.

Neither the kids nor Carrie had been outside the apartment since he parked there at dusk, but he'd expected them to stay behind the locked door. Rambo or no Rambo, Monica's roommate had to be nervous, Ned reflected as he munched on the last of his fries. Monica, despite her bravado, had seemed worried and had been about ready to change her mind and go back home tonight until Ned made his offer of a stakeout.

The other single guys had agreed immediately to a rotating watch over Monica's apartment. They all had a secret desire to be heroes, Ned thought with a smile, even him. He hadn't missed the flash of admiration in Emily's eyes when he'd mentioned what he'd be doing tonight. She might fear for his safety, but she was glad he'd stepped in to help protect the women and children.

The top was down on the convertible, and Ned settled down in the back seat with his legs propped on the side and stared up at the stars. He thought of his comment to Emily about possibly making love in this car, and he chuckled. In principle the idea sounded fun, but in reality they'd be horribly uncomfortable, with neither of them having any place to put their long legs.

No, they could find much better places to enjoy themselves than in this car, Ned concluded, such as his bed surrounded by pillows, or her large mattress, or a soft leather couch, or standing by the kitchen table... As his memories became more erotic he regretted climbing aboard that train of thought. Wanting Emily was pretty fruitless at the moment.

With an effort he pushed Emily from his mind and started thinking about his book, which he wouldn't be able to work on tonight. He was sorry about that. He hadn't realized the writing sessions would be so much fun. The book would be a novel, he'd decided, and creating the characters and devising a plot reminded him of the make-believe games he'd loved as a kid. At first he'd struggled to free his imagination, but lately the ideas were coming faster.

He couldn't believe that people earned money for doing something that seemed so little like work, but Emily kept assuring him that he very well might make a living at his writing business. He wondered if he'd ever have found the courage to try without her. Ah, Emily.... Once again his mind was full of her; his body beginning to ache with yearning. Thank goodness the next day was Friday and he'd be able to hold her again.

Ned drifted into semiconsciousness thinking of the look of exasperation he'd seen on her face as he'd left the bar tonight. He'd probably see that expression often in their life together, at least until she figured out that the daredevil part of him that worried her so much was also one of the traits that drew her closer. He wished she were closer right now.... He wished...

A loud swear word coupled with furious barking woke Ned up immediately and he swung his legs back into the car and listened.

"Let me the hell in there, dammit!" As the barking continued a doorknob rattled and a fist pounded on wood. Jake was home.

Ned leaped from the car without opening the doors and rounded the corner of the building. "Hi, there, Jake," he said casually, keeping any threat from his tone. "Is there a problem here?"

Jake slowly turned his head, but there was no surprise in his jowled face. He was apparently too drunk to question Ned's sudden appearance. "You bet there's a problem. Won't let me into my own damn house!" On the other side of the door the barking subsided to deep growls.

"From what I hear, this isn't your house anymore," Ned said, moving forward cautiously, poised on the balls of his feet. "If you need the price of a motel, I'd be glad to loan you a few bucks."

Jake scowled and hunched his shoulders. "Don't need no motel, buddy. Got a perfickly good bed in there, and I'm sleepin' in it tonight." Without warning he lunged against the door and Rambo went crazy on the other side, seeming just as anxious to destroy the barrier. "I'll kill that dog!" Jake shouted.

The door held, but Ned wasn't sure how many of those battering charges it could withstand. Jake weighed at least two-fifty, and from the looks of him, he'd had enough booze to dull the pain of ramming against a door several times.

Ned moved closer. "I wouldn't try going in if I were you, Jake. Why not sleep it off somewhere else? Monica doesn't want you here anymore, and that's the way it's gonna be."

"Who says?" Jake wheeled around and for the first time seemed to consider eliminating the irritation of Ned before he started in on the door again.

From the corner of his eye Ned saw a piece of curtain pulled aside and a little red-haired boy with wide blue eyes looked out before he was snatched away. The dog's growl was persistent, like a powerful motor left to run. Ned flexed his hand and arm muscles. Jake wasn't getting into that apartment. "I say," Ned commented quietly.

"You?" Jake laughed drunkenly and pitched his voice to a falsetto. "The Bookworm?" he asked, and made a mincing gesture with one beefy hand.

"Yeah," Ned replied, stepping to his right and circling to put himself between Jake and the door.

"Get away from there," Jake muttered. "Get your nose out of my business and stick it in a book, where it belongs."

"This is my business," Ned said easily. "Monica's my friend."

"She's my damn wife!" Jake roared. "And I'm goin' through that door!"

He barreled forward and Ned put all of his one hundred and ninety pounds behind his right fist as he brought it up under Jake's chin. Ned heard bones crack and figured it might be Jake's jaw or his own hand, or maybe both. Jake went down like a felled ponderosa, just as police sirens wailed in the distance.

Ned's hand began to ache, and he rubbed it as he gazed down at Jake, who was moaning groggily and holding his jaw. Ned decided that he might have trouble working tomorrow, but the pain and inconvenience would be worth it. "That was for Monica, you son of a bitch," Ned said.

Behind him the door opened a crack. "Who's out there?" called a woman. "Back, Rambo!"

"I'm Ned Tucker, one of Monica's friends," he said, turning toward the door.

"And Emily's right?" She opened the door a few inches more, and she was clutching Rambo's choke chain. Although the dog obviously wanted out, he obeyed Carrie's command and stayed beside her.

"Yes, Emily's friend, too," Ned replied, thinking that "friend" didn't quite cover it. "You must be Carrie."

"Yes. I called the police and I guess that's them coming now."

"I guess."

"Rambo would have taken care of him if he'd broken down the door," Carrie said. "I know he would."

"I'm sure he would," Ned confirmed, smiling at her. "To tell the truth, I've wanted a crack at this guy for a long time."

Carrie nodded. "I can imagine. Would you like some coffee or something? After the police leave, I mean."

"What I'd like," Ned said, laughing, "is a bowl of ice cubes. I think I broke my hand."

FIRST THING the next morning Monica called Emily and told her about Ned clobbering Jake and bruising his hand, which turned out not to be broken, after all.

"I hope he stayed home from work today," Emily said.

"I'm sure he didn't, knowing these ironworkers. Jake's working too, sure's the world. I called the emergency room to find out about both of them when I got home and found out that Jake's jaw had a hairline crack, but it isn't broken. He'll hurt for a while, is all."

"I was afraid of something like this."

"So was I, although I was glad when Ned volunteered, all the same."

"I suppose I was, too." Emily took a deep breath. "Listen, Monica, there's something I might as well tell you. Pretty soon everybody will know, including Ned."

"What's that, Em?"

"You know the guy who owns the construction company working on this job?"

"You mean Dan Johnson?"

"Yes."

"Well, I don't know him exactly, but I've heard of him, anyway."

"He's my father."

There was silence at the other end of the line.

"I figured if the guys knew about it, they'd never accept me at the bar," Emily continued, rushing into the condemning silence, "and I wouldn't be able to write my paper on ironworkers."

"You've got that right," Monica said.

"I'm sorry that I had to deceive everyone, including you, but I couldn't think of any other way."

"Why'd you pick this bar, where your dad's workers came in? Why not study another one?"

"Because—because Ned's brother was a student of mine and told me about Ned. I was fascinated by that information, and it led me to think of doing the study."

Monica's voice was almost a whisper. "Bookworm doesn't know?"

"Not yet."

"Oh, Em, sweetheart. You're in big trouble."

Emily's stomach clutched. "But—"

"One thing I know about Bookworm is that you have to be straight with him. I was worried how he'd take the news that you're a college teacher doing some study, but he swallowed it okay. But Em, this . . ."

"I know." Emily massaged her aching temples and blinked back her tears. "I love him, Monica. If he won't forgive me, I don't know what I'll do."

"When are you gonna tell him?" Monica asked gently.

"Soon. I have to. You see, my brother promised me he'd clear up the safety violations on this job, but he hasn't, and I'm worried sick about those guys. So I'm calling my father. He and Mom are on a cruise, but they have to come home, because..." She choked back a sob.

"There, there." Monica's voice came soothingly over the line. "I figure Bookworm will understand. I can see you're tryin' to do what's right. But you sure got yourself tangled in a mess, didn't you, honey?"

Emily laughed through her tears. "That's an understatement, Monica."

"Just remember that I'm still your friend, no matter what."

"You don't know how much that means." Emily sighed. "And now I'd better go. I have that ship-to-shore call to make, and Ned will be coming over here tonight, so I wanted to clean the apartment."

"I hope Carrie didn't leave a mess?"

"Oh, heavens no. I just want to make the place look, well, romantic."

"Soften him up a little for your announcement, maybe?"

"I guess. Monica, this will be the toughest thing I've ever had to face. My whole future with Ned is on the line."

"You'll pull through," Monica said.

"But will *we* pull through, Ned and I?"

Monica hesitated. "I'll keep my fingers crossed that you will," she said.

NED WARNED Mando at the beginning of the day that his right hand wasn't in great shape. He didn't mention that it hurt like hell every time he used it and his grip was weaker than usual. Somehow he managed to work, mostly by thinking of the night ahead with Emily. Once in her arms, he'd forget the pain in his hand.

Near quitting time the pusher decided they might as well shake out another load of iron and have it ready for Monday morning. Ned was cautious as the crane operator brought in each load. The twisted wire chokers that held the bundles of iron looked worse than ever, and he felt slightly handicapped today, anyway.

As the last load rumbled to the planked floor, Ned sighed with relief. "Okay, partner," he called to Mando. "Let's untie these suckers and we're home free."

"Yeah, for one more day," Mando said, reaching for the choker to loosen it.

Ned's laughing reply turned to a shout of warning as the frayed choker snapped and struck like a cobra, opening a three-inch gash in Mando's cheek. "Dammit!" Ned cried, racing to his startled friend.

Mando raised a gloved hand toward his face.

"Don't touch it," Ned warned.

"But I'm bleedin', man," Mando said quietly. "I can feel it."

"Let it bleed. Come on, we're going to the first-aid station." Ned threw an arm over Mando's shoulders and hurried him toward the elevator, ignoring the shouted questions of Smiley and Rooster as they passed by. Ned didn't speak again until Mando had a sterile butterfly bandage over the cut. "Now we go see Danny-boy," he said, setting his mouth in a grim line.

They found him in the construction shack and his expression when he saw Ned and Mando was wary. "Something happen up there?"

"You're damned right," Ned snapped. "We want to report a job-related injury, and this man needs a trip to the emergency room for stitches."

"Stitches?" Danny stood up and rounded the desk. "Looks like that butterfly will do the trick."

"The hell it will." Ned swore heedlessly, no longer caring about his job. "You just don't want a claim on your insurance, or proof of your shoddy standards. Mando goes to the emergency room."

Danny faced Ned and flexed his shoulders. "Listen, Tucker," he said. "You've acted like you run this place long enough. I make the decisions around here, not you."

"Is that right?" From his superior height Ned looked down on him tauntingly. Maybe Danny would take a swing at him, and then he could swing back. Ned wondered if this time he really would break his hand, but he didn't care about that, either. "I understand you take orders from your daddy. Maybe I should be talking to him."

Anger glittered in Danny's pale blue eyes. "My dad leaves everything to me."

"Oh, yeah? I'd like to hear that from him. I'd like him to tell me Mando isn't going to the emergency room." Ned gestured to the telephone on the scratched desktop. "I'm not leaving here until you call him."

"Nice try, Tucker," Danny jeered. "You want me to call him in the Bahamas? That's how much he trusts me to run things, buddy. He's out of the country, taking a cruise. You're gonna have to deal with me, and I say no emergency room this time."

Mando growled and stepped forward but Ned put out his arm and held him back. "What did you say?" he asked dully, staring at Danny.

"No emergency room."

"Not that. About the cruise."

"You don't believe me?" Danny stuck out his chin. "Want the name of their travel agent, buster?"

Ned felt as if rattling guns were operating in his head as he tried to deny what logic told him had to be true. Emily Johnson. Dan Johnson. Emily's parents were on a cruise, she'd said. *Dear God, let it be a coincidence,* he prayed, yet knew that it wasn't. All this time, through all this loving, she'd lied to him. She was Dan Johnson's daughter. Everything made sense—sickening, terrifying sense.

"Well," Danny said, balancing on the balls of his feet. "I seem to have shut you up at last, Tucker."

Ned gazed at him while noise continued to thunder in his head. This scumball, who was responsible for Mando's slashed cheek that easily could have been a gouged eye, was Emily's brother. A primeval cry of betrayal lodged in Ned's throat.

Mando glanced at him uneasily. "Let's go, man," he said, grasping Ned's arm.

Ned looked at him and shuddered. "Yeah. Let's go. I'm taking you to the emergency room, whether this jerk-head will use company insurance to pay or not." He turned back to Danny. "First thing Monday, my report goes in to OSHA."

"Brave words, but you'll never do it. Jobs are too hard to come by in this town, and you need the money."

"You're right." Ned realized that he'd become deadly calm. "I do need the money, but some things are more important than money. I doubt you'll understand that, though."

"You're stupid, Tucker," Danny said as fear edged his voice for the first time, "but not stupid enough to risk getting blackballed."

"I wouldn't be so sure," Ned replied. "I doubt if you could find anyone dumber than me. Come on, Mando. We'll get you taken care of, and then I'm buying us both a drink. Maybe several drinks." Ned thought about the woman who would be serving those drinks, and despite the heat in the construction shack, his body, his mind, his heart grew ice-cold.

CHAPTER SEVENTEEN

EMILY REALIZED that something had happened on the construction site from the moment the ironworkers came into the bar. The jovial banter was gone and instead the men communicated in low, intense tones. Shaking with apprehension, Emily approached Smiley. When he told her that a snapped choker had opened a gash on Mando's cheek, she was relieved that it hadn't been something more serious. Maybe her call to her father hadn't been too late to forestall disaster.

Ned would be furious, of course, because of the near miss for his friend. Emily understood that a flying choker could put out an eye and had come close to doing so today. Her parents had promised to be home as soon as they could reserve two seats on a plane, but her father had warned that it might be Sunday or even early Monday before they could make it.

She'd been surprised at a certain resignation in his tone, as if what she was telling him wasn't totally unexpected. Had he turned his head and refused to acknowledge the problems, knowing that Danny was cutting corners to boost profits? Emily wanted to believe that her father was guiltless, but in fairness she couldn't place all the blame on Danny, not when her father had spent so many years in the business and should know what was going on.

Mando's injury also shone a harsher light on the prospect of Emily making her confession to Ned, which she'd planned to do this weekend, possibly even tonight. She trembled to think of his attitude toward Johnson Construction after his friend nearly had been blinded because of the company's negligence. She felt certain Ned would be ready to contact OSHA, but if she could convince him to wait, her father would soon straighten everything out and Ned wouldn't have to assume the role of whistle-blower.

Yet what chance did she have of convincing him to hold off once he knew who she was? Virtually none, she admitted as she served the men in the bar and waited for Ned and Mando to appear. Smiley had said that they'd taken the elevator down to the first-aid station and that had been the last he'd seen of them, but he expected them to come in for a cool one tonight, of all nights.

While Emily was carrying a tray of drinks to Smiley and Rooster's booth, Ned and Mando walked in. Mando for once looked vulnerable with a square white bandage taped to one cheek. Ned was another story. Emily had never seen his expression so dark, and for the first time since she'd met him, he avoided her gaze. The only possible explanation for his behavior struck her with a vicious slap and she almost dropped her tray. He knew.

Danny, she thought wildly. He'd finally betrayed her, even though he couldn't be aware yet of the phone call she'd made this morning, couldn't yet know that their parents were on the way home. She continued toward Smiley's booth, which put her on a collision course with Ned and Mando, but somebody from the other side of the room called to them and both men stopped to answer a question.

Emily delivered the round of drinks and collected the money right away. She wasn't ready to face Ned yet. She needed to stop this shaking before she confronted the agony of his disillusionment. Hurrying back to the bar, she left her tray there and muttered something about a quick break before heading back to the bathroom. Once there, she closed and locked the door.

She stood in the darkness and took deep breaths, but each one ended with a sob. The worst had happened— Ned had discovered her secret before she'd had a chance to tell him. Would he ever listen to her explanation now? Tears seeped from her tightly squeezed eyes and she grabbed a handful of toilet tissue to wipe them away. She longed to run, to leave the bar and never come back.

The odds were against their love now, and she knew it. But if she gave up, defeated by those odds, she'd never know if their relationship might have been salvaged. She had to be strong. If their future together could be saved, she was the one who had to save it.

Gulping down her despair, she stiffened her spine and swiped at her eyes once more. She would face him and endure whatever he said, whatever his accusing gaze implied. She would trust that when the fury was drained from him, he would still love her. She had no choice but to hope that.

By the time she returned to the smoky bar Ned already had his Budweiser and was straddling a chair he'd pulled up to Smiley's booth. Mando had squeezed in beside Rooster. Nobody seemed interested in pool tonight. Ned smoothed a folded piece of paper on the table, took a stubby pencil from his shirt pocket and began to write, pausing to read sections to the men at the table. They nodded and added their comments as Ned returned to his writing task.

Someone called to Emily from the booth next to Smiley's, and she walked over to take the order. As she passed Ned, he didn't glance up. Not even the slightest body movement indicated his awareness of her, and she felt as if she'd been locked out of the Garden of Eden. Once again she longed to run away, but she stayed and served the drinks as they were ordered.

Eventually Rooster called for another drink. Emily's heart pounded as she walked toward the booth, toward Ned's rigid back. She gripped her tray until the plastic edge bit into her fingers.

"Anybody else ready for a refill?" she asked after taking Rooster's order.

"Why not?" Smiley said. "Seems like as good an idea as any, considerin'. Mike, how about you?"

"Yea, I'll take another," Mike said, draining his glass.

"Me, too," Al said, "and I'm buying whatever Mando wants. He needs it."

"I'll have another Bud." Ned spoke without taking his attention from the paper in front of him.

Everyone stared at Ned, including Emily.

"Two beers for Bookworm," Smiley commented, shaking his head. "Now we know we got troubles."

"Oh, we've got troubles, all right," Ned said. He addressed his statement to Smiley, but Emily knew the words were meant for her. "But so has Johnson."

"You mean both Johnsons," Rooster added. "I'd like to see Danny-boy and his daddy wigglin' on a hook together."

"At this point anybody named Johnson is on my list," Ned replied in a deceptively quiet tone.

Smiley was the first to respond. "Hey, let's not get carried away, Bookworm. Don't forget your best girl here is named Johnson." He chuckled. "Don't go throwing her in with those other two scum bags."

Emily held her breath. Would Ned announce what he knew in front of everyone? Doing so would sound the death knell to her study, but at this point she didn't care. Yet if Ned cared, if he at least showed her the small consideration of not embarrassing her in public, perhaps he still retained some tenderness that could serve as a place to begin rebuilding.

Ned glanced up at her for the first time, and she quailed at the pain and anger she saw reflected in his eyes. "I guess you're right, Smiley," he said, looking away again. "Emily doesn't belong in that category."

Tears gathered in Emily's eyes. "I'll get your drinks," she said quickly, and turned away. He hadn't revealed her secret, but the bitterness in his reply told her that if anything, he considered her worse than her father and brother. At least they had never pretended to be someone they weren't.

Monica met her at the bar, took one look at her face and grabbed Emily by the shoulders. "What is it?" she demanded.

"He knows," Emily said, biting down on her trembling lower lip.

"Oh, Em. God, I'm sorry."

"I'm not giving up, Monica. I'll make him listen to me. I love him too much to let him go."

"I wish you all the luck in the world, Em. If there's anything I can do—if you want me to talk to him—"

"No." Emily shook her head and picked up the tray of drinks. "I have to handle this." She gazed at Monica in a vain search for hope in her friend's face, and found none. "You think I'm finished, don't you?"

"I hope not, honey, but with someone like Ned . . ."

"Yeah." Emily took a deep breath and walked over to the booth full of serious men. She'd vowed to make Ned listen to her, yet she didn't have any idea how she'd manage that. If he chose to leave the bar tonight and never contact her again, how could she stop him?

Ned gave her the answer, as he downed his second beer and ordered a third. He took time out from his drinking to ask if someone was scheduled to cover Monica's house that night, but by the time that was determined he was well into his fourth can of Bud.

The married men of the group eventually went home, but Mando and Rooster remained. Ned put his papers away as the three men settled into the booth and ordered another round. Emily concluded that Ned planned to get roaring drunk.

Watching for her opportunity, Emily caught Mando alone when he was returning from the bathroom. He still intimidated her, but she was concerned about Ned and he was, after all, Ned's best friend.

"Excuse me, Mando," she said, touching his heavily muscled arm. "I'm worried about Ned. I've never seen him drink so much."

Mando's grin flashed from under his mustache. "That gringo can put it away pretty good when he wants to."

"Has he ever done this before?"

"Only once," Mando said. "The time he almost killed himself on the iron."

"The time you saved him."

Mando's dark gaze moved over her face. "He told you about that?"

Emily nodded.

Mando scratched his head. "Well, I can see why he got drunk that night. Most of us don't like thinkin' about dyin'. But I can't figure tonight." Mando touched his bandage. "This ain't nothin' to get tanked up about."

Emily swallowed. "Will he—do you think he'll keep drinking?"

"He talked about stayin' until closing time. If he does, somebody has to take that gringo home and put him to bed." He glanced at Emily. "And you ain't got the muscles," he added with another grin. "So I guess I'll hafta do it. I've had enough beer for one night, anyway."

Emily glanced toward the booth. Ned had noticed them talking and was staring in their direction. "I appreciate you taking care of him," she said to Mando. "If you end up driving him home, I'd like to follow in my car and stay with him."

Mando cocked his head. "He won't be much fun when he wakes up."

"I don't care. I want to make sure he's all right."

"Okay. I guess you can do what you want, seein' how you're his girl."

"Thanks, Mando." Emily squeezed his arm and walked away feeling grateful that Ned hadn't told his best friend about Emily's duplicity. If he had, Mando wouldn't have allowed Emily within a mile of Ned. As it was, she'd have her chance to talk with him alone. That was all she could ask.

By closing time only Mando, Rooster and Ned remained in the bar. Emily had lost count of the number of beers Ned had consumed, but he seemed to have won his battle over pain from the evidence of his and Mando's loud laughter. Mando had kept his promise to stop drinking, and Rooster had followed suit. Both men politely waited for Emily to finish up her work before they positioned themselves on each side of Ned and guided him outside.

Mando drove Ned's Pontiac and Rooster followed in Mando's truck. Emily in her station wagon brought up the rear of the little caravan. She was impressed with Mando's and Rooster's efforts to keep Ned from coming to any harm. They gave him their complete loyalty. If Ned openly turned against her, so would they, she realized.

The two men hauled Ned up the stairs and into his apartment, with Emily trailing behind. She stayed in the living room when, despite Ned's laughter and mumbled protests, they undressed him down to his underwear and heaved him into bed.

"That should do it," Rooster said as they came out of the bedroom. "I'm glad I'm not the one who's gonna be around when the beer wears off."

Mando glanced at Rooster and chuckled. "I bet Ned's glad, too. You'd make one ugly nurse."

"You're not so pretty, yourself," Rooster said. "Anyway, Bookworm's got a nurse, so let's beat it and go pick up my car."

"Thanks, both of you," Emily said. "You're good friends."

"He's done the same for us," Rooster replied with a shrug as they went out the door. "Well so long."

"Goodbye." Emily closed and locked the door. Then she switched off the lights in the living room and walked into the bedroom, where Ned, wearing only his briefs, lay sprawled across the hastily pulled back sheets.

He was already asleep. The eyes that had gazed at her accusingly throughout the night were closed, and for a moment she could pretend that nothing had changed between them, that Ned had drifted off to sleep after they'd made love, and that he would take her in his arms when he awoke. Her heart ached with the sweetness of what had been and what might never be again.

She undressed, leaving on only her panties. After some searching through dresser drawers, she found one of Ned's tank tops, a white one, and pulled it on. At last she turned out the light and crawled into bed beside him. "I love you," she whispered, kissing his cheek. He moaned softly in his sleep, and the sound tore through her. She had hurt him, hurt him terribly. Somehow she had to make everything all right again. Wrapping her arms around him, she settled down for a long night of sleepless waiting.

WHEN NED FIRST STIRRED, light showed faintly through the miniblinds of his bedroom. It was, she realized, looking at the bedside clock, his normal time to wake up. She'd dozed intermittently during the night, but her sleep had been crowded with horrible dreams of man falling from open girders. Sometimes the victim had been Ned, sometimes her father or her brother. She couldn't remember ever feeling so exhausted.

Ned's eyes fluttered open and stared into hers. At first they held a welcoming light, but that seemed to fade as he remembered what had happened the day before.

"Ned, I'm sorry," she said, meeting his gaze unflinchingly. "I love you, and I'm sorry."

He closed his eyes and shuddered. "You love me," he said, his voice hoarse from his night of drinking. When he looked at her again, his gaze was tarnished with sorrow. "How could you possibly love me? Love tells the truth, Emily."

"Everything important about me has been the truth."

His laugh rang bitterly in the dim room. "God. You say that as if you believe it."

"I do," she insisted. "The truth about me is that I'm a scholar, and I care about other people, and I love you. The rest is only an accident of birth. It's not important to who I am."

"Oh, no?" He raised on one elbow and winced. "Then if it's so damned unimportant, why didn't you tell me right away? Lord, but my head hurts."

She laid her hand against his hot forehead but he brushed it away.

"Please. Don't touch me as if you care what happens to me. That's a joke."

"It's not a joke!" Emily sat up as anger replaced her guilt. "Because of you I went to Danny and told him to clean up the construction site. When I found out he ignored me, I called my father yesterday and asked him to cut short his cruise and come home to straighten Danny out."

He gazed at her. "You think your father doesn't know about any of this?"

She avoided his accusing stare. "I'm not sure. He hadn't kept an eye on things for some time, and I—"

"He knows, Emily. Don't be naive. Your sugar daddy knows what's going on."

"Don't call him that!"

"Why not? Oh, I forgot, you have an aversion to the truth, don't you?"

"Stop it!"

He ignored her distress and continued. "And did you tell your father that you've been making love—" He paused and corrected himself. "I should say *going to bed* with an ironworker?" he finished softly.

"No, I didn't tell him I've been making love to an ironworker," she said, her voice shaking, "and I *have* been making love to you. If you're too blinded by your idea of honesty to understand that kind of love, then—"

"What kind is that? The kind that allows me to reveal myself completely, while you keep your secrets? Emily, I opened my soul to you." His jaw clenched. "In return you gave me lies."

"Would you have opened your soul to me if I'd been honest and told you who I was?" she cried, holding out both hands.

He stared at her silently.

"Of course you wouldn't!" Tears streamed down her cheeks and he watched her cry with no expression on his face. "You almost dumped me when you found out I was a college instructor. If you'd known that I was Dan Johnson's daughter, you'd never have gone out with me again!"

"Which would have been better all the way around."

"I refuse to believe that." She scrambled from the bed. "But I can see there's no use talking to you now, so I'll go." Hampered by her tear-blurred vision, she searched for her clothes.

When she found them, she pulled off Ned's tank top and reached for her bra. As she did, her glance swept across the bed, and she saw the unguarded look in his eyes—hungry, raw, hurting. She paused, the garment dangling from her hand. She took a step toward him. "Ned..."

"Dammit." His eyes glistened with unshed tears and his voice shook. "It's not fair for you to look like that.

You were the most beautiful, compassionate woman I've ever known. And dammit, I still want you!"

"Then don't end it," she said, stepping nearer. She could see that he was aroused. Perhaps he was right, and it wasn't fair for her to win him back with sexual attraction, but she was desperate.

"I have to." The light in his eyes was tortured.

"No, you don't."

His hands clenched into fists and his voice was low and tight. "If I took you now, it would be lust, Emily, lust and rage. I wouldn't trust myself to be gentle, to be careful. Chances are, I'd hurt you."

"I don't believe that."

"That's because you don't know the depth of my despair. I warn you. Go away."

"But I—"

"Go away! I don't want you here."

With a sob she grabbed her clothes and fled into the living room. She barely remembered dressing and running outside; the drive home was a blur of pain as his words of rejection repeated themselves over and over.

Once inside the apartment, she looked tearfully at the candles she'd placed in each room in preparation for their romantic night together. In her bedroom, exotic scents wafted from the perfumed sachets she'd tucked beneath the pillows. On the bedside lay a leather-bound volume of Browning that she'd planned to give him.

She'd created a seductive rendezvous, a celebration of their love. And then, when he realized fully how much she cared, she would have told him gently about her father. Surely the truth coming from her wouldn't have created the havoc that it had when Ned discovered it on his own.

Lying on the bed, she curled into a ball, too numb to cry as his words continued to pound in her head. *I don't want you, I don't want you, I don't want you.* Monica had been right. She was finished.

CHAPTER EIGHTEEN

ON MONDAY MORNING Ned arrived at work exactly on time, so that neither Danny nor his father would have a legitimate reason such as lateness to fire him. He'd tucked his report to OSHA in his lunch box. He would take it to the government agency's downtown office after work that afternoon.

Throughout the day he operated in a robotic trance, not allowing himself to think about anything except the iron he was connecting and the report he would deliver when he finished working. He had only one discussion with anyone all day—when Smiley told him that Jake was picking up his wages at quitting time and leaving town for good. Otherwise Ned talked to no one, and his buddies respected his silence. During his lunch hour he retreated to a faraway beam and submerged himself in Tolstoy's *War and Peace*.

The men attributed his taciturn behavior, he knew, to his concern about losing his job once the report was turned in. He let them think what they liked, but he didn't give a damn about the job anymore. If Johnson Construction fired him, and they probably would, he'd find something out of state and send the money home to his mother and brother. Ned had always loved Tucson, even during the boiler-room season they called summer, but since Friday the town had lost its appeal.

At quitting time Mando chanced the first personal question of the day as he and Ned stood side by side putting away their tools. "Goin' over to Suds and Subs after you turn in the report?" he asked casually.

"No." Ned made his mind a blank and refused to think of the bar and the person who worked there.

"The guys want to buy you a drink. They figure they owe you, for what you're doin'," Mando pointed out.

Ned looked at him. "I can't, Mando," he said simply.

Mando studied him for a long moment. "It's the woman, isn't it?"

Ned realized that nobody but Mando would have had the courage to pry like this, or the insight to hit the target. "Yeah, it's the woman," he admitted, and glanced away, embarrassed by the catch in his voice.

Mando took off his goggles and wiped the sweat from his eyes. "Come on and have a drink, then," he said. "By the time you get there, she'll be gone."

Ned stared at him. "What?"

"Rooster and Smiley and me, we'll get her fired, just like that." Mando snapped his fingers.

Ned frowned and looked away. "No, I don't want her fired. She needs the job."

"What do you care?" Mando picked up his lunch box.

Ned gazed at the plank floor, unable to answer the question. He shouldn't give a damn whether his friends wanted to get Emily fired or not. Having her out of the bar would simplify his life considerably.

"Listen, man," Mando said. "If she's messed with you, we don't want her around. We'll take care of it."

"No, Mando," he said, unable to turn his friends loose on her, despite how she'd treated him.

"But—"

"Leave her alone, dammit," Ned said roughly and saw the sting of his words on Mando's face. "Please," he added gently.

"Okay, you're the boss." Mando shook his head. "But I never thought I'd see some woman run you like that."

Ned's stomach clenched. He wanted like hell to take a swing at someone, but Mando was the wrong someone. "Careful," he warned. "I'm not in the best of moods today."

"So we noticed." Mando unhooked his tool belt. "Well, see you around. *Via con dios.*" He started toward the stairs but turned back. "Here comes Danny-boy," he said in a low tone. "Watch yourself, gringo. Don't go doin' somethin' stupid."

Ned grimaced. "Can't seem to help myself these days."

"Try," Mando suggested, and walked away. He nodded once in Danny's direction before descending the stairs.

Ned had been half expecting a visit from Danny all day, either to fire him or ask him to forget the report. Ned stayed where he was and waited for Danny to come to him. Danny and Emily didn't look much alike, Ned thought as the man approached. Then again, maybe they did if he concentrated on the lower half of Danny's face, the mouth and the rounded chin. The same features on Emily were soft and inviting, but on Danny they merely looked soft.

"Got a minute, Tucker?" Danny asked, crossing the plank floor. His white shirt was immaculate. Something about that white shirt, which wasn't even stained with honest sweat, angered Ned even more.

"I've got just about a minute," he replied.

A muscle tightened in Danny's jaw. "I thought I'd mention that you won't have to make any reports to OSHA. I talked to my dad last night and he's okayed some new cable and a supply of safety goggles." Danny's smile seemed forced. "You know how it is, crossed wires. Dad thought we had the stuff and I thought we couldn't afford it. Just a mix-up."

"Bull." Ned looked Danny straight in the eye and enjoyed watching him flinch.

Danny hesitated, and when he spoke again, his conciliatory attitude had begun to disintegrate. "You're gettin' what you want, Tucker. Why not take it and shut up?"

"Because it's too little, too late, Johnson." Ned clenched and unclenched his hands. "You should have listened to your little sister."

Danny's face twisted with anger. "My sister doesn't run this place. I do."

"More's the pity."

"Yeah, you'd like that, wouldn't you?" Danny advanced toward Ned. "Probably had that in mind, all along—marry the boss's daughter and move right into management of the company."

A red haze spread over Ned's vision, but he held himself in check. "No way in hell," he said.

"Oh, yeah, deny it, but I know the truth. The thing is, the plan won't work," Danny said with a sneer. "My sister would never marry some jerk who hangs iron for a living."

Ned's rage boiled like lava, but he dug deep and found the strength not to hit this imbecile. If anybody started swinging, he vowed, it would be Danny. "She'll never get the chance," he said, swallowing the bile that rose in his stomach, "because I'll never ask her."

"Oh, yeah?" Danny's body twitched.

"That's right." He dared the shorter man with a glance. "I wouldn't take your sister on a silver platter."

Danny swung and Ned ducked. The force of Danny's lunge carried him past Ned, and at that moment both men remembered where they were. Ned grabbed Danny at the same time that Danny reached out, and their arms locked just as Danny lost his footing. As easily as melted butter off a knife he slipped over the side, slamming Ned to the plank floor.

Self-preservation propelled Ned's other arm around a pillar as Danny's weight swung free twenty stories above the street. The effort to hold Danny and hang on to the pillar threatened to split Ned down the middle. Blood roared in his ears and his mouth tasted like rust. He closed his eyes against the pain as Danny struggled to hold on.

From below them Ned thought he heard a shout pierce the eternity of tortured muscles and gasping breath. His fingers grew numb, then his arm, then his shoulder. Was he still holding Danny or had the man plummeted like a discarded toy to his death?

More shouts and the sound of feet pounding up the stairway echoed off the iron. Ned held on, but the weight and the end of his arm shifted, slipped...slipped again...oh, God. An agonized wail tore the air as Danny lost his grip.

Ned's throat opened in a companion cry of horror as he pictured Danny's death, smashed on the pavement like an insect against the windshield of a car. Emily. Emily would be at work. Emily would see. He had to go down there, take her away from it. Somehow he had to pry his arm free and get to her.

"Hey, man, take it easy, gringo." Mando's voice seemed far away, but someone was helping him loosen his grip on the pillar.

"Emily," Ned croaked. "Got to help Emily. Her brother—she shouldn't see—"

"Nothin' to see," Mando said quietly, easing Ned to his feet.

"Danny...Danny's..."

"Danny's the luckiest son of a bitch in the world," Mando said, still partially supporting Ned as they started toward the stairs.

"Can you beat that?" Rooster said, bounding up the stairs toward them. "Have you ever seen anything like that? How's Ned?"

"If he didn't dislocate somethin', I think he's okay," Mando answered. "What's the word on Danny-boy?"

"He's sitting on the sidewalk cryin' like a baby. The ambulance is comin', but he won't need nothin'."

Ned tried to shake the buzz from his ears. "He's not dead?"

"Not last time I looked," Rooster said.

"What happened?" Ned shook off Mando's support and stood weaving like a drunk.

"Damnedest thing I ever saw," Rooster replied. "On the way down, he landed on an air hose that was dangling over the side. That sucker stretched all the way to the sidewalk, like some rubber hand, or somethin'. Danny rode it all the way down and stepped off like he'd been at some amusement park. 'Cept he didn't look too amused."

Ned stared at Rooster. "You're making that up."

"God's truth, right, Mando?"

"That's right. I saw him hit the air hose while I was ridin' the elevator up there to get you, gringo."

Ned began to shake with relief. "Do you—could we sit on the steps a minute?" he asked as his knees started to buckle.

"No problem," Mando said. "I was thinkin' of taking a rest myself."

Ned sat down and buried his face in his hands to cover the tears that were dampening his fingers and palms. He tried to remember what had caused Danny finally to take the first swing. Then he remembered—his comment about Emily, that he wouldn't take her on a silver platter. Danny had lashed out in defense of his sister, and had almost died for it. Yet the words that had enraged Danny had been spoke by a man who claimed to love Emily. What kind of a man would do something like that?

"Hey, gringo, I got an idea," Mando said. "You know that report?"

"Yeah," Ned replied, letting his hands dangle between his knees while he kept his tear-streaked face down.

"If I was you, I'd tear it up. Somethin' tells me you won't need no OSHA people to straighten out Danny-boy."

"That's right," Rooster said, sitting on Ned's other side. "I heard him cryin' about guardrails, 'cause of course one shoulda been on this floor, and he might've been saved by it. He's seen the light, that Danny-boy. He's been shown the way and the truth. So why risk gettin' a reputation for nothin'?"

Ned sighed. "I guess you're right."

"Feel like headin' down now?" Mando asked.

Ned took a deep breath. "I think so."

"I'll go on ahead," Rooster offered, "and get the drinks served up. I don't know about you guys, but I'm one thirsty man."

Mando gazed at Ned after Rooster left. "Speakin' about the bar, and a certain woman who works there, wanna explain what you were babblin' about when I pried you loose? Sounded to me like Emily is Danny-boy's sister. That true?"

Ned glanced at Mando. "Can you forget what I said? I swore to myself I wouldn't tell anyone, but I guess when I thought Danny was dead..."

"Sure, I can forget. I can forget anything." Mando rubbed his chin. "But I can't help thinkin' she's some spy for her old man, and I don't like that."

"No, she's not." Ned massaged his aching eyes. "Listen, Mando, if I tell you what she's doing at the bar, you have to swear to keep it to yourself."

Mando looked offended.

"Okay, sorry. I know you won't blab. Here it is— Emily's a college instructor in sociology, and she's writing a paper on the social interactions of ironworkers."

"No kidding?" Mando frowned. "Social actions? How could she, when there's no women to speak of in that bar?"

"No, not that kind of social interaction." Ned smiled faintly. "The kind between all of us, the guys who work together."

"Now, wait a minute, man—"

"Friendship, Mando, friendship," Ned said quickly.

Mando let out his breath. "Whew. For a second I thought we were talkin' about guys who like guys."

"We're not."

"Good." Mando shook his head and glanced at Ned. "How long've you known about this?"

"A while. But I didn't find out she was old man Johnson's daughter until Friday, when I finally had the brains to put some information together."

"I'm gettin' the picture. You're ticked at her for not tellin' you."

"I don't think 'ticked' covers it, Mando. I feel completely betrayed."

Mando took off his hard hat and scratched his head. "Yeah, well, I can see how you would." Then he looked at Ned. "But I was here when you thought her brother died, and I can tell you somethin', gringo. She's still in your system, but good."

Ned stared back at him, unable to find a reply.

"I got another idea," Mando said.

"What's that?"

"Go to the bar, have a drink with the guys. You'll see her and settle this one way or the other. Right now you're just runnin' away. I don't like seein' you do that, buddy. It's not like you."

Ned considered what Mando had said. "I guess you're right again," he replied finally.

WHEN THE SCREAMING SIREN became loud enough to worry them, Monica and Emily turned to each other and in unspoken agreement walked toward the front door of the bar.

"Probably some car wreck," Monica said over her shoulder, "but I have to make sure. I'm mad as hell at Jake, but I don't want him to get killed on the iron. This is his last day on the job."

"We don't want anybody to get killed," Emily said, fighting against what might be unnecessary fear. "But I'm sure you're right. It's a wreck, I'll bet."

"Although I didn't hear a crash."

"No, me neither."

Monica pushed open the heavy wooden door and held it for Emily. "My God," she whispered, shielding her eyes from the sun. "There's a crowd at the site." She began to run as best she could in her three-inch heels, and Emily followed. Eventually Emily's long-legged stride left Monica behind.

Emily stumbled once on a crack in the sidewalk but she stayed upright and kept going. *It's a bad dream,* she thought. *People always run like this in a bad dream, and then they wake up.* But she wasn't asleep. The heat from the sidewalk was too intense, the fading wail of the siren too real as the ambulance drove through the crowd and parked opposite the construction site.

Emily fought her way through to the inner edge of the circled onlookers, past members of the other building trades and people from the offices nearby. She caught snatches of their comments. "A miracle," a woman in a suit murmured. "He should've been history," added a carpenter.

No one's dead, she thought, but that didn't end the roiling in her stomach. Dead was the worst, but that left permanent injury, paralysis, disfigurement. *Who? My God, who?* Tensing herself against the blast of horrible reality, she focused on the spot where the paramedics gathered. Her heart caught in her throat when she saw Danny sitting on the curb with his face in his hands.

He looked incongruous and small sitting there, she thought in that split second, crumpled and broken-hearted; the same way he had when he was six and his ice-cream bar had fallen off the stick. But far more was at stake than ice cream, judging from the concern on the faces of the paramedics.

"What happened?" Emily asked the person next to her.

"He fell from the top, but got caught on an air hose that lowered him down as sweet as pie. He walked away from it without a scratch, but then he sorta collapsed."

Emily recognized the voice and realized Mike was speaking to her. "Nobody else was hurt?"

"Guess not. Bookworm tried to hold on to him, but I guess Danny-boy couldn't maintain his grip."

"Ned…" Emily whispered and went numb. He could have been pulled down. The air hose would never have caught both of them.

"Rooster says Ned's okay," Mike assured her. "Don't be scared. We'll all be in drinkin' and laughin' before long. Don't worry."

Monica squeezed in beside them, panting. "What is it?" she asked, straining to see through the people blocking her view. "What happened?"

"Danny was almost…killed," Emily said unsteadily. "He fell but an air hose saved him. I guess he's okay."

Monica gripped her arm. "Oh, Em, honey."

"Ned—" Emily swallowed. "Ned was the one trying to hold on to him up there."

"Wow." Monica rubbed Emily's shoulders. "You okay?"

Emily nodded. "I think so." The paramedics were helping Danny to his feet and she gasped at the waxen color of his face. His eyes moved wildly in their sockets as he tried to struggle free of the paramedics.

"No, no hospital," Danny said, shaking his head. "Let me go…let me go home."

"You've had a tremendous shock to your system, Mr. Johnson," one uniformed woman said. "I think you'd better be checked out by a doctor first."

"No." Danny raised a shaking hand to brush the woman aside. "I just need—" His darting glance settled on Emily and he uttered a strange, sobbing sound.

Without thinking she responded to his inarticulate plea. "Let me through," she said, pushing past Mike.

"Wait, Emily," Mike said, catching her arm. "You don't belong—"

"Yes, I do." She pulled away from Mike. "I'm his sister."

"His *sister*?"

Emily didn't bother to answer as she rushed forward and put her arms around Danny.

"Just a minute," one of the paramedics said, taking her arm as if to pull her away. "This man is in shock."

"He's my brother," Emily said. "Give us a moment, please."

Danny was shaking like a cornered rabbit, and she hugged him close and repeated the soothing phrases they'd used with each other as children. They had been buddies once, she and Danny, before the fierce rivalry had taken hold and separated them. Once they'd shared candy and toys, comic books and secrets.

Deep within her lay a love that had been forged through years of shared history, and she gave it now, even as she wondered what part she'd played in this terrible drama that nearly had cost two lives. Gradually Danny stopped quivering and was still.

Emily drew back and gazed into his ashen face. "I think you'd better go with them, Danny," she said gently.

"Okay." He looked completely beaten.

"I'll come, too, if you want."

"Okay."

With her arm around his waist, she led him to the ambulance, but as they neared it, Danny stopped and looked frantically around him. "What about Tucker?" he said. "Is Tucker hurt?"

"They say he's fine," Emily answered. A sixth sense made her glance toward the gate in the wire fence just as Ned and Mando walked through it. For a brief second she met his gaze, but she was too far away to read his expression. She longed to go to him, to wrap her arms around him, too, and assure herself by the solid feel of his body that he was safe. Yet she feared he wouldn't allow that ever again.

"We have to go, miss," the paramedic said, urging her forward.

"All right." Emily looked away and helped the paramedics get Danny into the ambulance. Just before she climbed in after him, she glanced back to the spot where Ned had been, but he was gone.

CHAPTER NINETEEN

EMILY CALLED her mother and father from the telephone in the hall outside the emergency room. Within twenty minutes her father walked through the double doors at the end of the corridor.

"Mom didn't come?" Emily asked as she went to meet him.

"She wanted to, but I talked her out of it." His tired gaze flickered over her Suds and Subs uniform but he made no comment. "We'll all go back there when they finish checking Danny over. How is he?"

"I think he's okay, Dad. Shook up real bad, but okay."

A shudder rippled through her father's large frame. He reached nervously for the pipe in his breast pocket, stared at it, and put it away again. "Do you know how it happened?"

"Sort of. I guess Ned planned to deliver a report to OSHA this afternoon after work. Danny tried to talk him out of it, and then they..." She folded her arms tight around her body. "They had a fight. I think it was—" She paused. "Correction," she said softly, "I know it was about me."

Something close to a growl sounded deep in her father's throat. "I told you he was trouble. I told you never to get involved with him."

"No, Dad." Emily unfolded her arms and faced him, head back. She thought of what Ned had risked today, what all the men risked every day, and gained courage from their bravery. "Ned's not the one to blame. The job was unsafe. Danny knew it and wouldn't change anything, even after I begged him to." She swallowed and clenched her fists until her nails made dents in her palms. "You knew, too, didn't you?"

His gaze wavered, and he glanced past her down the hall, as if searching for an answer to her question. "Emily, you have no idea what this business is like," he began.

"That's no answer, dammit." She saw him wince at her use of a swear word. She'd never sworn in front of him before or defied him so blatantly. "Did you know that the chokers were frayed?" she persisted in a strained voice. "Did you know safety goggles weren't issued, and guardrails were late in going up? Why wasn't there a guardrail on the twentieth floor, Dad?" she said, almost weeping. "Why?"

He glanced at her, his blue eyes dull with pain. "I wanted to keep you out of it. You're supposed to be a teacher." He gestured sweepingly with one hand. "Better than all this."

"I'm not! I'm not better than any of it!" She stared at him through her tears. "You knew, didn't you?" she whispered. "You knew what Danny was doing."

His mouth twisted. "How else do you think we got the damned contract? It's dog-eat-dog out there, companies underbidding, cuttin' corners, scramblin' for every little piece of business—"

"Dad, we're rich! We don't have to scramble like that anymore!"

He rubbed a hand over his haggard features. "Yes, we do, Angel," he said softly.

"What do you mean?"

"I'm in debt. Big debt. So's Danny." He stared at the polished tile floor.

"But…but Mom told me the house was paid for, and the cabin, and you're always taking trips, and helping with my rent, and…" Emily tried to think of more evidence to stack against this statement she didn't want to hear. Her parents in debt? The idea sent large-scale tremors through the foundation of her security.

"I've borrowed against the house and cabin to stay in business," her father said, looking at her with a resigned expression. "Your mother doesn't know that, and you'd best not tell her."

"But how? How did it happen?"

He sighed and gazed down the hallway again. "This and that. I was doing well, but not that well. Your mother deserved things—trips and better clothes. Then Danny married Gwen and naturally figured Gwen needed things, too. He asked me for a bigger salary, then a bigger one after that. I started turning over more of the job to Danny, because of all he was gettin' paid." He smiled wanly. "Then I had time on my hands, and your mother wanted more trips."

Emily cringed as she thought of the money she'd accepted for college, the monthly allowance that helped with her rent, the red Corvette her father couldn't afford, but had given her anyway. "You should have told me. I'd have put myself through college. Listen, it's not even too late. Maybe it won't help much, but I can begin paying you back."

"No!"

The force of his response stunned her into silence.

"I'm prouder of putting you through college than of anything I've ever done," he said, glaring at her. "Don't take that away from me. I've pushed you up there, Angel, higher than any of the rest of us, and no matter what happens, that schooling is yours. You've made it!" His voice shook as he continued. "Except that now you want some damned ironworker."

Emily welcomed his tirade as she struggled to collect her shattered illusions. She'd thought in standing up to him and his prejudices that she was fighting someone protected by material success and the satisfaction of having made a secure place for himself and his family. Instead her father's world was in danger of collapse, and in a desperate attempt to avoid that he'd mortgaged not only his home, but his integrity.

She hadn't realized that financing her escape from the blue-collar world had become his only source of pride. No wonder he'd reacted so strongly when she'd threatened to deprive him of that comfort by her liaison with Ned. For years she'd felt the weight of her father's dreams for her, but they'd never oppressed her until now.

She stepped forward and touched his arm. "I appreciate what you've done for me. I've loved every minute of school, and my teaching is enormously fulfilling. I'm not planning to give that up."

He looked as if he wanted to believe her. "What about Tucker?"

"I'm afraid Ned and I are finished," she said, and saw the triumph in her father's expression. "But if he should change his mind and want me back, I'd go in a minute," she added gently. "I love him, Dad."

Her father's triumph disappeared. "He's not the kind of guy I want for you, Angel."

"Yes, he is. You don't realize it, that's all. Ned is intelligent, kind, creative and honest. He's also very brave. There are plenty of college-educated men I know that I couldn't describe that way." She squeezed his arm and gazed earnestly into his face. "After paying good money to improve my mind, you ought to listen to what I've learned," she said with a tiny smile, "and I've learned that you can't judge someone by how many years of school they've had."

His expression reflected the heavy debate taking place in his head. "I want some guy who'll appreciate you, give you nice things," he insisted stubbornly.

"Dad, the nicest thing any man can give me is loyalty and devotion, and I've discovered that has nothing to do with college degrees. I've met people this summer who've made me proud to be their friend, and I'll have to be pretty special myself to stay equal with them."

"Hah. Why those bums, they—"

"They're not bums. Well, I know of one," she amended, remembering Jake, "but mostly they're terrific people. Don't let this thing you have about education blind you, Dad." She watched as he wrestled with his prejudices. He'd worshiped formal schooling for a long time because he'd never had it. She'd picked up many of his attitudes, which was one reason she couldn't dog-ear pages in a book. This summer had opened her eyes to her own preconceived ideas.

"You know, it doesn't make much sense," he said at last. "You've put in all these years of school, and you're telling me what you've learned is that school doesn't matter. Is that what I sent you there to find out?"

Despite herself, Emily chuckled. "It matters," she said. "It's just not the only thing that matters. That's all

I'm saying. And I didn't learn that in college. I learned that this summer, working at a bar.''

"Humph. That bar.'' He inspected her outfit again. "Two college degrees and you're flitting around dressed like a—like that. It's a disgrace, Angel.''

"I'm not crazy about the outfit, either, Dad, if it makes you feel any better.''

"Not much. All those punks watching you . . .'' He grimaced.

"They've treated me like a lady the whole time.''

"They'd sure as hell better! If I hear of any—''

"Don't worry,'' Emily said, figuring that her days in the bar were over, anyway.

"I just thought of something,'' her father said, as if following her train of thought. "If all the guys saw you riding off in the ambulance with Danny, won't they figure something's funny?''

"I expect they all know who I am by now,'' Emily said. "I told Mike, so he probably spread the word. That's the end of my summer project.''

Her father shook his head. "I knew it'd turn out to be a mess,'' he said, but his tone had lightened.

Emily reached up and kissed his lined cheek. "It's been part of my education,'' she said.

"Humph,'' her father said again and gazed down at her, the familiar fondness gleaming in his eyes. "So this guy you're nuts about, this Tucker, is history, huh?''

"I think so.'' Emily glanced away as sorrow overwhelmed her.

"Want me to talk to him?''

Startled, she studied his expression to see if he was serious. He was. "Oh, Dad.'' She hugged him as a lump rose in her throat at this unexpected generous offer. He had been listening to her. "You're wonderful,'' she said, gazing into his face. "And if I thought that would help, I'd take you up on it, but I don't think talking with you would change his mind. He's a great guy, but he's also... well, stubborn."

"Maybe you'd best not link up with him, then. We've already got a big pile of stubborn people in our family, including you."

Emily hugged him again. "That's true." She paused. "What are you going to do?" she asked hesitantly. "About the money, I mean?"

Her father's chest heaved. "We're gonna make some changes. I'm gonna work closer with Danny, make sure he's back on the right track. I hope we won't lose money on this job, but if we do, that's the breaks. He's gotta put the clamps on Gwen, stop spending so much on her, and I—I guess I'd best tell your mother a few things."

"She'll be fine, Dad."

"Yeah, I know. She's quite a woman. When you were telling me all that stuff about loyalty and devotion, I thought of her. I guess I know what you're talking about."

"I thought you would, if you gave yourself a chance." She peered over his shoulder as a nurse came out of the emergency room and beckoned to them. "I think they're ready for us to take Danny home," she said, stepping out of his embrace.

"Good." He walked beside her down the hall. "We'll go home and have a good meal. That always—"

"Dad, I can't."

"Why not?"

"If you don't mind, I'd like you to drop me off at Suds and Subs."

"I sure do mind! Why go back there now? Those mugs will just give you a hard time."

"Maybe, but I owe them an explanation."

"You owe them diddly-squat! Don't go back, Angel."

"I have to, Dad, and if you won't drive me, I'll take a cab."

Her father snorted. "Don't get that way. I'll take you." He glanced at her and sighed. "Like I said, a pile of stubborn people in this family."

FOR THE FIRST TIME since the day she was hired, Emily walked in the front door of Suds and Subs. Monica saw her immediately and hurried over. "How's your brother?" she asked in a hushed tone.

"Fine, but why whisper? The secret's out, right?" From the corner of her eye Emily saw Ned sitting with Mando and Smiley, Rooster, Mike and Al. He was looking directly at her.

"No secret's out unless you've been spillin' the beans," Monica said. "Ned's not talkin', and I told Mike I'd break his head if he told anybody. Far's I know, he hasn't."

Emily paused. "What about the way I hugged Danny and left with him?"

"If anybody asks, I've been tellin' them you're studying psychology at school and you know how to handle shock cases, like Danny-boy was after he fell."

Despite her agitation at being here, in the same room with Ned, Emily couldn't help but smile at Monica's creative storytelling. "So I could go on as before, with the study and everything."

"That's right." Monica looked pleased with herself. "It's all fixed."

Emily gazed around the smoky room at the people she'd learned to care for, and at the man she'd learned to love. Mike, who must be bursting with his discovery, would keep her secret, and so would Monica, who enjoyed gossip as much as anyone. And Ned. She didn't have to wonder about him. He'd never betray her.

She glanced back at Monica. "Thanks for protecting me," she said. "I'll never forget it."

"That's what friends are for."

"I know." Emily took a deep breath. "That's why I'm telling everyone, anyway."

"You are?" Crestfallen, Monica gazed at her. "And then I guess you'll quit?"

"If that's what everyone wants me to do, yes."

"Aw, Em."

"I have to tell them, Monica. They're my friends, and I can't deceive any of them anymore."

"But you're like a scientist, aren't you?"

"I'd rather be a human being."

Monica shook her head. "Boy, am I confused."

"That's okay." Emily put her arm around Monica and gave her a hug. "It happens to all of us, especially me. But for once, I'm not confused." She walked to the bar and asked Bailey for a glass and spoon. Then she turned around and clanged the spoon against the glass until everyone in the bar stopped talking.

"Sorry to interrupt your relaxing time, especially today, when I'm sure everyone needs to relax," she said, and most of the men laughed. "But there are a couple of things I want you all to know." She paused briefly and then plunged ahead. "First of all, I took this job because I'm an instructor in sociology at the U of A and I planned to write a paper on how ironworkers interact with each other after work."

She looked primarily at the men she didn't know well, because that was easier, and she noticed many weren't comprehending what she'd said. "In other words, my study was about the patterns you fall into when you come here—the leaders, the jokesters, how everyone chooses a place to sit and stays with it, even though—"

"You're *studyin'* that?" a man called from Monica's side of the bar. "Who the hell cares?"

"Sociologists do," Emily replied. "They want to learn more about how people relate with each other, and why."

"Sounds like that lady that went into the jungle to study gorillas," said another man. His comment was followed by uneasy laughter.

"I guess it does," Emily admitted, "and after working here for a while, and becoming friends with many of you, I've decided that I owe you the courtesy of telling you what I'm doing, instead of hiding it."

The men mumbled among themselves for a few seconds before Rooster spoke for the first time. "You wanna keep doin' this study?"

"I'd say that's up to all of you." She glanced at Bailey. "And my boss, of course."

Bailey looked slightly dazed. "I don't care, I guess," he said finally. "So long as you serve the drinks without spillin' them."

Several men laughed, and more mumbling followed before someone suggested they vote on whether to allow Emily to continue her project.

"Before you do that, you'd better hear what else I have to tell you," Emily said. She swallowed. This part would be much rougher.

"Well, out with it," prompted Rooster impatiently.

"Most of you know my name is Emily Johnson," she said as her palms began to sweat. She allowed herself a glance at Ned, expecting a stony expression. Instead he was smiling. Smiling! Bravely she continued, sending her confession directly toward Ned. "I am Dan Johnson's daughter," she finished.

This time the room was completely silent. Several mouths dropped open and many pairs of eyes glared at her with hostile intent.

"I guess we don't have to vote," someone said. "We don't want no Johnsons in here." Murmured assents followed.

Emily dropped her gaze. She could have expected nothing more, considering the mood of the men today. Eventually after their anger wore off a little, after her father instituted the changes he'd promised, she might have met a different response. But she couldn't wait days, maybe weeks. For her own sake, she had to stop the deception now.

Then Ned's voice broke the awkward silence. "Wait a minute."

Emily glanced up in surprise. He'd left the booth and was striding toward her, his face still streaked with dirt and sweat, his shirt torn from the accident. He was the most beautiful human being she'd ever seen.

He stood beside her and faced the men. "Before you make the decision to throw Emily out, you ought to know that she went to bat for us. She stood up to her brother and told him to make changes, and when he wouldn't do it, she called her father home from his vacation."

"Hey, Bookworm, why should we believe you?" asked one man. "You're sweet on that gal. You'd say anything for her."

"Watch your mouth," said Mando, rising from the booth and coming to stand by Ned. "Don't go callin' my buddy a liar."

"That's right," Rooster said, walking up to stand beside Emily. "And this lady's just fine with me. I don't care if she's related to the devil himself."

"She might be," someone shouted, to the accompaniment of more laughter.

"I'm for her, too," said Smiley, also leaving the booth to stand with them.

"That goes for me," Al added, following suit. "And me," Mike said as he joined the crowd surrounding Emily.

Emily felt tears push at the backs of her eyes. "Thank you," she managed to choke out.

"Aw, let's have her stick around," someone said from Monica's side of the room.

"Yeah," agreed another. "We've had enough of this talkin' anyway. It's time to get back to serious drinkin'."

After a chorus of shouted agreement, Ned turned to Emily. "I think that's your answer,"

She didn't trust herself to speak but just gazed at him and prayed that the expression she saw in his eyes meant what she hoped it did.

"I just talked Bailey into lettin' you off for the rest of the evening," Monica whispered, hurrying up beside her. "Here's your purse," she said, thrusting it into Emily's hand. "If I was you, I'd hightail it out of here before he changes his mind."

Emily glanced questioningly at Ned. "Would you—"

"Yes," he said, and steered her toward the front door.

When they stepped outside, late afternoon shadows from the tall buildings covered the nearly deserted street, but the air hung dusty and hot around them. Reaction to all that had happened was beginning to make Emily's knees rubbery, and she was glad for Ned's firm hold on her arm.

"We'll take my car," he said, propelling her down the sidewalk.

Opposite the construction site she slowed and gazed upward to the twentieth floor. "Ned, you almost—"

"But I didn't," he said, wrapping his arm around her waist and hurrying her past the giant skeleton. "That's all that matters."

Within seconds they were in his car headed north, toward her apartment. He took her hand and held it tight in his.

"Thank you for defending me back there," she began, still not certain where she stood with him. "They were ready to condemn me for my name."

His grip tightened. "Yeah, well, I understood that. Once upon a time, so was I."

"But not now?"

"No, not now."

"Because of my confession at the bar? I saw you smiling."

He glanced at her. "God, that was great. I was so proud of you. But no, not because of that. I—even if you hadn't come back to the bar, I would have looked for you tonight. I was prepared to go to your folks' house if necessary."

"You were?"

"Yep. You see, when I saw you holding Danny, comforting him, something loosened up in me. I realized how much you loved him and your family. Your love for them was pulling on one side—I was pulling on the other."

"Yes," she said, her heart full.

He laced his fingers through hers and brought her hand to his lips. "In a way," he said, kissing her fingertips, "you were going through emotionally what I've just been through physically, coming near to being torn apart. No wonder you didn't want to tell me who you were and let yourself in for that kind of pain.''

The tension dissolved in her with each word of understanding and she relaxed against the seat. ''Oh, Ned.''

''And as far as I'm concerned, the tug-of-war is over,'' he continued. ''I intend to make peace with your family and I sure hope they'll be willing to accept the olive branch from me.''

''I think they will,'' she said, laying her head against the seat and turning to gaze at him with love. ''After all, you tried to save Danny's life.''

''I can't tell you what I felt, when I thought...''

She gripped his arm. ''Let it be for now. The worst didn't happen.''

''Too close for comfort. Way too close.''

''I know.'' She rubbed his arm.

''He's really okay, though?''

''Yes. Once he has a few more hours past the scare, he'll be even better. By the way, I had a talk with dad at the hospital, and believe it or not, he offered to intercede for me to try to bring you around.''

Ned chuckled with surprise. ''He did?''

''Yes, and I told him you were too stubborn to listen.''

Ned held her hand against his thigh. ''Yeah, and I was, too. But not anymore. Your dad and I are going to be friends, Emily. I'm determined that it will happen.''

Emily laughed with delight. ''Then I guess it will. I'm quickly learning about your determination.''

''Good, because I'm also determined that we'll be married this summer.''

Her chest constricted. ''This summer?''

"Too soon? Do you think that your parents—"

"No," she said as joy overpowered all other reservations. "They'll probably be fine. Anyway, this is our decision. Their opinion really doesn't matter." She smiled when she realized the truth of that. "It doesn't matter! Do you know what it means to me to say that?"

"I know what it means to me," he said, his grip tightening. "God, I love you."

"And I love you. But Ned, are you sure about getting married now? I thought you wanted to wait until your brother graduated."

"I can't," he said, grinning. "I want you too much. And we'll make out okay financially, even if I'm still helping Curt and Mom, if I'll give up my grandiose idea of how we'll live."

"Ned, it doesn't—"

"Yeah, but I wanted everything to be perfect—a house, good money coming in, the works. Finally I realized that having you with me every day is perfect enough. So what do you say?"

"I say yes! I don't care where we live, or what we eat, or drive. Surely you know that by now."

He turned into the parking lot of her apartment complex. "Yes, I do," he said, parking the car and smiling at her. "Finally I do."

"The sun's setting," she murmured. "Want to stay out here and watch it?"

"No," he replied, reaching for his door handle.

In her bedroom he hesitated for the first time since they'd left the bar. "I should take a shower," he said, "after the kind of day I've had, and the way I—"

"Don't you dare." She finished throwing off her own clothes and tossed back the covers on the bed.

"But, Emily."

"Don't you understand, you dirty, sweaty, wonderful man? I love you like this. Now take off those clothes and come to bed."

"Ye-e-es, ma'am," he drawled, following her orders and climbing in beside her. "Anything else, ma'am?"

"Kiss me."

"Anyplace special?"

"Everyplace special."

"That I can do."

She breathed in the manly scent of him as he covered each breast with kisses. Her eyes misted at the tender touch of his hands, hands that at other times could close like a vise over giant beams. She caressed the corded muscles of his arms and back and felt the strength capable of heaving those beams into place—or saving a life.

"You are so brave," she whispered.

He kissed his way back to her lips and gazed into her eyes. "No more than you."

"I'm not brave."

"Ah, but you are." He cupped her face with one hand. "Revealing your identity this afternoon. That took courage."

"Yes, but I had you there. When you were on the twentieth floor, you were alone."

"No. You were with me." He gazed intently into her eyes. "After it was over, I realized you always would be, no matter how hard I tried to push you away. I was fighting a losing battle, trying not to love you." He nuzzled her throat and ran his tongue along her collarbone.

"I'm glad you lost the fight," she murmured, shivering with delight under the assault of his lips.

"Wasn't much of a battle," he mumbled between kisses.

"Neither is this," she said, gasping. "Please, Ned— love me."

"I do."

"No, now. You know...."

"Yes, I know," he said, sliding up beside her and smiling gently. "After all, that's my job—making good connections."

"Prove it."

"As often as you like," he said, moving over her and uniting them in heat-forged splendor.

Harlequin Superromance.

COMING NEXT MONTH

#390 A PIECE OF CAKE • Leigh Roberts
Lucius Donovan was shocked to discover he was the
father of a bouncing baby boy. Thea Willits hadn't
said a word when she'd abruptly ended their live-in
relationship. Determined to set things right, he
moved in next door. But winning Thea back would
be no piece of cake....

#391 CATHERINE'S SONG • Marie Beaumont
The Cajun motto, "Let the good times roll,"
signified only *wasted* time to restoration architect
Catherine Nolan. But then she met Blackie
Broussard, who valued the dreams he wove in song
more than any bridge he'd engineered. Soon
Catherine began questioning her own values, because
being held in Blackie's arms somehow felt like
coming home....

#392 RINGS OF GOLD • Suzanne Nichols
Tori Anderson just wanted Michael St. James to do
what he did best—help her recover from her injury
so that she could get back on the ski slopes before
the next Olympics. But racing again might put Tori
in a wheelchair for life. Could Michael convince her
to accept a gold ring instead of a gold medal?

#393 WITH OPEN ARMS • Suzanne Ellison
Stockbroker Camille Blaine had a great job, a slick
condo and a designer wardrobe. Then she met Linc
Stafford, a dead-broke widower with a passel of
kids, a senile grandfather and a sizable collection of
rescued animals. Suddenly, life in the fast lane no
longer seemed so appealing....

A compelling novel of deadly revenge and passion
from Harlequin's bestselling international
romance author Penny Jordan

Eleven years had passed but the
terror of that night was something
Pepper Minesse would never
forget. Fueled by revenge against
the four men who had brutally
shattered her past, she set in
motion a deadly plan to destroy
their futures.

Available in February!

February brings you . . .

Harlequin Presents...

PENNY JORDAN

valentine's night

Sorrel didn't particularly want to meet her long-lost cousin Val from Australia. However, since the girl had come all this way just to make contact, it seemed a little churlish not to welcome her.

As there was no room at home, it was agreed that Sorrel and Val would share the Welsh farmhouse that was being renovated for Sorrel's brother and his wife. Conditions were a bit primitive, but that didn't matter.

At least, not until Sorrel found herself snowed in with the long-lost cousin, who turned out to be a handsome, six-foot male!

Also, look for the next Harlequin Presents Award of Excellence title in April:

Elusive as the Unicorn
by Carole Mortimer

HPI243-I